A DISTANT LIGHT

THE DISTANT LIGHT SERIES, BOOK 1

LORRAINE SOLHEIM

The Distant Light Series, A Distant Light, Book 1

By Lorraine Solheim

Published by: Lorraine Solheim

Copyright © 2021 by Lorraine Solheim

Cover Design by Moonstruck Cover Design & Photography

Formatting by: E-book Formatting Fairies

ISBN 979-8-9852453-1-8

This book is licensed for your personal enjoyment only. It may not be re-sold or given away to other people. If you would like to share this book with others, please purchase additional copies. Thank you for respecting the hard work of this author. To obtain permission to excerpt portions of the text, please contact the author at:

lorraine@lorrainesolheim.com

This is a work of fiction. Names, characters, places, and incidents are the product of the author's imagination. Any resemblance to actual persons living or dead, business establishments, events, or locales is entirely coincidental.

To my husband. And my many friends who have encouraged me to keep writing. This book is for all of you. And to the late Kaye Coppersmith for her guidance and patience.

CHAPTER ONE

Boston

Catherine looked down at herself from the interior of the ambulance more as an observer than a participant. How could she be lying on a gurney yet at the same time suspended above the EMT as he performed CPR?

Her face was shrouded in an angry shade of purple, unrecognizable. Her right eye reminiscent of a prizefighter who'd suffered through one too many rounds. Her favorite cream-colored pantsuit, blood-soaked.

Minutes later, the doors flew open, and Catherine, still outside herself, floated to a team of doctors and nurses poised to take over.

"Paddles!" a doctor said in a loud, authoritative voice. He placed them on Catherine's chest. "Clear!"

"What are you doing?" Catherine asked, struggling to capture their attention. "I'm not dead." Then her surroundings faded, replaced by a tunnel emitting a warm, inviting glow. Serenity blanketed her.

"Catherine," a familiar voice said.

"Mom? Is that you?" Catherine said, eager to see her late mother.

"Mom, I'm so sorry I wasn't there for you when you passed. Can you forgive me?"

"Nothing to forgive. It was meant to be. But it's not your time."

"Not my time for what?"

"To cross over. More to do. Fix what's wrong."

Catherine stepped farther into the light. "Please, let me see you."

"Our choices define us," her mother said.

In the deepest recesses of her soul, Catherine sensed this was true. She reached out. "I want to stay with you."

"Not your time. More to do."

She yearned to remain in the warmth of her mother's loving light. "Please, just a little longer."

"Go back."

"I've made a mess of things. There's nothing much to return to."

Silence.

"Mom? Don't leave me!" she cried out. "I love and miss you so much."

Like exiting a dream, the light she'd entered moments before shrunk to a pinpoint and disappeared.

Two days later

CATHERINE'S NOSE stung from the sharp smell of disinfectant. Her fingers recoiled at the scratchy sheets, so unlike the Egyptian cotton she was used to.

Someone patted her hand.

"Mom?" Catherine murmured, and struggled to open her eyes. Her right eyelid wouldn't cooperate.

Through her unbalanced vision, a nurse came into view.

Catherine's mouth and throat felt dry as unbuttered toast. Her temples throbbed with an incessant drumbeat, and her abdomen cried out with searing pain. "Where am I?" she rasped.

"The ICU surgical unit at Mass General." The nurse handed her a small bowl of ice chips. "You've been sedated and on a ventilator with a tube in your throat for the past two days. But you're okay now. Do you remember what happened to you?"

Catherine tried to clear the drug-laden cobwebs from her mind. She scooped up a few ice chips and spooned them into her mouth. She closed her eyes and rewound her thoughts. Footsteps. A dark alley, the smell of restaurant trash and cat urine. The unending kicks to her body. Tremors wracked her. A stream of cold sweat trickled down her back. The smell of her attacker's hands and breath assaulted her as if he stood beside her. The memory of the metal blade ripping into her felt all too real. She opened her eyes to obliterate the images and thrashed her head from side to side. "N-o-o-o."

"It's okay," the nurse said. She patted Catherine's hand again. "You're safe, Miss O'Malley."

Catherine's pulse and breathing slowed. The tension gripping her shoulders eased.

"You've had a rough go of it. From what I understand, you came close to bleeding out and arrested in the ambulance. The trauma team had to shock your heart back to a normal rhythm. Then they rushed you into surgery to stem the bleeding from the knife wound and repair the damage it did to your liver. She gave a half-hearted chuckle. "Must've had an angel watching over you."

Catherine recalled hearing her late mother's voice.

Not your time. Choices. More to do.

The nurse adjusted Catherine's pillow. "Is there someone you'd like us to notify?"

Snapshots of people who once loved her kaleidoscoped in Catherine's mind. Her father and mother both dead within a year of each other. Her ex-boyfriend, a bittersweet memory. And a collage of friends who'd drifted away like fallen branches in a rolling stream completed the grim picture in her mind.

Her face warmed. Tears spilled down her cheeks. Her lips quivered. In the past, there'd be no question that Jack, the man she'd loved beyond measure, would rush to her side. Never far from her thoughts, it had now been two years without him. She had loved him then. And she loved him still.

The nurse touched her arm. "But surely, Miss O'Malley, there must be *someone*."

∼

The next day

CATHERINE WATCHED as the nurse rolled a supply cart over to her bed.

"Time to change your dressing." She carefully peeled away the gauze from the ten-inch incision stretching from Catherine's rib cage to her pubic bone.

"How long will it take for me to fully recover?"

"Your doctor should be here any minute and will answer your questions."

As if on cue, a man wearing a white coat entered the room.

"Catherine, meet Doctor Davis." The nurse finished the dressing, closed up the cart, and moved it out of his way.

He gave Catherine a compassionate smile. "Good morning."

Catherine warmed to his kind demeanor and noted that the young doctor appeared to know his way around a gym. "Good morning. How long before I heal, so I can return to work?"

"A month or so. Your body needs to repair itself, not only from the surgery, but from the numerous blows you took during the attack."

Catherine squirmed when she recalled the man kicking her. "That long?"

The doctor nodded. "You're young and appear to be in good physical shape. The surgery to repair your liver was successful, so that helps." He focused on her face, shook his head, and his tone softened. "But still, you've been through a lot."

Catherine envisioned her office. Her desk littered with contracts and design layouts. Her inbox overflowing. Her phone ringing. "I can't be out of work that long. I have clients and an upcoming conference to attend."

He pulled up a chair and sat. "Tell me, what kind of job is so important that you'd place it above your recovery?"

She closed her eyes. Due to her abdomen's vibrating pain and a headache that wouldn't quit, Catherine wasn't in the mood to engage in personal banter. But when she opened them, he stared at her, awaiting her reply.

"I'm not suggesting I get out of bed and run a marathon. I work in advertising," she said with an edge she hadn't intended. "My brain gets overworked, not my body. Most days are spent at my desk, creating print advertisements, television commercials, and renewing client contracts. When I'm not doing that, I attend business lunches and board meetings."

Searing pain burned her throat. Truth be told, it wasn't unusual for Catherine to dash from one meeting to another. She'd flit around the office counseling her staff or finish a project late into the night so a coworker could leave early to enjoy their child's birthday. Or, she'd be on a plane, shoehorned into a coach seat, flying off to who knows where to attend a client meeting.

"Doctor Davis, I appreciate what you're saying, but my clients can't put their businesses on hold while I take my sweet time getting back on my feet."

"And your body can't heal any faster than it can. It takes time. If you don't give it the care it needs, trust me, you'll come to regret it."

"But you don't understand. My customers depend on me. I make pulling a company out of the red and having it land in the black look like a visit to Starbucks. Have you seen the commercial for Chug-a-Lug? The one with the talking giraffes?"

He chuckled. "My kids love it."

"That's one of mine. The company was on the verge of bankruptcy, and my commercial helped put them in a profit position within six months. I had a hand in saving the jobs of one hundred and twenty people."

The doctor stood. "Is your job stressful?"

Catherine nodded. She had to admit, she'd experienced her share of stress. Those times when she'd wanted to tell everyone to leave her alone, let her take a few moments to kick back, and luxuriate in the view her office afforded. Maybe pop a chocolate in her mouth. "It keeps me on my toes."

Doctor Davis bobbed his head and straightened. "Exactly my point. *We're* good at what *we* do, too. And it's my job and the nurse's job to help you recover, which won't happen if you don't follow our instructions." He leaned on the side rails. "As I've said, you'll need a few easygoing weeks, or you and your body will never be friends again." He patted Catherine's arm. "I'll check on you later. In the meantime, get some rest, and please, think about what I've said."

The next day

CATHERINE BRISTLED at the sight of the lone potted plant sitting on the windowsill. Why couldn't Rusty, her boss, find time to deliver it in person? Hadn't he always considered her his star performer? And why hadn't any of her coworkers called? After all she'd done for them?

Her thoughts were interrupted when a man stepped around the half-opened door to her room. "Miss O'Malley?"

"Yes."

"I'm Detective Rodriguez. If you're feeling up to it, I have a few questions."

"Come in." Catherine pressed a button, raising herself to a sitting position. She watched the way his well-worn suit allowed him to maneuver a heavy chair next to her bed. His slicked-back dark hair matched his eyes, and she noticed his clean and neat fingernails when he pulled a small device from his pocket. "I'll be recording our conversation."

"Okay."

"The nurse made me promise not to wear you down. So, if at any time you need a break, just let me know."

Catherine strained to sit up a little straighter. She gulped a breath and blew it out in short bursts, wincing at the pain in her abdomen.

He leaned forward in his chair and spoke into the recorder. "Detective Rodriguez. Interview with Catherine O'Malley." He laid the device on the table that crossed over her bed. "Okay, let's start with the time of the attack."

She looked up at the ceiling and thought. What time had she left the office? No later than usual. She returned her attention to the detective. "Around nine-thirty."

Rodriguez raised an eyebrow. "That's pretty late for the business district. Why were you on that stretch of Atlantic Avenue at that time of night?"

Catherine ran her hands along the covers, ironing out a line of small wrinkles. "I was on my way home from work."

"Where are you employed?"

She cleared her throat, still sore from intubation. "Fitzpatrick & Associates. It's an advertising firm."

"What do you do there?"

"I'm responsible for some of our largest and most demanding clients. Thus, the late hours."

When he nodded as if he understood, she doubted he even had a clue.

"Is it typical for you to work that late?"

If she volunteered that what she'd been working on could have been accomplished from home, or even the next day, it would elicit a stream of questions she didn't feel like answering.

"Yes."

Rodriguez's gaze traveled to her hand. "Are you married?"

Catherine tucked her hand under the sheet. "No."

"Significant other?"

She shot him a look. "No."

"Is there anyone you can think of who might wish to harm you?"

Catherine shook her head. "No."

"Do you think you can identify the assailant?"

She gave a deep, weighted sigh. "No. He grabbed me from behind and dragged me into an alley. He also wore a ski mask, so the only distinguishing feature I recall are his eyes."

"Well, that's a start." The detective reached into his pocket and pulled out three photos. "Perhaps one of these will help jog your memory."

Catherine shuffled through the first two pictures, then stopped and stared at the third. She grimaced. The man's mismatched eyes captured her attention. One green, one blue. Sure, he was the man who attacked her, she pointed at the last picture with a trembling hand. "That's him. I see his eyes in my sleep."

"The victim has identified suspect 7358." Detective Rodriguez gave Catherine a nod and a knowing look. "He was found a half block from the scene rifling through your purse, blood on his hands, and scratches on his neck. The DNA found under your nails will put the final nail in *his* coffin."

Anxious to be rid of the photos, Catherine handed them back as if they had burst into flames.

Rodriguez turned off the device and slid it into his pocket. "He had two priors and was released from prison less than a month ago after serving time for assault and battery. Thanks to the Massachusetts three-strike law, this will send him away for life. So, you won't have to worry about him anymore." The detective stood. "You'll be hearing from the district attorney for a formal statement. And you may be asked to testify." He handed Catherine his card. "If there's anything else you think might be helpful, please give me a call."

CHAPTER TWO

Minutes after settling into the back seat of a rideshare, Catherine questioned her decision to return to work a week and a half sooner than Doctor Davis recommended. Despite the prescribed Oxy she had popped before she left, each bump along Boston's cobblestone streets caused an increased level of discomfort. She stared out the window to keep from thinking about how drained she felt. The pain raced around her abdomen like a car on the Indianapolis speedway.

Like Ebenezer Scrooge, she, too, had been forced to rethink her past. And like the ghost of Christmas past, hadn't her late mother hinted that Catherine's view of life had been through the wrong prism?

Our choices define us. More to do. Fix what's wrong.

As her ride sat in traffic, Catherine recalled the many nights she'd stayed late at the office to avoid going home to an empty apartment. Those days were over. If nearly losing her life had taught her anything, it was that her time on earth was too short not to live it to the fullest.

When the car pulled in front of the Fitzpatrick & Associates office building, she was so anxious to relieve the cramps gripping her upper abdomen that she needed to restrain herself from opening the door before the car came to a stop.

The driver must've noticed how gingerly she'd settled into the back seat, because he hurried around and offered his hand. He assisted her with a gentle pull out of the car. "Have a good day."

Catherine gave him a smile that came up short. How sad that she couldn't recall the last time she'd had a truly good day. "Thank you."

She looked around at the bustling streets. Like her former self, people were on the move, oblivious to their surroundings, their eyes or ears glued to their phones.

Inside the building with its shiny marble-floored lobby, Catherine made her way toward the bank of elevators. She pushed the button and watched the displayed floor numbers descend. *Hurry up.* Then, as if the elevator had heard her silent plea, the doors slid open. Relief rained down when no one approached. After the doors closed, she grasped the brass bar encircling the elevator to steady herself.

It would just take a few moments to reach her destination, and she needed every one to regain her strength. Floor thirty-five rolled into view. She headed for the Fitzpatrick & Associates backlit sign. *You got this*, she thought.

Catherine took a deep breath, forced a smile into place, and pushed open the door. As she rounded the corner, she called out to her assistant Marge, "I'm back!" Her prior assistant, who she'd adored, had retired two weeks before the mugging, so Catherine hadn't gotten a chance to know Marge before her forced convalescence.

"Catherine, what a surprise," Marge said, a few nervous decibels louder than necessary.

Catherine glanced toward her corner office and the view it offered of Boston Harbor. *What the heck?*

Tom Sinclair, a junior colleague at the firm, sat on the edge of Catherine's desk as if he owned it, talking to her boss, Rusty.

The two men shifted their attention towards her. Tom's eyebrows shot up as he slipped off the desk. The boss grasped Tom's shoulder, tilted his head toward the door, and led the way, with Tom fast on his heels.

"Catherine, how are you?" Tom asked.

"What a surprise," Rusty said, mimicking Marge.

Catherine's heart broke into pieces, when one by one, the sea of familiar faces outside her office turned and looked away. She'd hoped her coworkers would rush to her side and offer a myriad of explanations about why they'd been MIA during her time away.

"Figured my inbox must be overflowing," she said with an air of casualness nowhere close to how she felt.

Rusty nodded again at Tom, and the younger man made a beeline to a nearby smaller office. Then he looked at Catherine. "Of course, we're happy to have you back. But are you sure you're ready?"

She had attempted to camouflage her fading facial bruises with makeup. She knew that even a hint of yellow peeking through would be jarring. Still, this wasn't the greeting she'd expected. She thought for sure he'd bubble over with relief to have her back in the mix. Even insist that he'd have sent the company car for her if he'd known she was returning. After all, wasn't this the man who made her feel guilty when she'd requested earned time off?

Catherine, we need you. We can't get this project done without you!

And she'd always acquiesced. So what had changed?

"Absolutely! I am so ready." Catherine sucked in a breath and lowered herself into her high-backed chair. It felt good to sit. She scanned her office. Photographs of Tom's family peppered her desk, while hers were stacked in a corner of the credenza. She leaned forward and raised an eyebrow. "Is this still my office?"

Rusty paused a little too long. "Of course. We've just been crazy busy since your incident, and Tom graciously agreed to step in and pick up the slack. It made things easier to have him occupy your space, that's all. I must say, you did a great job training him. He slipped right in. What a trooper!"

Incident? Trooper?

Catherine stared at the man she thought she knew, realizing the conversations she'd had with Rusty during her three-week recovery were his way of appeasing her. *We're struggling without you, but please take all the time you need to heal,* he'd said. What a joke. Why hadn't she picked up on that? And Tom had jumped at the opportunity to take over her accounts and move into her office. These new revelations collided with her mother's words, urging Catherine to fix what was wrong in her life. Why had she let her career take over any semblance of a personal life, including the one relationship that meant the world to her?

CHAPTER THREE

A week later

Catherine expected that over time, her days at the office would become manageable, but the opposite had proven true. Her inability to focus (due to overwhelming fatigue) and her numerous bathroom visits (thanks to the gallons of coffee she consumed in an attempt to alleviate it) meant she accomplished only seventy-five percent of what she once did with ease. So, when Marge marched into her office with yet another stack of documents for her to review, Catherine inwardly winced.

Marge pulled a folder from yesterday's unfinished mound and placed it in front of her. "Rusty wants your comments on the Chug-a-Lug contract as soon as possible."

"Okay, I'll get right on it as soon as I get some coffee."

Did Marge just roll her eyes? she thought to herself.

"I'd get it for you, but it'll make me late for the staff meeting," Marge said, and headed for the door.

"Staff meeting? It's not on my calendar."

But Marge was gone.

Catherine threw down her pen and made her way to the conference room.

The chatter inside the wood-paneled room that smelled of lemon polish quieted when she walked in, and she took her usual seat catty-corner from Rusty.

"Good morning," she said, refusing to let the silence intimidate her.

Tom, who Catherine had taken under her wing and taught the advertising ropes, nodded from across the table. "I thought you'd be reviewing the CAL contract." He tapped his finger on the face of his watch. "I need it in less than an hour. I'm flying out this afternoon to present it."

Catherine fought an urge to lunge across the table and wipe the smirk off his face. How on earth could she have so misjudged his character and his loyalty to her? She turned and glared down the table at her assistant. "Unfortunately, Marge forgot to mention that."

Rusty cleared his throat. "It's not Marge's job to remind you of important deadlines. You, more than anyone, should be aware of the importance of due dates. After all, you negotiated the CAL contract last." He then removed his glasses and laid them on the table. "Tom should've already had it so he'd have time to review it and make whatever necessary changes he sees fit."

He couldn't be serious. Other than F&A's attorneys, no one had ever changed her suggested wording. And now Tom, a subordinate, had permission to edit her work?

Rusty dipped his chin and lowered his voice as if the rest of the room couldn't hear him. "Look, Catherine, perhaps you returned too quickly, so if all this is too much for you, then maybe..."

Her face grew hot, and her stomach slipped into a knot. How *dare* he belittle her in front of everyone. Had he forgotten all that she'd accomplished for this company? The many times she'd made him look good? He couldn't deny the enormous role she'd played in the mega bonuses he'd received. And this was her thanks? Oh no. Not today. Not tomorrow. Not ever! Catherine pushed back her chair and stood.

Her pulse raced as she placed the palms of her hands on the table for support. This was what her mother meant.

She scowled at Tom. "My office will be yours again by the end of the day. However, I suggest you keep in mind your wife and children, because I promise you, Rusty won't give them a second thought. He'll do his best to keep you from enjoying what's truly important. He'll balk at the mention of you attending school plays or anything else that matters. Vacations will never be convenient. And God forbid someone attacks you after you leave here one night, because you stayed late to help a coworker. I promise you, not one of these people—" she glanced at each person seated at the table—"will be there for you. And if you're fortunate enough to return after a prolonged absence, you can rest assured, there will be another hungry *you*, just waiting to take your place."

Everyone appeared frozen in place, as if someone had hit a pause button.

Catherine pushed her chair against the table, walked to the door, turned, and swept her hand to encompass the room. "Hard to believe I ever saw this part of my world, and all of you, as worthy of my dedication." She shook her head. "What a sad and unfortunate mistake that was."

FIGHTING BACK TEARS, Catherine closed the door to her office, slid into her burgundy leather chair, and swiveled around to face the expansive window that afforded a spectacular view.

The morning fog had lifted, and the city stretched before her like a king's ransom. Oh, how she'd enjoyed her roost far above the hustle and bustle of the city. She recalled times when the city lights had so captivated her that she'd lost all sense of time, only to arrive home to find a note from Jack saying he'd waited as long as he could.

Her vision blurred when the scene in the conference room replayed in her mind. How could she have let this job consume her, and in the process, let Jack go? How could she have allowed it to be everything, when, as it turned out, it was less than nothing?

Catherine swung her chair around to face her desk. If she needed to have the CAL contract ready for Tom, she'd better corral her thoughts and get down to business. Not that she gave a hoot that he wouldn't have what he needed for his trip, but she wouldn't give her colleagues, including Rusty, the opportunity to tarnish her name by blaming her for Tom's lack of preparedness.

Catherine eyed the fat stack of folders alongside the CAL contract and vowed to finish what was on her desk before she left. So she pushed up her sleeves and plowed through the agreement. The only thing that thwarted her progress were the restroom visits and the much-needed jolts of caffeine. When it was finished, she called Marge to deliver it to Tom. It soon became evident that other than the CAL contract, the remaining pile of documents was nothing more than busywork. Something a junior colleague, like Tom, could've handled.

Rusty's message couldn't be any clearer than if he'd written it on a chalkboard. She was yesterdays' news as far as he was concerned. Catherine choked up thinking about how he'd treated her. How he'd used her *incident*, as he'd referred to her near-fatal attack, to replace her with someone whose salary was sure to be a fraction of hers. And in the process, make himself look good by increasing the company's bottom line. She stood up, glanced around the office she'd come to adore, stuffed a few personal items in a box, and carried her belongings out the door.

CHAPTER FOUR

After leaving F&A, Catherine struggled with how to right her life. Should she look for another job in Boston? Move elsewhere? Thinking about it, she determined that landing a position like the one she'd left behind would be more of the same. She needed to break free. Make a fresh start. Maybe start her own business, a long-held dream. But where should she go? That was the elusive answer to her question.

Her mind wandered back to Jack. She remembered the many times he'd borrowed his friend Rick's plane to fly them to Nantucket. Could Nantucket, the place where he'd summered at his grandparents' house on the outskirts of town be the answer? Would this be starting over, or would she be embarking on another disaster? And there was the fact that Jack often visited when his schedule allowed. What would happen if she ran into him? Would he still have feelings for her? Would he be able to accept that she'd never stopped loving him?

Her thoughts wandered to other times he'd talked about the tiny island, the grandparents he adored, and the memories he'd collected at their seaside cottage. She'd gotten caught up in his feelings and fell in love with the island, too. But had she really? Was it the island, or Jack?

To start over, she'd convinced herself she'd have to exorcise her thoughts of what could have been, and stare down the ghosts that still haunted her. Perhaps, at the same time, she'd start a new business and launch a new life.

~

September, a month later

CATHERINE LEANED against the Hy-Line ferry's railing. Her shoulder-length auburn hair blew gently in the breeze as the ferry sidled Nantucket's Straight Wharf. She shielded her eyes from the sun and scanned the crowd lining the dock, waving at the arriving passengers. She could smell saltwater and Rosa rugosa, the bountiful island flower that filled the air.

Although Jack's grandparents had always invited them to stay in their home, she and Jack had always maintained a monthly standing reservation at the Sunny Skies Bed and Breakfast on Union Street. The owners always treated them like family. And after all she'd been through, feeling like she mattered to someone would be a welcome change. So, she'd booked a month at the inn and tried not to second-guess her decision.

She gathered up her rollaway bag, made her way onto the ramp leading to the dock, and began her trek. The cobblestone street she'd once considered quaint now felt like an obstacle course, thanks to her achiness and rolling bag. After several stops along the way, Catherine righted her suitcase and bumped it up the five Quaker-style friend-ship stairs of the inn.

At the top, she imagined giving herself a shoulder pat. The pause allowed tugging skin around her abdominal incision a moment to ease while she gazed at the surroundings. Nothing much had changed. Sailboats and pleasure craft bobbed like apples in a bucket. The briny air, along with the view, brought to mind vivid memories. Tears stung her eyes when she thought of the night Jack arranged for a private sunset sail around the island. The streaks of purple and pink that tinged the sky had provided the perfect backdrop for a romantic evening. The memories buoyed her, like the lifejacket he'd insisted she wear, even though she'd assured him she was an accomplished swimmer.

Perhaps the man yielding the knife had done her a favor. If not for him, she wouldn't have heard her mother direct her to fix what was wrong and see her life through a new set of lenses.

Catherine squared her shoulders and reached for the doorknob. When her phone rang, she pulled it from her purse. "Rusty" displayed across the screen. What did he want? And whatever it was, after the way he'd treated her, the chance that she'd accommodate him was less than zero. She wrestled with what to do. Before the call slipped into voicemail, she answered. "Yes?"

"Catherine." He sounded relieved. "How are you?"

"Rusty, we both know you couldn't care less about my well-being, so why are you bothering me?"

A beat of silence. Then another.

"Let's just say I've seen the error of my ways." He lowered his voice, as if confiding a secret. "Let me buy you lunch and apologize in person."

Catherine leaned against the railing. "I'm not interested in an apology. Your actions during my recovery and return to the office told me everything I need to know. More than any insincere words you might throw my way now."

"Catherine, you know how life is in our business. We have to keep moving. Slowing down isn't an option."

"I almost died," she said through clenched teeth. If she thought a passerby wouldn't hear her, she'd let a few expletives fly. "Sometimes we *have* to slow down. I didn't understand that before, and for your sake, I hope you never have to learn that lesson the way I did. Now excuse me. I have to go."

"A raise. A promotion. Anything you want. You name it."

Catherine exhaled. "What I want is for you to leave me alone."

"Lunch is all I ask."

"I'm out of town."

"Permanently?" The question came in a strained voice, almost as if someone had their hands around his neck.

"I don't see why my location should concern you. It made no difference when I was nearby and needed assistance in the worse possible way."

"But—"

She disconnected the call, tossed the phone into her oversized purse, and turned the doorknob. The wooden door's familiar squeak comforted her as she stepped inside. The interior's warmth transported her to happier times and banished the anger evoked by the call.

The walls, once a rose color, were now soft yellow. Other than that, not much had changed. Here too, time had stood still. The rich mahogany front desk where she and Jack had so often registered still sat nestled under the curved staircase. The wood-burning fireplace in the parlor that ran the length of its far-left wall beckoned.

"Marry me," she heard Jack say, as if he were here now, rather than on that chilly November day, long ago. "You can choose the names of our first two children, but I draw the line at Prince or Madonna."

She placed a hand to her face as a tear streaked her cheek. She'd given up so much for so little. If only she could turn back time.

"Catherine?" a woman said.

Helen and Bill, the longtime proprietors of Sunny Skies, had slipped in while Catherine walked down memory lane.

"Oh my goodness, Bill, Catherine's here!" Helen said, her hands covering her cheeks.

"Helen. Bill." Catherine gave them each a hug. "So good to see you."

"I have to say we were beyond excited when we saw your online reservation," Helen said. "What's it been, three years?"

Catherine followed them to the registration desk, dug in her purse, and pulled out her credit card. "Just about."

"Where's that handsome boyfriend of yours? Still flying the friendly skies?"

"I wouldn't know." Catherine's cheeks flushed. "We aren't together anymore."

Helen lowered her eyes and ran the card through the machine.

When she lifted her gaze, her cornflower blue eyes, always so expressive, showed a sadness Catherine hadn't expected.

"I'm so sorry. I always imagined you two together, raising a family." Helen shook her head. "You might remember how I enjoy happy endings. When things don't work out," she continued, touching the area of her heart, "it kind of hurts in here."

Bill wrapped his arms around his wife's shoulders. "There, there, honey. Just because the ending isn't what you had in mind doesn't mean Catherine hasn't had a better one."

Helen seemed downhearted enough, so now was not the time for Catherine to point out Bill's misconception. Anyway, she was not interested in rehashing her breakup with Jack. At least, not while the memories that danced in her head were far sweeter than she could have imagined.

"Did you come over on the ferry, or did you fly in?" Bill asked, changing the subject.

"Ferry."

"You should have let us know. Bill would've picked you up." Helen handed Catherine back her credit card. "I'm sure maneuvering the streets with your suitcase was no easy feat. But then again, you've always been a determined sort."

"Here." Bill grabbed her suitcase. "Let me haul this upstairs for you." He checked the key Helen handed him. "You're on the second floor, first room on the right. You may recall, all the rooms on that side of the house have a spectacular view of the garden and harbor. Sound good?"

Catherine gave a thumbs-up.

"Okay, then. Up we go."

She followed Bill slowly up the stairs, and he unlocked the door. Then he placed her suitcase on a padded bench at the foot of the bed. "Can I get you anything?"

Her gaze settled on the plush comfy bed. "Not that I can think of."

"We serve lunch until two. And dinner is at five-thirty."

"I won't make lunch. I plan to unpack, read a little, and maybe take a nap."

"Sounds like a plan," he said, and quietly closed the door behind him.

Catherine laid back on the inviting four-poster bed covered with a fluffy white duvet and spread her arms out like a snow angel. She closed her eyes and was whisked away to the first night she and Jack had spent there in adjoining rooms one floor above.

After he had unpacked, and given her a kiss that left her wanting, he'd headed downstairs to commandeer a table in the garden and order them each a glass of wine.

The intensity of the memory stirred the same butterflies that had set up camp in the pit of her stomach that very night.

Catherine opened her eyes, sat up, and ran a hand over one of the four plump pillows encased in soft percale and trimmed with eyelit. Tears tumbled down her cheeks.

Why had she let Jack slip away?

She got up and went to the window, kneeled on the window seat, and pulled back the French lace curtains. She looked down at the garden, where, weather permitting, she and Jack had spent countless hours discussing their future. When she opened the window now, the scent of the Rosa rugosa clinging to a nearby trellis reminded her of the sweet life she'd once enjoyed.

She turned and admired the room she'd call home for the next month. A beveled glass vase on the dresser held a bouquet of lavender and pale-green hydrangeas, the last of the season, plucked out of the Sunny Skies garden earlier that day. How nice it would be to curl up with a book in the plush, navy-blue armchair with a matching footstool tucked in a corner. She ran her hand along the cream-colored dresser opposite the bed with a flat-screen TV perched above.

Inside the bathroom, vanilla-scented candles lined a shelf above the tub, similar to those she'd lit years earlier. Catherine leaned her head against the doorframe and smiled when she recalled soaking in a similar antique claw-foot vessel amid a mountain of bubbles. After, she'd wrapped herself in a soft, waffle-design bathrobe like the one now hanging from a hook.

She pressed her lips together and nodded. Her decision to stay at

Sunny Skies felt right. She unpacked her suitcase and then grabbed an apple from a bowl of fresh fruit on the dresser. After taking a bite, she picked up a walking map of downtown and climbed onto the bed. Propped up against the fat pillows, she glanced at her phone and saw a voicemail notification from Rusty. What was wrong with him? Hadn't she made herself clear? She clicked on the message.

Rusty's booming voice invaded the sanctity of her room. "Catherine, call me." He paused. "Please."

She rolled her eyes and contemplated whether she should turn off the phone for the duration of her trip. Rusty wasn't known to give up easily when he wanted something.

CHAPTER FIVE

The next morning

Catherine's mouth dropped open at the cornucopia of breakfast items Helen had assembled in the dining room. Warming trays along with plates and silverware lined one sideboard. On another, carafes of coffee and hot water for a large selection of teas sat alongside assorted muffins and a variety of bread slices. There were also Danishes and an assortment of jams Catherine assumed were homemade by Helen.

She grabbed a plate and heaped on a sizable portion of fluffy scrambled eggs, then hovered the tongs over the crisp bacon. After a few lobs of mental tennis, she decided to indulge and dropped two strips on her plate, then scooped up a third and forced herself to move along. Before taking her plate and a mug of decadent-smelling coffee to the table, she reached for a cranberry and walnut muffin.

Helen emerged from the kitchen, wiping her hands on her apron. "Good morning. We missed you last night at dinner."

"After my nap, I awoke reinvigorated. So, I decided to take a walk and check out downtown. Later, when I couldn't stand listening to my stomach complain any longer, I stopped for a slice of pizza, sat on a bench, and people-watched while I ate." Catherine scooped up a forkful of scrambled eggs. "Oh, my goodness, Helen." She patted her lips with her napkin. "I'd forgotten how delicious your eggs are."

Helen smiled. "Why, thank you. The secret's in the egg whites." She pulled out a chair. "Mind if I join you while you eat? I could use a break after the rush of guests this morning. And besides, I'd like to catch up."

"Please." Catherine motioned to a nearby chair. "I'd love the company."

"So, tell me, how did you arrange for us to enjoy your company for an entire month? As I recall, you could hardly squeak out a weekend stay, years ago."

Catherine fiddled with her fork, not sure how much to confide. She trusted the older woman, but she'd rather not endure a myriad of questions and the embarrassment of Helen learning how empty her life had become. "I needed a break."

Helen bobbed her head. "Good for you. Respites are necessary."

"It's more than a respite." Catherine slumped, expelling a breath. "I've resigned."

Helen clasped her hands on the table and leaned toward her. "Well, that's a surprise."

Catherine sat up straight. "I've learned that sometimes, we have to step back, slow down, and reassess."

"So true, but remembering how much your career meant to you, I can't help but wonder what brought about this change of heart. Was it your breakup with Jack?"

"Not entirely. It's a long story."

Helen reached over and covered Catherine's hand with her own. "We don't serve lunch on weekends, so as long as you don't mind keeping me company in the kitchen while I clean up from breakfast, I'd love to hear it."

Catherine teetered on the edge of rejecting Helen's offer. But over the last few months, she was the first person who'd offered to listen to her story. Besides, Helen had never been judgmental. Catherine followed her into the kitchen. "If you're sure, I could use a friendly ear."

∽

DESPITE COMMERCIAL-GRADE APPLIANCES and granite counter updates, Helen's kitchen didn't match what Catherine considered restaurant-grade. A ruffled valance of green gingham hung over the window above the farmhouse-white porcelain sink. Like the ones in the foyer, the walls were a pale yellow, and along with the white wooden cabinets, they helped to brighten the space. "This is so homey," Catherine said. "I'm reminded of making Irish soda bread with my granny."

"I like it." Helen chuckled. "And with as much time as I spend here, that's important." "Don't get me wrong; I'd be lying if I said I don't love every minute of it." She pointed to the round rustic wooden table in the middle of the room where Catherine suspected Helen and Bill shared their meals. "Please have a seat. Thanks for gathering up your plate and such. It wasn't necessary, but I do appreciate it. As much as I hate to admit it, I find myself slowing down." She finished loading the two stainless steel dishwashers and turned them on. "I'm about to pour myself a cup of tea, will you join me?"

"Sounds good."

Helen placed a steaming mug of brewed green tea spiked with lemon and ginger in front of Catherine. Then she pulled out the chair opposite her and sat down. "So, what's this about resigning from your job?"

Catherine lifted her mug, blew on the liquid, took a sip of the aromatic blend, and swallowed. "It all started when a man mugged me on my way home from work one night."

Helen reached over and placed her hand on Catherine's forearm. "Oh my, were you hurt?"

"Yes. He stabbed and beat me. My heart stopped in the ambulance, and they performed CPR. I almost bled to death and underwent surgery to repair damage to my liver."

"Goodness gracious, you're lucky to be alive." Helen's face was etched with concern. "It must still be very traumatic."

Catherine sighed. "It's hard. What's made it worse, I've had no one to talk to about it."

"What about your mother? As I recall, you two were *very* close."

Catherine's eyes moistened. "She passed away two years ago, right after Jack and I broke up. It was very sudden."

"Heart?"

Catherine nodded. "She never knew she had a heart condition, and certainly no indication of one that would take her life."

"I'm so sorry for your loss."

"Thank you," Catherine murmured. "I miss her every day."

Helen dipped her chin. "When were you attacked?"

"A few months ago. It truly changed my outlook. Things that seemed important before the mugging no longer held that distinction."

Helen cocked her head to the side, her voice laced with compassion. "Do you want to talk about it?"

Did she? Should she plunge into full disclosure? Would Helen think she was crazy if she mentioned hearing her mother's voice?

"As I said, my heart stopped in the ambulance, and I required CPR."

Helen leaned back in her chair. "How scary to have to go through that alone." Her face brightened. "But look at you now. The picture of health. You must've had an angel watching over you."

Catherine recalled her nurse saying the same thing. She lowered her voice, as if imparting a secret. "I saw the light that some people mention. My mother said it wasn't my time."

Helen made the sign of the cross. "I've heard of that but have never known anyone who experienced it." She nodded her head. "That's what triggered your decision to leave your job, wasn't it?"

Catherine gazed at the sun streaming through the window. "Yes. She also said that our choices define us. It made me take stock, and I soon realized I should never have allowed my career to consume me. So, I decided to take her advice and fix what was wrong."

"Boy, oh, boy. Talk about an eye-opener." Helen leaned in. "You've been given a second chance. Not many people can say that. Do you have any idea what you're going to do with it?"

"That's why I'm here. With all the time Jack and I spent on-island, I figured where better to start over? I'm hopeful a month will give me enough time to sketch out my future."

"Speaking of Jack, may I ask if you've heard from him?"

Catherine closed her eyes and shook her head. Then she opened them and locked them on the older woman's eyes. "No. I've toyed with calling him, but I haven't worked up the nerve." She paused. "Have you heard from him? I know how much he enjoyed staying here."

Catherine held her breath. Did she really want to know? What if Helen launched into a dissertation about Jack's new life?

"Indirectly. A friend of his stayed here for a weekend a year or so ago. Jack referred him. He was a nice man. I think his name was Rick."

Catherine exhaled, both relieved and disappointed. "Rick's a close friend and a fellow pilot. Jack borrowed his plane several times to fly us here when we visited his grandparents." She stirred her tea. "I've considered trying to see them while I'm here, but I don't know if I'm ready. I always liked them, so part of me wants to try. Then again, I'm scared that I'll find out that Jack has moved on."

"I remember the Chandlers. Unfortunately, both passed away within six months of one another about a year ago."

Catherine squeezed her eyes shut. "Oh, that's too bad. I bet Jack was devastated. He loved them so."

She put her cup down. If she didn't steer the conversation in a new direction, her emotions were bound to surface. "To answer your earlier question about what I might do, I've always dreamed of owning a store. It may be a pipe dream, especially here, where I suspect rents are outrageous, but it's an ideal location for the type of merchandise I'd carry."

Helen peered at her over the rim of her cup. "And what would that be?"

Enthusiasm welled up in Catherine, a sensation she hadn't experienced in a long time. "I've always had a penchant for all things nautical. During my teens, I collected miniature lighthouses and attached all kinds of romantic notions to them. Guiding lights bringing sailors home to their waiting families, that sort of thing."

"So, you'd have yourself a lighthouse store?"

"No. I'd carry an eclectic mix of high-end collectibles, antiques, anything that hints of the sea."

Helen sat back, her hand to her chin as if deep in thought, then pushed back her chair and stood. "Hold tight to your dream. You never know what can happen in a place as magical as Nantucket. And for what it's worth, consider calling Jack. Who knows, you might be surprised."

Later that day

AMAZED AT HOW liberating it was to confide in Helen, Catherine felt lighter. The near-constant tightness in her shoulders, relaxed. Despite the sadness of learning about the Chandlers' passing, Catherine headed downtown to check out the stores with a renewed sense of purpose.

She marveled at the treetop canopies lining Main Street that would soon morph into vibrant autumn hues. A fall chill filled the air. Unlike the handful of shoppers now peering into windows, carrying bags filled with newfound treasures, a few weeks earlier, summer crowds would've crammed the sidewalks.

After poking in and out of stores for several hours, Catherine located an empty bench and sat down. Across the street, a middle-aged woman stood outside Nantucket Realty, chatting with a younger, dark-haired bearded man. She laughed, and his hand rested on her shoulder. Then Catherine's phone rang, disrupting her thoughts. She pulled it from her purse and eyed the display. *Rusty*. She should've known he'd try again when she didn't return his call.

"Why do you keep calling?"

"I want to make things right," he said. "If it makes you feel any better, I acted like an idiot. Treated you like crap. I see that now."

Catherine rolled her eyes. "Look, Rusty, you've apologized. So let's leave it at that."

"I understand where you're coming from—"

"Oh no, you don't," Catherine's voice rose, and people nearby, including the couple across the narrow street, turned to look in her direction. She lowered her voice. "I dedicated myself to F&A. Developed a client list longer than other senior executive's twice my age. Raked in more money for the company than you or anyone dreamed possible, and you didn't have the *common decency* to check on me while I fought for my life." She drew in a deep breath. She would not allow him to burst her mood and define her day. "Now I have to go."

"Catherine, wait. Don't hang up. Hear me out. Please."

"Make it quick. I'm busy," she lied.

"Let me know when you're back in town, and I'll clear my calendar so we can meet."

Her voice rose again. "Why on earth would I do that? What could you possibly have to say that you can't tell me now?"

He let out a long stream of air. "Okay, look." His voice sounded strained. "This isn't how I wanted this to play out, but since I can't convince you otherwise, you leave me no choice."

Catherine leaned back against the bench. "Two minutes."

"Your clients are up in arms. They can't stand dealing with Tom."

Catherine didn't try to stifle her laugh. She'd wondered how long it would take them to see through Tom. That bit of knowledge alone made the call from Rusty worthwhile. "And why should I care?"

"Because caring is what you do. It's who you are. It sets you apart from the others. I see that now, and that's what made you so successful."

"Thanks for the reminder," Catherine said, her voice laced with sarcasm. "Too bad it took you so long to realize it."

"You have every right to be upset. Like I said, I was a jerk."

She was really starting to enjoy this. "Uh-huh."

Rusty paused. "I *need* you to come back. I'll make it worth your while. You'll be named partner. You worked hard enough. You deserve it."

"You're right. I did. But it's too late. I'm moving to Nantucket and plan to open a retail establishment."

She wondered what had prompted her to say that.

"You can't be serious. A store? Come on, Catherine. You can't possibly expect me to believe that."

She threw back her head and laughed. "Do you think I care what you believe?"

"Something like that won't keep your mind engaged. You'll be bored in no time. Be sensible. Please, at least consider my offer."

Sensible? Who did he think he was?

"There's nothing to consider."

Based on the deafening silence, so unlike Rusty, Catherine suspected he knew that once again, he'd bungled things.

"I'm hanging up. Oh, and Rusty?"

"Yes?" he replied, his voice ripe with optimism.

"Just to be clear, don't call me again."

CHAPTER SIX

Catherine's body sent her signals that it needed a nap after she'd traipsed in and out of stores for the past five hours. Rusty's call had only added to her need to escape the streets. What if he was right that a retail establishment wouldn't challenge her? No. It didn't matter what he thought. She hadn't come across one vacant store all afternoon, however. Maybe owning a store *was* a pipe dream. Taking him up on his offer would be easy, considering his revelation that the clients wanted her back. That alone would ensure he wouldn't dare mistreat her again. She'd be in a position of power, something she'd never given a thought to in the past. Now that she saw Rusty for what he truly was, it would be a significant coup.

She climbed the stairs to the inn and pushed open the door.

"I'm so glad you're back." Helen rushed over from the front desk. "I would've called, but I didn't want to bother you."

For a strange reason, Catherine's mind made a quantum leap to thoughts of Jack. Might Helen have done some sleuthing and found out that he'd been living at his grandparents' house? "What's going on?" Catherine silently prayed that she'd hear "Jack" tumble from Helen's lips.

"I'm so excited I could burst." Helen took hold of her hand. "Come sit with me in the parlor."

Catherine had looked forward to heading upstairs and burrowing into the soft, inviting bed. But Helen couldn't contain herself, and now her excitement had sparked curiosity in Catherine.

"I'm a big believer that things happen for a reason," Helen said when they settled onto the couch.

Maybe she *had* found out something about Jack. Catherine leaned forward. "Uh, yeah. Me, too."

"I'm sorry." Helen took a deep breath and exhaled to slow herself down. "Let me start over." She paused, gathering her thoughts. "There's a store on Main Street called Special Treasures."

Catherine forced a pleasant expression of maintained interest onto her face. So much for news about Jack. "Yes, I saw it today. It's lovely."

"Well... Linda, the owner, and I are friends." Helen's eyes twinkled. "We met for lunch today while her husband, Hal, handled the store. She'd been conflicted in recent weeks and wanted to share some news."

"O-k-a-y," Catherine said.

"When her only child and her family relocated from Maine to Chicago, Linda was lost. So, she and her husband decided to pull up stakes, too, went in search of something new, and landed here."

"I don't mean to be rude, but how does this affect me?"

Helen's face lit up. "They're moving back to Maine, and Linda plans to sublease the store! Although I didn't say anything about your hopes of opening one, I think the location would be ideal."

Catherine sat up straighter. Thoughts whirled in her mind. "It's situated right in the heart of things."

"It is, but it gets better. Upstairs is a furnished studio apartment, currently used for storage. Linda said it could easily accommodate a single person or even a couple."

Catherine went from being half-dead on her feet to wanting to jog back into town and check out the store with fresh eyes. But reality moved in and shoved aside her enthusiasm. "That sounds wonderful, but that location, not to mention the upstairs apartment, is outside anything I can afford."

"That's what I thought, too, but Linda's willing to take a loss and reduce the rent for the right occupant. You see, she too, moved here to realize her retail dream. Linda always wanted a store that sold dolls of all kinds, and now that she does, and the store has been wildly successful, she'd like someone who'll match her original intent and keep the space flourishing."

Catherine's enthusiasm deflated like a leaky balloon. "I'm not interested in selling dolls."

"She understands not everyone will want to maintain her merchandise, so if the renter isn't interested, she said she'll sell off her inventory. It's about handing the space off for the remainder of the lease to someone who'll want to make their dream come true, much like she did."

AFTER CALLING LINDA, Catherine learned that Tina Benton at Nantucket Realty represented her. Catherine then dialed the realtor and arranged to meet her at Special Treasures.

Along the way, she took note of the handcrafted signage gently swinging in the breeze over storefront doors. She couldn't help but envision what her sign might look like. A centered lighthouse surrounded by a curling blue wave etched with sea spray, and above, the name printed in an arched design.

Since she was early for her meeting, Catherine checked out display windows that captivated her. What was it, besides their merchandise, that set apart the ones that had more traffic? All stores featured high-end inventory nestled among seasonal bursts of color. She made a mental list of store windows she might wish to emulate from a design standpoint. When she passed the local newspaper office, her thoughts jumped to what came naturally—advertising. By the time she approached Special Treasures, her excitement had peaked.

From across the street, she studied the building that might

someday house her dream and the place she'd call home. She crossed the road. The store next door, the Double Scoop, a 1950s-era themed ice cream parlor, was lined with round metal stools covered in red vinyl material, cozied up to a long red-and-white speckled Formica counter. The young man behind it wore a white cloth apron tied in the front, and on his head sat a paper triangle hat.

How nice to have a quaint store as a neighbor, she thought. If an ice cream shop could be successful, she should be able to make her store a success, too. And maybe down the road she and the owner of the Double Scoop could come up with a reciprocal agreement to throw business to each other.

She crossed the street and peered into the Special Treasures window display. Dolls appeared so real that Catherine couldn't believe they weren't breathing. One baby doll, so lifelike, that if she didn't know better, she'd swear it slept soundly inside the antique buggy displayed in the middle of the faux front porch.

A bell dinged overhead when Catherine opened the heavy door to go inside. The interior mimicked a room in a Victorian house. A side window featured a lace curtain. Shabby chic bedroom chests and bureaus acted as display cases. Their drawers pulled open to showcase an assortment of doll clothes and other infant necessities. A white chair rail circled the space, and perched above were floating shelves with merchandise that could be seen but not touched.

An older woman who Catherine assumed was Linda was assisting a customer. She watched her slide a step stool into place and carefully hand down a baby doll from the top shelf. The customer admired it from several angles and nodded her head in approval. A moment later, the cash register's digital readout indicated a sale of over five hundred dollars. Catherine was both shocked and pleased. Five hundred dollars for a doll? Must be a collectible or antique. She smiled. The price point boded well for what she had in mind.

The sound of approaching footsteps broke her concentration and suddenly transported her back to the night of the attack when the same *click-click-click* indicated something wasn't right. She took a deep breath now, calmed her racing heart, and clenched her fists.

Breathe. This is Nantucket, Catherine told herself. She turned to see a middle-aged woman walking toward her. She let out a breath and narrowed her eyes. The woman looked familiar. But how was that possible? Had they met during a past visit with Jack?

The woman smiled widely and held out her hand. "Catherine? Tina Benton."

Catherine extended her hand and remembered that she was the woman she'd seen the day before with the handsome younger man. "Tina, so nice to meet you."

"Likewise."

The warmth of the space ignited Catherine's imagination. She envisioned how she'd reimagine the rectangular area. She'd fill it with merchandise steeped in history, like miniatures of old-world sailing ships and nautical antiques. When she spotted a wooden side table at the back of the store, home to coffee and hot chocolate and a platter of cookies, she decided to copy the idea.

After the customer left, Tina walked over and hugged Linda. "Have you settled into your decision?"

"It's been tough, but knowing you'll help me in my search for someone to take over has lifted the burden of worry about rental details."

Tina smiled and patted Linda's shoulder. Then she glanced toward Catherine. "Meet Catherine O'Malley. She's looking to move to our tiny slice of heaven and follow her dream."

"Sounds like me."

Tina winked. "Exactly what I was thinking."

Catherine and Linda shook hands. Then the older woman made a gesture that took in the store. "Welcome to *my* dream. I never imagined abandoning it so soon." Linda sighed. "In hindsight, Hal and I made too hasty a move. We'd lived all our lives in Maine and thought this would be a nice change. Don't get me wrong; we love it here, but we miss our friends and family more than we ever expected." Her welled with tears." When I'm alone with my thoughts, I feel isolated and lonely."

Catherine understood only too well how she felt. Unlike Linda, though, she hadn't left much behind. "You have a beautiful store. Such lovely merchandise."

Linda pulled a tissue from her pocket and wiped away the tears. "I hope if you decide to assume my lease, you'll consider purchasing my display cases, cash register, things I'll have no use for."

"You're not planning to open another shop in Maine?"

Linda half-chuckled. "Oh my, no. My daughter and her family have returned from Chicago, and coupled with my friends, I'll be very busy."

After Catherine walked the store with Tina, she asked, "Can we see the upstairs?"

"Of course. It's mostly storage, but it'll be cleared out and refreshed for the new renter."

Once up there, Catherine saw beyond the clutter, envisioning a space she'd transform into a cozy nest. She poked around the stacked boxes. Although modest, the kitchen featured an apartment-sized stainless-steel refrigerator, a compact four-burner stove with oven, and overhead cabinets. A microwave and coffee maker consumed most of the small granite countertop. Tucked in a corner outside the kitchen was a bistro table with three chairs. The walled-off bathroom contained a narrow stall shower, sink, and toilet, all almost new-looking. The rest of the living space housed a couch, which, when Catherine lifted one of the cushions, unleashed the secret that it was a sleeper. An end table with a shaded lamp stood next to the sofa, and a mounted flat-screen TV occupied the opposite wall. The other end of the room housed a full-size bed and dresser.

With a fresh coat of paint and a few personal touches, Catherine was sure she could call it home for a while. "Will the furnishings stay?"

"Yes, everything's included." Tina laughed. "Except for the clutter, of course."

Catherine gave a definitive nod. "How much is the rent? And how many months remain on the original lease?"

Tina showed her the sub-lease agreement.

Catherine could hardly contain her excitement. The rent, considering it included a living space, although it was not cheap, was actually quite a bargain. So much so that she thought there must be some sort of catch. And the remaining eighteen months fit with her timeline.

Catherine pointed to the spot reflecting the rent. "This seems quite reasonable. My friend Helen mentioned that Linda is willing to take a loss, so I assume this reflects her adjustment. I'm concerned about what it will rise to after the end of the term."

"Linda can tell you what her current rent is. I know that the owner's always been fair when it comes to renewal. I wouldn't expect it to be much more than what she's paying now. Let's go downstairs, and she can fill you in."

"So, what'd you think?" Linda asked when the two women returned.

Tina smiled. "As I've told you it would, the rent has spawned a question."

Linda nodded. "I understand that it's lower than what you might expect. That's because I've added a bit of a sweetener. If the owner raises the rent at the end of the lease, rest assured it won't be outrageous. But keep in mind that the amount I'm supplementing will disappear."

"If you don't mind me asking, what are you paying?"

Linda told her, and Catherine rolled it around in her mind. Would she be able to afford it after the lease term? Then again, could she even afford the lowered rent? "Is the owner in agreement with what you're proposing?"

"Yes, I've agreed to make him whole for the rest of the term." Linda glanced around the store. "In case you're wondering why I've added an incentive, it's because the last thing I want is to walk away, not knowing how long it'll take to rent, especially after it housed a hobby of mine and gave life to my fantasy. Truthfully, I never expected it to provide a livelihood, but it's turned into a rousing success. What's made it harder for me to walk away from should give you added assurance that you, too, can be successful. My decision to leave has everything to do with my desire to get back to friends and family, and nothing to do with the financial aspects of the business or this location." She glanced at Tina. "And now that I've come to terms with it, I don't want the burden of an unrented space weighing on me. And if I'm fortunate enough to turn it over to someone who wants to make a dream of theirs a reality, much like I did, then it will all be worth it."

Catherine restrained herself from bouncing up and down. She wanted to reach out and hug Linda. Instead, she shook her hand. "Well then, I'd say we have a deal." Happy tears and a huge smile radiated her happiness. "If my enterprise doesn't work out, at least I'll have given it a try."

CHAPTER SEVEN

One week later

*E*ver since Catherine had given in to her impulse and signed the lease on the Main Street retail space, her sleep had turned erratic. Her emotions shifted like the San Andreas fault line. Whenever excitement crept in, fear and worry, nudged it aside. What had she been thinking when she'd signed the lease? Her store wouldn't open until after the last of the summer tourists abandoned the island. Other than the swell of tourists who returned for *Christmas Stroll* for a few days in winter, she'd be totally dependent on locals to jumpstart her venture. And if that wasn't bad enough, there was the issue of what to name the place. Night after night, she'd stared at the ceiling for hours, wracking her brain to come up with something.

"Why is dreaming up a name so difficult?" she mumbled as she stepped into a pair of slacks and pulled a long-sleeved top over her head. Advertising and creating something catchy were what she did best. Wasn't it?

She ran a brush through her hair, stuffed her room key in her pocket, and stomped down the stairs. A jolt of caffeine and a shot of protein would help clear the remaining sleepy cobwebs from her mind. But as she descended the last of the stairs, it hit her that there was little chance the dining room would be empty at nine-thirty. This presented another problem. If she opened her mouth, anyone within earshot would hear how irritable she was. Her mother called it "clipping her words" when she used one-word responses, which telegraphed that now was not the time to engage her.

In the lobby, she glanced around. Her suspicion was spot on. Only one seat remained at the dining room table. And that one was smack dab in the center, surrounded by people chirping about the weather and their plans for the day. Catherine rolled her eyes. She thought back to when she'd attended customer events, had to mingle, swallow the innate shyness or edginess she harbored, and plunge forth with a bright smile. But that was then. This was now. She wouldn't wear a smiley face and pretend she was something she's not. Those days were over.

Catherine did her best to seem preoccupied when she entered the dining room. She grabbed a cup of coffee, painted a dollop of cream cheese on a poppy seed bagel, and scooted across the hall to the parlor before anyone could toss a "good morning" her way. In the privacy of the parlor, she took her first sip of coffee and let the brew settle in her mouth, savoring it before swallowing. Well on her way to a rousing second-guessing party about the lease she'd signed, she saw Helen enter the dining room wearing a smile so big it could traverse the Grand Canyon. Catherine watched her buzz around, chit-chatting with guests, and then Helen glanced across the hall and cast a questioning look her way.

Before Catherine could look away, she rushed over.

"What are you doing over here all alone?"

"I'm a little irritable, and wouldn't make good company. Best I keep to myself."

Helen frowned.

"I overslept."

"Sleeping in isn't the end of the world."

"It is when there's so much to do."

"Haven't you been sleeping well?" Helen sat in a chair across from Catherine.

Catherine didn't want to get into what had kept her awake at night. She wanted to be left alone, but Helen sat there, still looking concerned.

"It's the store." Catherine looked down at her hands. "Maybe I acted too hastily."

"Too late for second thoughts."

Helen was right, of course. The lease Catherine had signed gave her forty-eight hours to change her mind without incurring a substantial financial penalty, and that timeframe had long since passed. Being reminded of that caused her anxiety level to spike.

"I can't come up with a name, for heaven's sake. Plus, I've only found a fraction of the merchandise I plan to carry." It was like a dam burst, and suddenly all the words Catherine had swallowed came gushing out. She threw her hands in the air. "Then, there's the store layout to design, but I can't start on that without knowing the merchandise I'll have." Her shoulders slumped, and she sighed. "Why can't I pull this together?"

Helen scooted the chair closer, leaned forward, and looked Catherine in the eye. "Going into business for yourself can be overwhelming. Trust me, I know. But you can't let it get to you, or it'll turn into a self-fulfilling prophecy."

Catherine, not known for crying in public, felt her chin tremble. Could Rusty be right about her venture? Maybe it wasn't for her.

Helen reached over and placed her hand on top of Catherine's. "You know, if there's anything I can do to help you, all you have to do is ask, right?"

It had been a long time since she had had a good friend. Someone willing to help her think through a situation. Even though Catherine considered Helen a friend, her upbeat personality was at odds with Catherine's current disposition, and it grated on her.

Helen checked her watch. "Once everyone finishes up and I clear the breakfast items, I'll be in the kitchen if you want to chat. Maybe if we put our heads together... You know what they say, busy hands, busy minds." She swatted the air and laughed. "Or something like that, anyway." Helen stood, leaned down, and lowered her voice. "Let me leave you with a bit of advice. If you're going to be successful, you can't wear your emotions on your sleeve. Customers will come to your store excited to see what you have to offer, and the last thing they'll want to come across is a grumpy owner. Even when a customer is unhappy with your service, you still have to paint on a smile." Helen sighed. "And finally, try not to overthink every aspect or dwell in a puddle of self-doubt, both of which I might add, you seem to be doing. You're intelligent, Catherine. I have no qualms that you'll figure all this out." Then she straightened. "As I said, I'll be in the kitchen if you want to talk."

Catherine's initial reaction was to lash out. Defend herself. But she gulped down her annoyance and washed it down with a good serving of pride. Helen was right, and a good friend. That's what good friends did. Tell it like it is. She reminded herself, if it weren't for Helen, she wouldn't have known about Linda's desire to sub-lease her space and wouldn't be anywhere close to realizing her dream.

AFTER A LONG TALK with herself in the confines of her room, Catherine popped into the inn's kitchen armed with a measuring tape, her phone, and a renewed attitude.

Helen dried her hands on a red checkered towel. "Where are you headed?"

"Special Treasures, to take measurements and a few pictures. Maybe that will help me formulate a layout and visualize what I'll put where."

"That's my girl." Helen offered a warm smile. "Sorry for being so blunt earlier. At my age, I'm no longer worried about offending others with the truth when they need it. Especially someone as special as you."

"No worries. I needed a good swift kick."

"At the risk of further sticking my nose into your business, don't forget about ordering a sign for your store. You'll need to contact someone soon if you want it finished before you open. As you've probably noticed, we business owners like our signs. So, the few craftsmen around who do that sort of thing are at a premium."

"But I haven't come up with a name yet."

"Doesn't matter. You will. In the meantime, line someone up. If you have a design in mind, you can start with that."

"I've had one in my head for a while," Catherine admitted.

"Well, there you go. Make a sketch and work from there. Later, when you come up with a name, you can add it. At least you'll have one less thing on your to-do list. And one less worry."

"Is there someone you recommend?"

Helen leaned in and bumped her shoulder against Catherine. "Do you like ours?"

"What's not to like?"

"I have his number somewhere, but since you're heading over to Main Street, stop by Nantucket Realty. Tina Benton can give you her brother Michael's number."

OUTSIDE THE REAL ESTATE OFFICE, Catherine was greeted by voicemail when she called the number Tina gave her. She left a message, disappointed that she couldn't speak to Michael himself, and headed over to Special Treasures.

There wasn't one available parking space outside the store, probably due to the large cardboard sign with black lettering draped across the front window. "Going out of business! 50% off! Everything must go! All sales final!"

With less than two weeks before Catherine assumed the lease, it was only natural Linda would be selling off her merchandise. The sign and the onslaught of customers made it real.

Butterflies swarmed in Catherine's stomach. She pushed aside her angst, remembered Helen's advice, smiled, opened the door, and stepped inside. The scene in front of her felt like controlled chaos. People were shoulder to shoulder, vying for Linda's attention.

With a pencil balanced behind her ear, Linda looked at Catherine, and the lines on her face eased. "Thank goodness," she mouthed and motioned Catherine over. "I'm so glad to see you." Linda ran her hand across her forehead. "As you can see, the last thing I need is another customer."

Catherine looked around. "Geez, this is a lot busier than I expected."

"I never imagined there would be such a crowd wanting to take advantage of my change of heart. If I had, I would've enlisted help." Linda rolled her eyes when the chimes on the back of the door sounded. "Oh, boy, just what I need," she whispered.

A scowling man entered the store and headed straight for Linda. A road map of lines crossed his brow, and his eyes were narrow slits. "Linda, what in blazes is going on?" he said over the hum of customers' voices. "I got back on-island and heard you've subleased your store. I had no idea you were thinking of getting out. You should've let me know. I've told you I want to expand Double Scoop."

A woman approached. "Excuse me, I need help with a doll that's on a shelf too high for me to reach."

Linda's gaze ping-ponged from the woman to the man and then to Catherine.

"I can try and help if you like," Catherine offered.

Linda's shoulders visibly relaxed. "Thank you. There's a cheat sheet next to the register with instructions on how to operate it, and everything has final sale price tags." Then, never losing her smile, she guided the cranky man away. "Jerry, let's step over here, so we can talk privately."

"Are you going to get that doll for me?" the woman huffed at Catherine.

Catherine, reminded once again of Helen's advice, squelched a look that would signal her displeasure. "Of course." She forced a smile, slid over a step stool, and handed down the doll to the woman.

Noisy chatter prevented Catherine from hearing what Linda and the man were saying. But he waved his hands in the air, and it looked like Linda was trying her best to calm him down.

The self-centered woman interested in the doll approached Catherine a couple minutes later, when she was up to her elbows, helping two other customers. "I'll take it," she announced, as if she was Catherine's only customer.

"Great." Catherine pushed away any unkind thoughts, choosing to remember the woman was helping to clear items from the store, which aided both her and Linda. "Give me a minute, and I'll meet you at the register."

Catherine broke free of the two customers and sidestepped a guy who appeared to be out of his element. When he attempted to gain her attention, she put a forefinger in the air and mouthed that she'd be right back.

The woman with the doll was tapping her fingers on the glass countertop when Catherine approached. "Sorry for the delay. Seems everyone has a question." She eyed the register and the cheat sheet. She hadn't been a cashier at the place she'd worked while in college, but how hard could it be? "I'll need a minute." She scanned the instructions. "Will this be cash or credit?" she asked with a false degree of confidence.

"Cash," the woman said.

Catherine's shoulder muscles relaxed, and she unclenched her jaw. Cash had to be less complicated than credit. Now, if she could just figure out how to ring up the sale. She glanced at Linda, still engaged, and returned her attention to the instructions that indicated she should enter the SKU number, then the price. But when she attempted to do so, the register beeped each time she pressed a key. She blew an errant lock of hair away from her eyes, then hit the clear button and tried again. Same result.

The woman crossed her hands in front of her and began tapping her foot. "Are you new?"

"Temporary help." A moment later, Catherine almost clapped her hands when she realized that she had to enter a PIN that Linda had written at the top of the instructions before proceeding with the sale.

How had she missed that? She keyed the number, then entered the merchandise SKU and price information. The final price, including tax, displayed on the screen, and the drawer slid open. Bingo. Catherine wrapped the doll in tissue paper and placed it into a shopping bag. "I hope you enjoy your purchase." She smiled with as much graciousness as she could muster. Before she could catch her breath and gave herself a silent high five, three more customers waved their hands in the air at her. She hurried over to one and let the others know she'd be with them shortly.

Catherine wiped her brow. "Okay," she said to the guy who looked like he'd made a wrong turn and ended up in Special Treasures instead of the hardware store across the street. "How may I help you?"

"If my granddaughter doesn't like this, can I return it?" he asked.

Finally, an answer Catherine was comfortable giving. The sign at the register and the one outside stated all sales were final. "I'm afraid not."

After attending to the other two customers, she offered them coffee and cookies from the table at the rear of the store. She would've purchased the table, but Linda never offered it. Pushed in a far back corner stood an antique chest Catherine also would've bought. It sported a small placard in lovely cursive writing that indicated it was not for sale.

Finally, the man who'd cornered Linda for forty-five minutes headed for the door, slamming it behind him.

Linda, on the other hand, didn't miss a beat. She maintained her smile, answered questions from the few lingering customers, then turned the dead bolt after they exited.

Catherine hadn't expected to work at Special Treasures, but she couldn't abandon Linda. And as frustrating as it had been, she harbored a sense of accomplishment for the first time in months.

She scooted herself back onto the edge of the front window display.

Linda flipped the door sign to "closed," slipped her arm around Catherine's shoulders, and gave her a gentle squeeze. "Thank you. I'm sorry I had to enlist your help."

"Who was that guy, anyway?"

"He owns the Double Scoop and can be a pill."

Catherine frowned. "Why was he so upset?"

Linda sighed. "According to him, my sale brought so many customers that his patrons had no place to park. He swears I cost him business."

Catherine's mouth dropped open. "What did he expect you to do? Reimburse him for lost sales?"

"He didn't venture quite that far. But he went on and on about the importance of sales at this time of year." Linda rolled her eyes. "As if I don't know that. Had I offered, I'm sure he would've jumped at some level of compensation, but I was able to assure him that many of my patrons likely wandered into his shop afterward for a treat." She quieted a moment. "But that wasn't the primary reason for his mood. He told me he'd expected first dibs on the lease. I tried to explain that I had no idea about his interest, but he kept ranting about how I must've forgotten because he's sure he'd mentioned it." Linda lowered her voice even though the store was devoid of customers. "Without coming right out with it, he hinted that maybe my age played a part."

Catherine shook her head.

Linda chuckled. "Honestly, I think it's *his* memory that's in question. Thankfully, he backed down when I assured him that the new store wouldn't pose any competition." She blinked. "It won't, will it?"

"Not in the slightest," Catherine said.

Linda wiped her brow. "Thank goodness."

"You'll have to give me some tips on how to deal with him. I don't think I could've hung on as long as you did without giving him a piece of my mind."

"As evidenced by the amount of time it took for me to get rid of him, I'm no one to offer advice. All I can say is to slather him with praise about his business savvy, and invite his opinion. His ego is the size of California."

Catherine would have to practice biting her tongue when it came to the guy next door. For now, she was anxious to take pictures and be on her way. "I'll keep that in mind. I hope I didn't make too many mistakes. I left a couple of notes next to the register so you can figure out how I handled a few of the complicated sales."

She scanned the store. Everything had sold except for two boxes of doll clothes Linda said she'd sell online. The only other things were the baby buggy, the cash register, two glass display cases Catherine had purchased, and the refreshment table and antique dresser that Linda didn't offer. The only item Catherine didn't know how she'd use in her store was the baby buggy. It reminded her of a childhood toy, so she had to have it.

"I guess that about does it." Linda looked around the near-empty space. "You have no idea how grateful I am that you stopped by. When the customers first started coming in today, there was light at the end of the tunnel. I was confident that I could handle things. But as the day wore on and the crowd grew, the light grew distant and then faded, sending me into a tailspin. Then you showed up, and I considered it a sign. Somehow I knew everything would be all right." Linda sighed. "You truly are a godsend."

It was interesting that Linda had used that analogy. Catherine, too, had witnessed a light the night of her mugging, and like Linda, it had changed things for her.

Hmmm, a distant light. Catherine rolled it around in her mind. The name of her store was suddenly as clear as hearing her mother's voice.

"I should be the one thanking you," Catherine said. "Not only did I get on-the-job training, you've just handed me the name of my store."

Linda cocked a well-arched eyebrow. "I did?"

"Yes. I've been struggling to come up with something. Then you mentioned a light at the end of the tunnel, and boom, there it was." Catherine tapped her forehead. "I don't know why I hadn't thought of it, but I'm glad your words inspired me. I plan to call my store "A Distant Light."

Linda's brow furrowed.

Catherine knew Linda didn't have a clue about Catherine's recent past, and she had no plans to share her trials and tribulations with a near stranger. "It'd take some time to explain, so let's say it'll be my way of honoring my late mother."

Linda gave her a broad smile. "How sweet. Glad I could help."

"Well, if there's nothing else..." Catherine slid off the window ledge. "I'd like to take a few pictures and some measurements. Then I'll be on my way."

"Of course."

Catherine walked across the store.

"I planned to leave these behind with a note, but since you're here..." Linda motioned at the coveted furniture. "I want you to have these."

Catherine's eyes widened. "Really? Are you sure?"

"I could see by the look on your face the first time you saw them that you adored them as much as I do. I decided to gift them to you then and there. Think of it as a little something to remember me by," Linda said with a sweep of her arm and a tear in her eye. "I only hope that you derive as much pleasure from this place as I have."

Catherine's eyes brimmed with tears, and she pulled Linda into a hug. "Thank you so much."

"You're welcome. In some small way, I hope I've helped you launch your dream."

CATHERINE INWARDLY WINCED when Helen appeared at the registration desk after dinner. A long relaxing soak in a warm bath to mull over some thoughts she had for the store was what she wanted, not a prolonged conversation.

"So, did you get a hold of Michael?" Helen asked.

With everything going on at Linda's, Catherine had forgotten about hearing back from him. She paused. "Come to think of it, he never returned my call."

"See, that's what I mean. These guys are busy, and Michael's extremely talented, so his carpentry skills are in high demand. Best to try again."

Catherine would prefer to call him with her feet up. But Helen had dialed the number and handed her the phone. Once again, the call went straight to voicemail. "This is Catherine O'Malley, *again*. I'd appreciate it if you would at least let me know if you're interested in working with me." She left her number for a second time, disconnected, and handed the phone back to Helen. "Done."

"Well, that should get his attention." Helen narrowed her eyes. "But I'm not sure if that's a good thing."

∼

CATHERINE CLIMBED out of the tub, grabbed a towel, dried off, and slipped into her pajamas. Between the patter of raindrops and the relaxing scent of lavender bathwater, her eyelids were heavy and her nerves calmed.

She padded into the bedroom to the sound of her ringing phone.
"Hello?"

"Uh, Catherine. This is Michael Benton. I got your second message. It sounds like you didn't receive my earlier voicemail. I'm available to meet tomorrow morning, if that works for you."

Darn. What must he think? She should've checked her phone before leaving her snarky message. A warm blush climbed up her neck into her cheeks. During her time at the store, she'd worked at being gracious, but she'd let that fall away after she left.

"Catherine?" Michael asked, breaking the awkward silence.

"Yes. Yes. I'm here. Tiring day. I'm sure you understand."

"We all have some of those. Best not to let it rub off on other people, don't you think?"

She pushed back her shoulders. Was everyone on Nantucket this outspoken? Maybe Michael had spoken with Helen and had picked up a few tips on being forthright before deciding to return the call.

"So, tomorrow?" he asked. "Will that work?"

"Yes. How about ten. I'm staying—"

"At Sunny Skies," he said. "I hope you have a pleasant evening and, for my sake, an even better morning. Good night."

Catherine disconnected and pulled up the voicemail. "Thank you for calling," Michael's pleasant voice greeted her. "I'd be happy to meet with you. Tina told me we had a new business owner in town. Let me know when it's best to get together. I look forward to working with you."

She paced the room, ran her hands through her hair, and puffed out her cheeks. Maybe she should cancel and work with someone else rather than risk the embarrassment of facing this man. Who was she kidding? He was a friend of Helen's, and Tina's brother. Catherine couldn't afford to have them both upset with her. She'd have to suck it up and make things right, regardless of how embarrassing it turned out to be.

The next morning

CATHERINE LINGERED over her morning coffee and the early edition of the paper in the dining room. A part of her dreaded having to face Michael, and. another part hoped he hadn't changed his mind. After all, her sign was an essential appendage to her store, and he was one of the best carpenters on the island.

Minutes later, she saw a man enter the lobby, and checked her watch. Nine-forty-five. Must be a guest.

He glanced her way and smiled.

Catherine couldn't help but think he would've made a perfect candidate for one of her previous toothpaste commercials. She guessed him to be about six feet tall. His chocolate-colored hair and beard, both entwined with slivers of silver, gave him a distinguished appearance usually afforded to much older men. And his tanned complexion seemed reminiscent of someone who spent a lot of time outdoors.

She caught herself staring, then buried her face in the newspaper before he had a chance to notice.

A minute later, he stood in front of her. He wiped his palms on his pants and extended his hand. "Catherine?" He smiled as if he were genuinely happy to meet her, her sarcastic comment long forgotten. "I'm Michael."

Up close, Catherine considered him more handsome than she'd initially thought, and it threw her off-center. She pushed back her chair and stood. Despite trying to maintain her composure, heat spread up her neck like a rash. She shook his hand. "Nice to meet you. I wasn't expecting you this early."

Michael's face reddened. He dropped his hand and looked at the splayed newspaper and half cup of coffee. "I can wait if you're not ready. I figured better to be early. And, well, I was ready to go, so I told myself I could wait if I had to."

Catherine smiled. Michael seemed nervous, too. Maybe what she had taken for a baiting comment last night was his way of reminding her that things worked differently here. She motioned for him to take a seat. "*I'm* the one who should be apologizing for not checking my messages. Then again, for piling on sarcasm. I'm so sorry. I've been edgy, and yesterday was especially trying." She gave a nervous laugh. "Forgive me. That sounds like I'm excusing my behavior, and that's not right."

"No worries." Michael flashed a smile. "Apology accepted."

Her breath caught at the deep sexy tone of his voice, which sent currents of excitement through her. She swallowed. "Thank you. Help yourself to Helen's amazing coffee."

"Thanks. I've already had my fill," Michael said, and then sat next to Catherine.

She cocked her head to one side and studied him. Where had she seen him before?

"Is something wrong?" he asked.

"I know this is going to sound like a tired pickup line, but you look familiar." She chuckled. "But that's impossible."

"They say everyone has a double. So maybe I do, too."

Catherine shrugged. "I suppose…"

Michael reached into his back pocket, pulled out a small notebook, and took a pen from his shirt pocket.

She couldn't shake the sense that she'd seen him before. Then it dawned on her. Michael was the guy she'd seen talking to Tina when she'd first arrived on-island. She snapped her fingers. "I saw you outside Nantucket Realty. Come to think of it. I had the same déjà vu moment when I first met Tina."

Michael nodded. "Yep, that was probably me. I usually stop by around lunchtime." He leaned in.

Catherine's pulse raced.

"I don't know if you're aware of it, but my sister is a world-class cook. Self-trained, I might add. On my fortunate days, she packs me lunch and gives me a break from takeout."

What an intoxicating combination of handsome and down to earth this man was. He made it hard for Catherine to focus. She reminded herself he was there to take on a job, and with her luck, he probably wasn't single anyway. "After you called last night, I made this sketch."

She pulled the drawing from her pocket, then smoothed out the folds on the dining room table. She took in the light scent of his aftershave, pine needles and Christmas, and fought an urge to close her eyes and revel in the thoughts swimming in her mind. "I'd like it carved from a flattened piece of driftwood if possible. Oval." She pointed to the centered lighthouse. "And this will be the design's prominent aspect. The wave should curl behind it, like this, and here above the wave, I'd like the name arched as I've indicated." She settled back against her chair.

Michael perused the drawing. "This is very good. Are you an artist?"

"I studied graphic design, and my professional background is advertising campaigns. I've always had a penchant for a sketch pad and pencil."

He chuckled. "Well, it shows. It will help shorten the time line for sure. I'm usually the one who has to lay out the design based on what the customer envisions. And it's not at all uncommon to struggle through several iterations. So this is a huge first step."

Catherine relaxed. "So, does that mean you'll work with me, even though you had a glimpse of my bad side?"

A smile lit his face, and he gazed into her eyes. "Absolutely," he said, his voice barely above a whisper.

She blinked slowly, afraid she'd lose herself in the pull of his magnetic hazel eyes.

Michael leaned back. "I have to admit I had a déjà vu moment myself. I was on Main Street yesterday and saw that Linda had a big sale going on. I peeked in the window and spotted the attractive salesclerk. Of course, I didn't know it was you until I walked in this morning. So, I saw your better side yesterday, and can understand why you were tired last night. Some of those people seemed very pushy."

Catherine stood.

"I'm—" They both said at the same time.

Catherine laughed. "You first."

He stood and stretched out his hand. "I'm looking forward to this. I love a challenge, and this will test my skill level."

She shook his hand. His rugged skin and firm grip sent a thousand points of electricity surging through her as she imagined him running his hands over her. He was right; it *would* be a challenge. But for Catherine, it would come in the form of keeping her mind on the project and not on him.

CHAPTER EIGHT

Returning to Boston brought the worst parts of Catherine's recent past to mind. Her breakup with Jack. Working insane hours to tamp down her loneliness. Her brush with death. But she couldn't put off packing her clothes and personal items any longer. By the time she'd ferry back to the island laden with the detritus of everyday necessities, Tina Benton would be there to hand over the keys to the store and efficiency apartment.

And then her odyssey would officially begin.

Catherine parted one of the inn's front curtains and saw Lexi, the plum-colored, dated Lexus SUV that Bill and Helen offered her, roll to a stop, with Bill at the wheel. He'd said the old girl had been riding bumpy and needed new shock absorbers, thanks to the cobblestone streets, so he'd insisted they have Lexi serviced before Catherine's trip.

Although she had been thankful for the offer and the chance to save a bundle on a rental, she'd initially declined, arguing that Helen would be without a vehicle for her endless trips to the market. Her menu creations, all made from scratch, required bushels of fresh fruit, vegetables, and endless pounds of meat, poultry, and seafood.

A DISTANT LIGHT

But they'd assured her they'd be fine. "No worries," Helen had said. "We'll stock up before you leave and we can use the van, if need be."

"Here you go." Bill handed Catherine the keys when he stepped inside the lobby. "She's had a bath, gotten a new set of shocks, and I filled her tummy."

Catherine hugged him. "Thank you so much. I promise to take good care of her."

"Honey, don't forget the cooler I packed for Catherine!" Helen called out from behind the registration desk. "It's in the kitchen, and too heavy for her to lift. Be a doll and slip it into Lexi's cargo area."

Catherine stepped behind the registration desk and gave Helen a hug. "You didn't have to do that."

"It's a little sustenance to keep you going while you're away. A few meals. All frozen and wrapped securely, along with an assortment of sweets, is all. We all need dessert." Helen winked. "Don't want you looking like a bag of bones when you return."

Catherine laughed. "Ha. As if that's about to happen."

SHE ACCELERATED when she passed her former office building. Further down, as she approached the place where the attack had occurred, her breath caught and her chest tightened. Her foot pressed harder on the pedal, causing the vehicle to swerve. Then instinct kicked in and she took her foot off the pedal, slowing the SUV, and proceeded on.

If her Nantucket experience didn't work out, would she ever be able to return?

A few minutes later, Catherine parked Lexi and got out.

"Good to see you, Miss O'Malley," the doorman said, then grabbed a rolling luggage rack. "Here, let me help you."

She opened the rear hatch. "Good to see you too."

He slid the cooler and her suitcase onto the rack.

Inside the lobby, the doorman handed her an envelope. "A man dropped this off about a week ago. I asked him if I needed to get in touch with you about it, but he said it could wait until you returned."

"Thank you." Catherine eyed the envelope. The handwriting as familiar as her own. Rusty. What now?

The elevator doors slid open on the top floor, and Catherine pushed the luggage rack into her condo. The apartment smelled musty. The sheets she'd draped over the furniture gave off a haunted house vibe. There had been a time when she'd looked forward to coming home, knowing that Jack would be waiting for her. Tears filled her eyes. Why had she let her career scuttle their relationship?

She was unloading the luggage rack when she recalled a voicemail from Jack that she'd saved all these years. After their breakup, his voice had helped her through some of her loneliest times. Catherine grabbed her phone and walked to the window with the picturesque view of Boston Harbor. She pressed play, and his voice filled the air. Should she swallow her pride and call him? Tell him she'd been a fool to let him walk away? But what if he'd made a new life for himself?

"Choices," she heard her mother say.

CATHERINE PICKED up the letter from the hallway table that the doorman had handed her two days earlier. She'd tossed it there, knowing it was from Rusty. Thanks to her manic efforts to finish packing in record time so she could return to Nantucket, she'd pushed its existence from her mind.

She tore open the envelope.

Catherine,
I'd like to see you when you return.
PLEASE!
I'll stop by at your convenience, or you can come by the office ANYTIME!
Rusty

A DISTANT LIGHT

LATER THAT NIGHT, Catherine sat in a Chinese restaurant she'd missed since leaving Boston. She pulled Rusty's letter from her purse. It had been a surprise, and not a good one. During their last conversation, she'd made her position clear. What else could he want to talk about?

The waiter arrived with her order of butterflied shrimp wrapped in bacon, alongside a tangy red dipping sauce and a side of pork fried rice. She thanked him.

He bowed his head and walked away.

Catherine bit into a shrimp dripping with sauce, satisfying her craving. She glanced at the letter again. Rusty must be desperate. She'd have thought that his bruised ego would've caused him to give up. Sure, her former clients were upset with her departure, but no one was indispensable.

After devouring the tasty shrimp and half of the fried rice, she stuck the letter in her purse and waited for the check. Whatever Rusty wanted, it was bound to be a waste of her time. On the other hand, maybe she could leverage his vulnerability to her advantage. In an earlier phone call, hadn't he mentioned working remotely? She glanced out the plate-glass window into the dim light of the setting sun. What if her store didn't turn out as she hoped? A part-time job would provide a comfortable cushion. Then again, was she willing to risk even a sometimes-assignment that could pull her away from what she anticipated for her future?

After paying, Catherine stepped outside and lifted her collar to the brisk Boston air. She looked up at the sky as if seeking answers from above. Her mother's words reverberated in her mind. "Our choices define us."

CATHERINE STEPPED off the elevator in front of the Fitzpatrick & Associates entrance, pushed on one of the double-entry doors, and stepped inside.

Aimee, the receptionist, greeted her. "Catherine, how nice to see you. Rusty said you might be stopping by."

"Did he now?" She mentally kicked herself for coming. He hadn't changed. Still smug and sure of himself. She took in the surroundings. Not long ago, she'd considered this her second home. Why had it taken a life-threatening trauma to see how off track she'd gotten? Her stomach lurched at the thought of seeing her former coworkers, people she'd once considered friends. Would they gossip that she'd come asking for her old job back?

Who cared? She no longer did.

Rusty stepped around the corner. His face lit up. "Catherine, I'm so glad you decided to stop by. You look fabulous. Time away has agreed with you." He ushered her toward his office. "No, interruptions please," he said to Aimee over his shoulder.

Rusty gestured toward a chair in front of his desk and closed the door to his inner sanctum. "Please, make yourself comfortable."

Catherine couldn't help but recall the number of times she'd sat in this very seat, taking direction or offering suggestions on how to revamp someone else's campaign that had withered and died. How many assignments had been deemed impossible by others, only for Catherine to develop a creative way to make it work?

"Is there something I can get you? Coffee? Water?"

She parked her thoughts. "No, thanks." She glanced at her watch. "I'm pressed for time."

He sat behind his desk, tented his hands, and leaned on his forearms. "I appreciate you taking time out of your busy schedule to stop by."

Catherine wasn't sure how to take that. Was he being sarcastic? Patronizing?

"First and foremost," he said. "I want you to know how very sorry I am for the way I treated you."

She nodded her head. "You've said as much."

He removed his glasses and placed them on the desk. "Trust me. I understand your need to regain your footing. The mugging was a heck of a scare. You're undoubtedly still in some level of shock. Anyone would be."

"Rusty, you don't have a clue what I've been through, so please don't pretend otherwise."

His eyes narrowed for a nanosecond.

Catherine leaned forward. "Look, I've given that night a lot of thought. Although the man almost killed me, perhaps he did me a favor by allowing me to see the trajectory of my life. My outlook has changed. And this"—she gestured with a sweep of her arm—"no longer fits with my new perspective."

"But—"

She held up her hand. On a roll and determined to have him hear her out, she continued. "I'm not finished. In my quest to make partner, I see now that I let the pendulum swing too far from who I am. I intend to chart a new path and enjoy every moment of what's left of my life, instead of watching days pass me by, surrounded by people who couldn't care less about anything or anyone but themselves." She paused. His incredulous expression telegraphed his shock at her frankness. "A friend recently pointed out that I have a second chance at life, and I intend to make the most of it."

Rusty blinked. "If you give me the opportunity, I can help with that." He reached into his side drawer, extracted a manila envelope, and slid it across the desk.

"What's this?"

"Something I'd like you to consider."

Catherine's thoughts swirled. What could it possibly be? A contract? A prorated bonus? An unexpected check would be nice. But as far as she knew, the company policy stated that if an employee resigned, the payout was forfeited. And Rusty would *never* offer money without something in return. So that left a contract.

"Didn't you hear what I said? I have no intention of returning, no matter what's in there." She pushed the envelope back with an air of confidence she didn't feel.

"I've made it so you can work from home, regardless of where that is. Think of it as an insurance policy. If your plan to go into business for yourself doesn't work out, you'll have something to keep you going for a while." He chuckled. "And who knows, maybe over time, you'll see that coming back isn't the end of the world."

She had to admit, what he said made sense. Catherine conjured her best poker face. "I doubt anything you've come up with will change my mind."

He fingered his glasses. "I don't expect an answer right now. Take it with you. Look it over. It's fair, Catherine. More so than in the past. Consider it a demonstration of how much I respect you."

Respect. Give me a break. As much as Catherine would have liked to laugh in his face, she refrained. Should she leave empty-handed? Proof of her final checkmate? Or do as he suggested and decide later?

Rusty picked up the envelope and extended it toward her. "Please look it over. You have nothing to lose. Keep in mind, though, my offer isn't open-ended."

∼

CATHERINE'S CLOTHES hung from a pole stretched across Lexi's backseat. She had filled four large cardboard boxes bought at UPS with items that she hoped would transform the efficiency apartment into a home. Bed linens, plump towels, her favorite bed pillows, and a few kitchen essentials, like her mother's cast-iron frying pan, seasoned to perfection. Sitting in the SUV's cupholder was a coffee mug she'd bought while on vacation with Jack in Switzerland, once stuffed with an assortment of chocolate, inscribed, "Give me chocolate or give me death."

Packing the framed photos of her late parents and those of her and Jack, all of which she'd covered with bubble wrap, had been a heartwrenching task. The memories they'd unlocked had sent her reeling, and served as another grim reminder of how empty her life had become.

Catherine closed the rear cargo door with a thud and frowned. The full trunk snuffed out her plan to haul any finds from Cape Cod antique stores back to Nantucket. She took one last look around at the surrounding street. Funny, she'd only lived on Nantucket for a short time, yet it felt more like home than Boston. Then she slid behind the wheel and told herself she'd stop at the Cape Cod antique shops anyway. If she uncovered something spectacular, she'd arrange to have it shipped. And time spent shopping would help her decompress from the stress she'd piled on rushing to get back to Nantucket, not to mention the aftertaste from her visit with Rusty.

CHAPTER NINE

While Catherine waited for Tina outside the former Special Treasures shop, she chalked up her anxiousness to pushing herself to the limit the last few days, and to Rusty, who wouldn't leave her alone. During her Boston visit, he'd laid a time bomb in her lap, and its ticktock was driving her crazy. Should she let it explode into nothingness or slowly defuse it?

"Catherine." Tina interrupted her thoughts.

She pushed away the strands of hair the wind had blown onto her face, and turned. What was it that she saw written all over Tina's face? Worry? Concern? Aggravation? What had Helen said about not wearing your emotions on your sleeves? It seemed neither she nor Tina had learned that lesson well.

"Sorry I'm late," Tina said. "I got tied up with a customer. Ah, doesn't matter." She waved a hand in the air. "You don't need to hear my troubles."

"No problem. I just got here."

"Helen mentioned you went to Boston." Tina eyed Lexi, parked at the curb. "Looks like a worthwhile trip."

Catherine nodded. "Should have everything I'll need for a while."

Tina reached into her pocket and dangled the keys to the store and the upstairs efficiency apartment. "These are yours."

Catherine stretched out her hand, palm up, and closed her eyes.

Tina dropped them into the middle of Catherine's hand. "Come on. The wind's picking up, and I think we might get some rain. Let's go inside and check things out."

Catherine unlocked the door and stared into the space that was hers for at least the next year and a half. Her breathing quickened, her palms grew sweaty, and her thoughts exploded like a Fourth of July display. How would she turn this into the picture she had of it in her mind's eye? Had she purchased enough merchandise? What if the customers didn't share her affection for the inventory? She swallowed, filled her lungs to slow her racing heart, and exhaled.

She'd make this work. She had to.

The cash register and display cases, including the antique baby buggy that Catherine had purchased from Linda, were all there, as well as the refreshment table and the antique dresser. And to Catherine's surprise, the floors had been sanded and refinished, and the walls had a new coat of creamy beige paint.

"You must be a mind reader. I was thinking of having the floor and walls redone."

Tina chuckled. "No psychic powers here. It simply needed freshening. The owner is very accommodating. I simply planted the seed."

Catherine stepped forward and hugged Tina. "Thank you for getting the floors done. For helping me work things through with Linda. For everything."

Tina hung on for a few seconds, then leaned back and locked eyes with Catherine. "In part, it's my job. The other part is a gesture of friendship. If I did have psychic insight, I'd see that we're going to be great friends."

"I think so, too."

Tina gazed out the window at the darkening sky. "Let's get your stuff unloaded before we get rained on."

Catherine had no problem loading all the boxes. No doubt, she could handle the opposite. But she reminded herself, Tina's suggestion was what friends do. "Thank you." She opened the cargo door. "I made sure to pack the boxes on the light side, but I forgot I used a luggage rack to get them to the car, and didn't think about the stairs."

After the last trek up to the apartment, Catherine wiped her brow, happy that she hadn't given in to her initial instinct to rebuff Tina's offer of assistance.

"Seems like all I do is thank you."

"Glad to help. You'll have enough to do with unpacking and setting up the store. The last thing you need is to pull a back muscle carting all those boxes. Oh, and before I forget, I had this grocery cart in my attic and figured it might come in handy since you don't have a car."

"Thanks, it *will* come in handy, since my only mode of transportation will be these." Catherine pointed at her feet. "And the bike I brought with me. But that'll be for exercise when the nice weather comes around, not lugging groceries."

"I also took the liberty of having my housekeeper give this place a thorough cleaning." Tina headed for the refrigerator. "And although it's not much, I picked up a few basics, so you don't have to run to the market today."

Catherine peered into the sparkling clean fridge to find milk, butter, and a six-pack of bottled water inside. Next to the toaster was a loaf of bread, a Cheerios box, and a bunch of ripe bananas.

She couldn't help but think how polar opposite Tina and Helen were from her previous coworkers, who she'd naively considered friends.

"What can I say?" Catherine's voice cracked. "Except, thank goodness for you and Helen. What would I do without you two?"

Tina grinned and gave her shoulder a squeeze. "One more thing to check off your worry list. I'm afraid you're stuck with us."

Catherine's pleasant smile left as her expression turned serious. "Is that someone knocking?"

Tina peeked out the window. "It's Helen, and by the looks of it, I'd say she's brought dinner."

Catherine shook her head. "Is there no limit to the woman's generosity?" She headed for the stairs and forced herself to keep her shoulders from slumping. She was torn between enjoying time with her new friends and her desire to lock herself away for a few hours, when her stomach growled and made her decision easy. She would enjoy herself with the two women who had proven supportive, asking nothing in return.

Displaying anything other than a happy face to Helen wouldn't do. Catherine conjured up a smile and opened the door. "What on earth have you done now?"

"Just a little something for dinner."

"A *little* something? That basket's big enough for a five-course meal. Come on in."

Helen stepped inside.

The overhead floorboards creaked.

Helen glanced up and bit her lip. "Oh dear, am I interrupting? I was hoping…"

"Tina's here. She came to give me the keys and ended up helping me move in. Let me take the basket." Catherine led the way up the stairs and into the apartment.

Tina waved when Helen entered.

Helen pointed at the basket. "I've brought dinner. I thought Catherine would be starving after a long day of unpacking, and the truth is, it gave me an excuse to get away for a while. I've brought plenty. I hope you'll join us."

"Plenty and then some, based on how heavy this is." Catherine hoisted the basket onto the bistro table and opened it. The aroma of turkey pot pie and fresh-baked bread filled her nose. She glanced sideways at her friends. How different they were. Tina, blonde, little more than five-feet tall, in her late forties. Helen, her silver hair cut in a pixie style to frame her wrinkle-free face, pushing her late-sixties. Yet both women shared one thing in common—their caring spirits.

Tina inhaled. "How can I pass up a Helen concoction?"

Helen rubbed her hands together. "Great. We girls can have a nice dinner and catch up." She lowered her voice. "Bill dropped me off so he could help with the basket, but I think it's because I packed a bottle of wine, and he didn't want me to drive after having a glass or two. He also volunteered to man the inn for an hour or so." She shimmied and waved her arms in the air. "I'm a free woman."

Catherine set out plates and silverware, pulled out her chair, and sat. "Well then, let's make the most of it. We all deserve a break."

Helen scooped out a serving of pot pie for herself after Tina and Catherine filled their plates. Then she raised her fork to her mouth and addressed Catherine. "When will the Cape Cod items you purchased arrive?"

Catherine swallowed her bite of pot pie. "The sea captain's desk should be here Friday, and the three clipper ships the following Tuesday."

Tina dipped a slice of crusty French bread smeared with honey-infused butter into the turkey gravy on her plate and turned her face to Catherine. "Have you found all the merchandise you plan to carry?"

"Pretty much." Catherine picked up her wineglass. "Although a woman at one of the antique shops suggested a couple of websites I should check out. So maybe I'll find something else that catches my eye."

"Speaking of eye-catching," Tina said. "I almost forgot, my brother said to let you know he should have your sign ready in a few days."

Catherine grimaced. "Gosh. It goes to show where my head's at. I'd completely forgotten about the sign. Glad he didn't."

Tina laughed. "Him forget? Not likely, considering the impression you've made."

Catherine's cheeks warmed, and she cringed. She could only imagine what Michael had said about her snarky attitude.

"Ha!" Tina leaned back and pointed at Catherine. "That's the exact color his cheeks turn when I mention you."

Catherine took another sip of wine. "Really?"

"Really."

Catherine stared at her plate. When she'd first met Michael, he'd bowled her over with his good looks and charming personality. And although she was intrigued by Tina's comment, Jack was the man she truly wanted.

Helen checked her watch. "Oh my, where has the time gone?" She pushed back her chair and stood. "This has been fun, but I should get going. Bill's generosity only goes so far."

Tina slid down from the bar-height chair. "I'll drop you off and save Bill a trip."

"Thanks. He'll appreciate not having to drag himself away from the Pat's game."

Catherine walked the women to Tina's car. The hugs she got from both of them felt as natural as a spring day. "Thanks again, ladies."

Helen slipped into the front seat and lowered the window. "No need for thanks. I thoroughly enjoyed myself. Maybe once you're settled, we girls can make this a standing date."

Catherine bent down and peered into the car. "Sounds like a plan."

Tina started the engine and looked around Helen to Catherine. "Let me know if you need anything."

"Will do." Catherine straightened and waved as they pulled away.

Splashes of light from the antique, wrought-iron lampposts that bordered the road bathed the area in a warm glow and added to the illuminated nearby storefronts.

Catherine stuck her hands in her pockets. So much had changed. A few months ago, she'd hopped around the globe as most Bostonians cross the street. Thinking it exciting at the time, she discovered now that she didn't miss it in the least.

She headed for the door, stopped, and turned. The view was nothing like what she'd become accustomed to. Instead of Boston Harbor and Faneuil Hall's lights, Nat's Hardware store next door to The Book Corner, then The Bean, a coffee shop, occupied her line of sight. She exhaled and let out a quivering breath. For the first time in a long time, she didn't feel alone.

THE LURE of Rusty's contract pulled at Catherine, much like the opioids she'd taken to quell her pain following the mugging. It'd been hard then to fight off the voices in her head, urging her to pop another pill. Now the compulsion to read and reread Rusty's offer was just as compelling.

Would she be able to run the store and spend her free time working from home, and be successful at both? Did she want to? No and yes. Though she had to admit, the offer was tempting. Signing it would erase any worries about how long it'd take before the store took off and threw profits her way. She knew it was petty, but she enjoyed the satisfaction of knowing that Rusty had to acknowledge her worth to Fitzpatrick & Associates. And, considering his oversized ego, that couldn't have been easy.

Catherine tried shutting down her thoughts and focused on the clipper ships arrangements in the front window. They'd arrived that morning. But instead of preparing A Distant Light to open on December first, her mind catapulted back to the pros and cons of Rusty's offer. Being practical, it would provide a guaranteed income stream. Pro. Without it, what if her venture didn't work out? Then what? Back to Boston to start over? No. She'd fallen in love with—as Tina called it—the tiny slice of island paradise and its relaxed pace. What if she agreed and couldn't do both and, in the process, A Distant Light failed? Con. That would hand Rusty the perfect opportunity to sport his I-told-you-so smirk. Big con. Unthinkable. If her retail venture didn't make it, it would mean leaving behind her new friends. Huge con.

She looked outside at the cloudless sky. "Choices," she heard her mother say.

∽

"Hello?" a man called out upon entering the soon-to-open store. "Anyone here?"

Catherine let out a yelp, clutched her chest, and turned to see who it was.

"Sorry. I didn't mean to frighten you," Michael said.

She swallowed hard. "Hi. I was in my own little world and didn't hear you come in."

He tilted his head toward the door. "You always keep that unlocked?"

"No. I'm expecting a delivery I can't afford to miss. And with the windows masked, I can't see the truck. Besides, this is Nantucket."

"You can't be too careful, even here."

Her face warmed. She looked down and brushed imaginary lint from her pants to tamp down the rush she felt. When she returned her gaze to Michael, he was staring at her.

A smile tugged at his lips.

"So, how's my sign coming along?" she blurted out.

"I finished it up last night and thought you'd be anxious to see it, so I brought it with me."

Catherine rubbed her palms together, relieved that Tina hadn't mentioned that the sign had slipped her mind. "Great."

Michael had positioned it against the wall behind him. Then he lifted it up for her to see. "What'd you think?"

Catherine's hand flew to her mouth. She scanned the oval-shaped piece of gray weathered wood with smooth edges. Its centerpiece was a striking lighthouse with lines carved to reflect a shining beacon. Thin yellow rays stretched beyond the curled wave background. "A Distant Light" was etched in black lettering and arched above the lighthouse. It was a work of art, far more than what she'd expected. "Oh, Michael, it's beautiful." Her eyes blurred. "You gave life to my sketch."

"Glad you like it. Let me know when you want it hung."

"Will do." She went in search of her purse. "How much do I owe you?" she asked over her shoulder.

He gave her that toothpaste advertisement smile of his. "Dinner."

Catherine knitted her eyebrows. "You want me to make you dinner?"

"No. I want to take *you* to dinner."

She put her hand on her hip. "Now, how does that qualify as payment?"

"Payment is in the eye of the beholder." He rubbed his chin. "Or is that *beauty* is in the eyes of the beholder?" He swatted at the air. "Doesn't matter. Both apply."

Jack's face suddenly flashed before her, and Catherine took it as a sign. "I'm flattered and appreciative, but I can't accept your offer. Now please, how much do I owe you?"

He shook his head and rolled his eyes. "It's just two friends having dinner."

"I know, but Tina must have mentioned that my hands are full getting the store ready to open." She hoped he'd make this easy for her and keep it to *just* friends.

He gave her a gentle smile. "Tina doesn't confide her friend's lives to me or to anyone, for that matter."

Catherine smiled, warmed by his need to clarify his sister's stance. After she nagged him into giving her a price, she cleared her throat. "So, as far as hanging the sign, I plan to open on December first. Could you be here the day before?"

Michael pulled his phone from his pocket and checked his calendar. "How about four o'clock?"

"That'll work as long as you don't need me here. I have an appointment."

CATHERINE PARTED the curtain behind the couch a fraction when she heard a thump on the outside wall.

Michael was prompt. He'd agreed to hang the sign the day before the grand opening, and here he was at the stroke of four, just as he'd said.

She felt terrible having lied to Michael about why she couldn't have dinner with him. Then again, about not being at the store when it came time to hang the sign. Her reluctance to be alone with him had nothing to do with him and everything to do with herself. She'd feared that Michael was a guy she could fall for, and if she did, that wouldn't be fair to him.

How could she pursue a relationship when her fantasy to reunite with Jack still existed?

Catherine watched Michael eye the door to the store while he stood in front of the ladder. She rummaged through her memory. Had she locked the door? Yes, she was pretty sure she had. *Please don't knock.* She let out a breath she hadn't realized she was holding when he turned and went to the truck, retrieving the sign and a bracket from the truck bed.

He muttered words she couldn't hear as he climbed the ladder and struggled to hang the wooden masterpiece.

The ladder shifted toward her window. Catherine covered her mouth, backed away, then slowly edged closer. He moved down the ladder. Halfway, the bracket he held fell to the ground. He then stomped the rest of the way to the sidewalk, straightened the ladder, grabbed it, and reclimbed the rungs.

What if he fell? Should she go downstairs and steady the ladder? But if she did, he'd know she'd been there all along.

After waiting forty minutes, she gazed at the sign as it swung in the light breeze. It looked amazing.

Michael closed his ladder and loaded it onto his truck.

Before he opened the driver's door, he glanced up at the window where she stood, shielded by the curtain.

Did he suspect she hid there like a scared rabbit? She winced. If he did, what must he think of her?

Then he raised his hand, gave a small wave in her direction, got in his truck, and drove away.

CHAPTER TEN

December 1st

Catherine loved the inviting vibe she'd created at A Distant Light. Every nook and cranny filled, yet no sense of clutter. She ran her hand over the antique baby buggy she'd bought and had restored. A handmade infant's quilt embroidered with a centered sailboat, and a crew of teddy bears lay folded over its side. The chest she'd purchased from Linda stood nearby topped with an Irish linen table runner. It showcased woven placemats of all shapes featuring nautical designs and an assortment of potpourri pouches that smelled like the sea.

Inside another case were pairs of women's silk pajamas decorated with tiny lighthouses, draped over the graduated open drawers. But her signature items, the ones she hoped would define her store, were three-masted ships in the front display window, a period piece steamship trunk, and an antique sea captain's desk that hugged a far wall.

She should take a picture and send it to Linda. Yes. That's what she'd do. She headed for the back counter, where a platter of macadamia nut cookies she'd baked the night before awaited. She

A DISTANT LIGHT

placed it on the refreshment table alongside a carafe of freshly brewed coffee, then checked her watch. Ten o'clock. She walked to the front door and briefly closed her eyes. "Wish me luck, Mom." Then she rolled up the shade on the back of the door and turned over the sign.

OPEN.

∽

CATHERINE CHECKED the wall clock for the umpteenth time since opening the store that morning. Three o'clock, and not one customer. And if an absence of foot traffic wasn't enough to shake her confidence, there was Rusty's looming deadline set to expire in a few short hours to consider.

She dropped onto a stool behind the counter and cradled her head in her hands. Maybe this was a mistake. Her expectations were too high. It was only the first day. She shouldn't jump to conclusions. She raised her head. Perhaps it wasn't the store's appeal, but a lack of pedestrians. She stood. Of course, that must be it. She went to the door and stepped outside. Although the sidewalks weren't bustling with potential shoppers, neither were they deserted.

Why weren't the people browsing other storefronts stopping by hers?

Back inside, she went to the rear counter, pulled Rusty's contract from a shelf below, and grabbed a cookie. With trembling hands and depression setting in, she nibbled at the cookie and re-read the document. The main elements buried in the legalese were term, deadline compliance, and a non-compete clause. The term: two years. Deadlines must be met or exceeded, or the contract was null and void. And the non-compete clause extended beyond the contract expiration to year three and forbade her from approaching F&A clients to further her interests.

The enticing aspect of the contract was the guaranteed income stream, assuming she met the deadlines. But ensuring she did could be a death knell to A Distant Light. What if Rusty set his usual unreasonable time frames? Catherine rubbed her forehead. Was she willing to risk jeopardizing her fledgling venture? And then there was the extended non-compete, which would preclude her from contacting F&A customers. What if her retail venture didn't work out and she decided to freelance?

On the other hand, what if she accepted the offer? Would Rusty be interested in renewing? Probably not. Would she? That depended. And what if she missed a deadline and had to endure the lecture that was sure to come her way? Did she want to risk being humiliated once again? No.

The door chimes grabbed her attention.

Catherine squared her shoulders and put on a smile. Finally, a customer.

Tina closed the door behind her.

Catherine's shoulders slumped.

"Good to see you too," Tina joked.

"Sorry. It's not you. It's me."

"What's bothering you?" Tina looked around. "This place is amazing."

"I haven't had one customer. Not one."

Tina nodded. "It's only your first day. And non-tourist season to boot. Don't let a few hours on a winter day serve as a bell weather of what's to come. You had to expect it would be slow until the summer crowds arrive."

"I did, but I didn't expect that *no one* would stop by. Considering the ton of money I've spent on advertising, I thought I'd at least attract some curious locals."

"Give it time. You have a website, right?"

Catherine nodded half-heartedly.

"Great. I'll post a glowing review." Tina looped her arm around Catherine's shoulders. "Come on. Pull yourself up out of the dumps. Trust me. Before long, we'll be laughing over your first-day worries."

"Boy, I sure hope you're right. It's hard not to think that maybe this vision of mine is a pipe dream."

"Don't go there. *Christmas Stroll* is this weekend. I'd be willing to bet that will help make up for a few slow days. And here." Tina picked up four placemats sporting a Clipper ship design. "Count me as your first customer." She dug into her purse and came up with her credit card and a crisp dollar bill. She handed them both to Catherine. "Frame the dollar as a memento of your first sale."

Before Catherine could respond, her cell phone rang. She glanced at the display. Rusty. She should've known he'd call.

"Go ahead and take that," Tina said. "I have to get going anyway."

"It can wait." Catherine finished up the sale and hugged her friend, a gesture she'd come to enjoy. "Thank you."

Catherine's phone then dinged a voicemail alert.

"You're welcome." Tina headed for the door. "Hey, I'll stop by tomorrow with lunch," she called out over her shoulder. "In the meantime, stay positive."

After the door closed, Catherine stared at her phone, then picked it up and clicked on the voicemail.

Rusty's voice filled her ear. "Catherine, Rusty here. I need your answer. Please call me as soon as possible."

CATHERINE ONLY HAD five minutes to call Rusty before the deadline expired. She paced the store holding the contract. What should she do? Mom had always said that she would know when something was right. So, if agreeing to the proposal was the way to go, wouldn't she have already responded?

She grabbed the phone and punched in Rusty's direct number.

"Talk about waiting until the last ship has sailed," he chuckled. "So, when should I expect to receive the signed original?" he said with his usual air of cockiness.

She walked over to the sea captain's desk, sat on the adjoining diminutive chair, and took a deep breath.

"Catherine?"

She squeezed her eyes shut. "I've decided to decline."

"What? You must be joking."

Catherine opened her eyes. The space that unfolded before her was everything she'd hoped it would be. She was proud to have had the strength to leave behind life as she'd known it and branch out in a whole new direction. At first, she hadn't been sure how to follow her mother's advice and fix what was wrong. But after returning to work, what needed fixing became clear as a mountain stream. Now that she was comfortable with her choice, why risk everything for a chance at some level of financial peace of mind, from a man she couldn't trust?

"F&A is forever in my rearview mirror. I'm building my future here."

"How can you say that when you're venturing into something as shaky as retail?"

Catherine bristled. Her spine stiffened. "If I were to accept your offer, there's no way I could do both effectively. One would suffer." She imagined him thinking that she was right and that he'd do everything in his power to make sure it wasn't her commitment to F&A. She saw him in her mind's eye running his hand through his hair, trying to figure out what he could offer up that would clinch the deal for him.

"You can take my offer to the bank, unlike your little retail experiment," he said. "Catherine, don't cut off your nose to spite your face, because if you expect this offer to still be on the table if you change your mind, you're mistaken."

Rusty hadn't changed. When all else failed, he intimidated and fell back on his best scare tactics.

"The only expectation I have is to make my store a success."

"And what if it's not?"

"I guess I'll cross that bridge if I get to it."

"Chances are you'll get there faster than you think."

She switched the phone to her other hand and shook off the pins-and-needles sensation that gripped it. Rusty's words erased any sense of self-doubt. Who the heck did he think he was?

"Let me remind you that you've been wrong before."

"Excuse me?" he coughed out.

"As I recall, you once said that my goal of making partner was unlikely. That F&A had no interest in adding to the established stable.

Yet, when you were forced to acknowledge my worth, the door that you previously slammed in my face magically opened."

"Things change."

Catherine stood, fortified by the sense that she had made the right choice. "None of what you're saying matters to me. The truth is, it hasn't for a while. That's what you seem to be missing."

"But—"

"Goodbye, Rusty. And please don't call in hopes that you'll change my mind. There's nothing left for us to discuss."

Although *Christmas Stroll* hadn't delivered as many customers to Catherine's doorstep as she'd hoped for, she'd take what she could get. It comforted her to hear the customers' comments, although some sounded surprised about the high quality of her merchandise and the vast array of selections. She prayed that word would spread and bode well for the remaining frosty months leading up to tourist season.

Around noon on day two of the annual event, the doorbell chimed, and three well-dressed women entered her store. She guessed two were in their early forties, and the third close in age to Helen.

"What a lovely establishment you have," the older woman said to Catherine after browsing for several minutes. "I've never seen so many collectibles and other high-end nautical pieces in one place except for my own store that I ran several years ago."

Relief rushed through her. "Thank you."

The older woman side-eyed Catherine. "If I were to buy everything that fancies me, you'd have nothing left, and my husband would divorce me." She glanced around the store and sighed.

"Splurge, Aunt Shelley," one of the younger women said. "You know you're not leaving the island without something expensive. And Uncle Vince is as likely to divorce you as he is to start eating grass."

Shelley laughed and shook her head. "You're right. Poor man." Later, she elicited her nieces as beasts of burden for four purchases they could carry with them, while she considered three others, including the sea trunk that she proclaimed was perfect for the foot of a guest bed that had gone wanting for years. "I'll need the trunk shipped." She handed Catherine her credit card. "Is that possible?"

"Of course." Catherine extracted a shipping form. "Where would you like it sent?"

The woman recited her Beacon Hill address.

"Ah, Boston."

"Yes, and I bet you hail from my hometown, too," Shelley said. "Am I right?"

Catherine smiled. "It's my accent, right?"

Shelley nodded. "Where did you call home?"

"A stone's throw from the Long Wharf."

Shelley turned to survey the store. "My nieces visit the island for a few days every so many months to browse the stores, and they're sweet enough to allow me to tag along. I have to say I'm enamored with your shop, and based on what my nieces are hauling around, I'd say they are, too." She gave a definitive bob of her head. "Yes, it's likely we'll be back."

Catherine handed the woman her credit card and smiled. "I'll look forward to seeing you again." She reveled in the fact that she hadn't been wrong in her choice of merchandise.

The door chimes sounded.

Michael's gaze swept the store, and he gave an approving nod.

His apple-red puffer vest over a flannel plaid shirt, corduroy pants that hugged all the right places, and leather work boots personified Webster's definition of masculinity.

Catherine's cheeks warmed, and her insides stirred. She finished the sale and confirmed the shipping address with Shelley.

The older woman tilted her head in Michael's direction. "Seems you have a visitor. I'll see what my nieces are up to."

Catherine watched as the trio formed a circle and whispered amongst themselves.

"Hi." Michael whipped out a bouquet of pink and white carnations with baby's breath wrapped in green tissue paper from behind his back. "Just thought I'd stop by and wish you good luck with all of this."

She reached for the flowers and brought them to her nose. "Carnations. My favorite. Thank you."

He lowered his voice. "So, how's it going?"

Catherine side-eyed the women, still deep in discussion, returned her gaze to Michael, leaned in, and whispered, "Well, until the last two days, I thought I'd be returning to Beantown."

He offered her a smile. "*Stroll* is a good indication of how things will be during tourist season. And besides that, it's a fun time."

Catherine laughed. "You sound like your sister. She stopped by yesterday with lunch and couldn't wait to say she'd told me so about the traffic this event would bring."

Michael smiled and shook his head. "Sounds like something she'd do. Bring lunch, I mean. And I bet it was homemade. Am I right?"

"Yes. A chicken sandwich smothered in peppers and onions. Delicious."

"I'd stack her up against any of the famous chefs. She's that good."

"Well, if that sandwich is any indication, I agree."

"I won't keep you. Enjoy the flowers." He stopped at the refreshment table and eyed the cookies. "May I?"

"Of course."

He grabbed one, bit into it, and flashed that killer smile of his. "Awesome."

She felt herself melt like candy left too long in the sun.

"By the way, Tina and I are going to watch Santa arrive at the wharf tonight, and we're wearing our ugly Christmas sweaters. Why not join us?"

Not anxious to agree to a quasi-date, even though Tina would be in tow, Catherine still wrestled with the notion of contacting Jack and didn't want to complicate the decision.

"I have a lot to do. Maybe next time—and besides, I don't have an ugly Christmas sweater." She forced a laugh.

"Well, if you change your mind, I'm sure Tina can supply one. I hope you reconsider. It's always a lot of fun."

After he left, the younger duo piled up their intended purchases on the counter and cooed over Michael's good looks.

Shelley winked at Catherine. "That's some boyfriend you have there." She placed a hand over her heart. "If only I were single and forty years younger," she said. "I'd give you a run for your money!"

Catherine swatted at the air. "Oh, he's not my boyfriend. The brother of a friend."

"Somehow, I don't think that's what *he* has in mind." Shelley's smile she'd been wearing suddenly did a one-eighty.

"Is something wrong?" Catherine asked.

Shelley shifted her gaze to her nieces, then back to Catherine, as if watching a tennis match.

"Are you having second thoughts about your purchases?" Catherine hoped the answer was no. The sea captain's chest was one of her most pricey items. And the last thing she wanted was to reverse the sale.

Shelley shook her head. "No, no, quite the opposite."

Catherine's shoulder muscles relaxed.

"Go on." One of the nieces coaxed.

Catherine frowned.

"Well, my nieces and I were saying it's such a shame."

"What is?" Catherine asked, confused.

Shelley lowered her voice. "As I said earlier, you have a beautiful establishment here. Such high-end, very desirable merchandise. And I should know."

Catherine was lost. What in the world was this woman trying to say? "I'm sorry. I'm not following you."

"Just spit it out, Auntie Shelley."

Shelley exhaled a long breath and dipped her chin. "I think I mentioned that my nieces and I visit the island every so often."

Catherine nodded.

"Well, over the years, we've come to know some of the shop-keepers."

Catherine wished Shelley would follow her niece's advice and get to the point.

"We would've been here the day you opened if it weren't for…"

Catherine's patience was wearing thin. She wanted to shake the words out of the woman, but she followed Helen's advice and kept a smile in place.

Even though the store was absent from any other customers, Shelley glanced over her shoulder. "We'd heard that the goods you're selling come from third world countries that employ child labor."

Catherine gasped and stepped back as if pushed. "Child labor? Third world countries?" The words echoed in her mind. "Did they say why they think that?" she asked, forcing a level of calm into her voice when she wanted to scream.

"No, but I got the sense that it's the talk of the town."

No wonder customers hadn't crossed her doorstep during the first few days. With the *Stroll* crowds, it would be impossible to taint everyone's mind. Thus, the few customers who had stopped in since it started.

"I assure you I'm not a gossipmonger. You seem like a lovely young woman, and I thought you should know, especially now that I see your merchandise is nowhere near what's alleged."

Catherine felt faint as she struggled to get the words past the tightness in her throat. "Thank you."

"I'm so glad we followed our instincts and decided to pay you a visit before we left this afternoon."

Catherine's stomach tightened. She struggled to catch her breath, reminded of the fear she'd felt during the attack in Boston. Moisture formed on her upper lip. Still light-headed, she lowered herself onto a stool behind the counter.

"Are you okay?" Shelley asked.

"I'm fine. Just stunned." She gave a weak smile. Who would spread such vicious lies? "I'm surprised. Where did you hear this?"

Shelley lowered her eyes. "I'm sorry. I'd rather not say. As I said, I'm not one to perpetuate gossip, and I'm not a troublemaker. But I couldn't leave and not say something after seeing the quality of your merchandise."

"I appreciate that."

Shelley reached out and touched Catherine's shoulder. "Although

I'm not comfortable offering up a name, I promise to make a point of stopping by where I heard it to set the record straight."

Catherine's heart pounded so hard after the women left, she heard its vibration in her ears. She tried to calm herself. What was the best way to handle this? She couldn't go running around town like a madwoman. She drew in a breath so deep her lungs felt like they were on the verge of exploding. Then she let out a whoosh and marched to the front display window, scanning the storefronts. Who would want to sabotage her? Other than her snarky attitude with Michael, she hadn't breathed an unkind word to anyone on the island.

She paused. *Michael? Don't be ridiculous*, she told herself. He'd brought flowers and invited her to *Christmas Stroll*. Besides, what would he have to gain by her failure? Nothing. But then again, maybe he didn't handle rejection well. She'd turned down his dinner invitation, and today shot down his request to join him at the wharf. A man as handsome as Michael probably wasn't accustomed to being rebuffed.

"Come out with us tonight," Tina said, before Catherine had a chance to say hello after answering the phone. "A bunch of us are going to the *Christmas Stroll* festivities. It'll be fun."

"I'd like to, but I have too much to do."

"Really? Like what?"

Catherine had tossed around whether to confide in Tina or Helen about her conversation with Shelley. Would they chalk it up to idle gossip or a misunderstanding? Advise her to let it go? She couldn't volunteer what she wanted to do, which was continue making an inventory of stores that lined the street and narrow down who might consider her competition. Then swoop in and nip this thing in the bud before it festered.

"For one thing, I have cookies to bake for tomorrow. And I should straighten up the store. It's gotten kind of picked over today." Even to Catherine, her excuses sounded lame.

"Listen, if it makes any difference, Helen and Bill will be there, too. They've arranged for one of their staff to watch over the inn. It'll do you good to get out. Give you a chance to unwind. Besides, tonight's the sort of night that'll generate memories to keep you warm all winter."

How could she create memories when all she could think about was who was trying to shut her down? "I don't have an ugly Christmas sweater."

"No problem. I have several. I'll stop by around seven and bring one with me."

Tina didn't make it easy. Catherine had to admit, it sounded like fun. Maybe taking a break would clear her mind. Help her think things through. "You win. But please don't make the sweater too ugly, okay?"

∼

CATHERINE LAUGHED out loud at the hideous sweater Tina brought her. It was a smorgasbord of misplaced Christmas designs. Lopsided decorated trees, gingerbread figures, brown felt reindeer encircling a house with smoke curling from the red brick chimney. And if that wasn't silly enough—on the back, a giant Santa face lit up when the concealed battery contraption randomly engaged.

Catherine slipped the sweater on over her turtleneck. Before long, they were out among the crowds of people that assembled along Main Street.

"Hey, let's stop and listen to the carolers." Tina started singing along.

While the strains of "Jingle Bells" filled her ears, Catherine took in the surroundings. Seven-foot decorated trees lined the street, and the scent of their pine needles filled the air. Closed to traffic, Main Street had been transformed into a stage. The storefronts, including Catherine's, were all ablaze with holiday themes, all vying to win the best storefront contest.

Tina tugged on Catherine's arm. "I'm so glad you decided to

come." She opened her arms wide. "It'd be a shame for you to miss all this. If *Stroll* doesn't put you in a holiday mood, nothing will. Come on. Let's get to the wharf and warm our inners with some hot chocolate."

~

CATHERINE SMILED when they arrived at the wharf. People mingled and children fidgeted, anxious for the arrival of Santa Claus. The air was filled with holiday tunes by a local musician. In spite of circumstances, she caught the holiday spirit and grinned.

When Tina and Catherine approached Michael, he stood and hugged his sister, then turned to Catherine. "Glad you could make it. You're in for a treat."

Catherine's jaw dropped. "I've never seen anything like this. Boston is always decked out, but this is different. Small-town America. One more thing to love about Nantucket." She glanced at Helen and Bill, seated on the bench next to Michael. Two throw blankets piled between them, topped with a thermos, eliminating that spot as a potential seat for Catherine. That meant sitting next to Michael, because Tina had strategically chosen the corner of the bench. Catherine inwardly squirmed when she realized the three of them would be shoulder to shoulder, knee to knee.

"Who wants hot chocolate?" Michael asked.

"Me." Tina raised her hand like a schoolchild wanting to gain the teacher's attention.

"We're all set," Helen said. "I made us hot toddies."

"Catherine?"

She lowered herself down next to Tina. "Sure."

"Before you get comfy, would you mind helping my little brother get our cocoa?" Tina asked. "Michael has a lot of talents, but juggling three cups of hot liquid isn't one of them." She patted the bench. "I'll stay and guard our seats."

Tina's setup was obvious. Based on the broad grin that had blossomed across Michael's face, he was totally on board. Catherine couldn't decline without appearing rude, so she let it go. "I'd hardly call him little."

He flashed that smile of his. "I guess I grew up when my sister wasn't looking." Then he gestured Catherine to join him. "Come on. The booth is right over there."

She felt herself dissolve into the light woodsy scent of his aftershave as they made their way to the booth. She noticed women sitting on the sidelines, following Michael with their eyes. Was that envy she read on their faces?

"So, have you always lived on Nantucket?" she asked, breaking the awkward silence.

"No. Tina and I are Providence natives. She moved here first, about ten years ago. I've only been here for two."

"What can I get you?" the woman at the concession stand asked.

Michael reached in his back pocket for his wallet. "Three hot chocolates."

"Whipped cream?" the woman asked.

Michael looked at Catherine. "Do you like whipped cream?"

"A lot."

"Yes, whipped cream for all, but the lady really likes it, so give her extra, please."

Catherine smiled, touched by his graciousness.

"What brought you here?" she asked.

"In my previous life, I was a commercial fisherman and decided it was time for a change. When Tina and I discussed it, she suggested I come here to think things through."

Catherine thought back to her own life-changing decision. Her personal life had shifted into neutral long before the mugging. Hearing her late mother insist that she fix what was wrong in her life had been the nudge she'd needed to kick-start her life.

"Why did you want to change careers?"

"Being at sea for long stretches was okay when I was younger. But over time, I started to feel there had to be something better." He shook his head. "No, that's not right. I guess I wanted something more."

Between his aftershave and golden hazel eyes, Catherine tried to focus on his story, afraid she'd lose herself in thoughts of what it might feel like held in his embrace.

Michael winked as if he could read her mind.

Her cheeks warmed, and she cleared her throat. "So, what attracted you to the sea?"

"The vast openness, I suppose. The challenges, the freedom, the true camaraderie among shipmates." He laughed. "Tina said I took to it because it's a far cry from our father's corporate world." He shook his head again. "But that's not it. Dad played no part in it." He chuckled. "No need to call in the shrinks." He pondered his next response. "Fishing is something I had to try. That's the whole of it." He waved his hand. "Enough about me. Mind if I ask why you gave up advertising to move here?"

"I, too, decided a change was in order. A slower pace, and at the risk of sounding histrionic, more fulfilling."

He looked her square in the eye. "Nothing histrionic about it. I get it."

"Here you go," the woman at the booth said, and slid the three cups in a cardboard tray across the counter. Her eyes fixed on Michael a couple of beats longer than necessary.

Catherine wondered if he noticed, or was he used to the attention? After he paid, they made their way through the crowd, toward their bench, and they laughed and gave a thumbs-up to those wearing similar, outrageous ugly sweaters. In spite of her doubts about going, she had to admit to herself, she was really having fun.

"Wow, Catherine," Helen said. "That's one tower of cream."

Despite the chilling temperature, Catherine's face flushed. She tilted her head in Michael's direction. "Don't look at me. It's his doing."

Michael grinned. "What can I say? The woman likes whipped cream. Who am I not to indulge her?"

Catherine settled into her seat, took her hot chocolate, and before she could take a sip, she saw a man rushing through the crowd toward them.

Michael straightened in his seat. "Do either of you know this guy?" he asked.

He looked familiar, but Catherine couldn't place him. Then she snapped her fingers. It was Jerry. The troublemaker who'd blasted Linda at her closeout sale.

"He owns the Double Scoop," Tina said. "I wonder what's got his pants on fire?"

"I think that's how he comes across," Catherine said. "He gave Linda an earful the day I was there helping out."

Before she could share any further insights, Jerry planted himself in front of her, hands on his hips. "You're the one who rented the space next door out from under me."

He left Catherine no room to stand. She raised her eyes and squared her shoulders. "I'd hardly call it that."

"I don't care what you call it," he said.

Tina stood. "Whoa, hold on, Jerry. I represented the previous renter, and I don't recall you expressing any interest."

"Ms. Benton, I don't believe I was addressing you."

Michael stood. "Hey, buddy, I don't know what your deal is, but we're here to have a good time. I suggest you take your misplaced attitude elsewhere."

Jerry scowled at Michael, who towered over him by six inches. Then he turned his attention back to Catherine, lowered his hands from his hips, and shook his finger at her. "Rest assured, you haven't seen the last of me. I'll be by tomorrow to finish this."

"Hey." Michael stepped forward. "That sounds like a threat."

Jerry took a tentative step backward and held up his hands. "No such thing. I simply want to finish our discussion in private, if you don't mind."

"There's nothing to discuss," Catherine said. "I've signed the lease, and I'm here to stay. So, you may as well get over it."

Jerry's eyes narrowed, and he backed up a little more, allowing her room to stand.

Wait. Could Jerry be behind the rumors spreading through town like fire in dry grass? Catherine wagged a finger at him. "I hope for your sake that you're not the source of the derogatory comments regarding my inventory that I've heard about." She dipped her chin and stared at him. "If I find out you are, you'll be looking at a lawsuit."

Jerry huffed out a breath, turned on his heel, and pushed his way through the crowd.

Michael held up his hand in a high five. "Way to go, Catherine," he said. "I've always admired feisty women."

Tina sent a questioning glance her way. "Derogatory comments? What's all that about?"

Catherine pasted a smile on her face. "I'd rather not get into it now. We're having such a good time. Let's just get back to doing that. We'll talk about it another time."

CHAPTER ELEVEN

The next day

Catherine flipped her door sign to "open" after returning from an early morning raid to scoop up a dozen bite-size fruit pastries from The Bean, across the street. She'd been too tired to bake cookies after the previous night's event. Santa's arrival had done her in.

She liked the added touch of providing refreshments, and in the summer, she'd add lemonade. Catherine found that people tended to spend more time in the store when they were sipping coffee or munching on a cookie, translating to increased buying potential. Until last night, she'd considered asking Jerry what he thought about her passing out coupons for discounted treats at his ice cream parlor. That was before he'd made a scene at *Stroll,* igniting her suspicion that he might be the one bad-mouthing her merchandise.

Catherine was arranging pastries on a tray when a middle-aged couple sauntered into the store. They headed to the antique captain's desk. The man examined the exquisite piece of furniture from different angles.

"May I help you?" Catherine asked.

"How much are you asking for this?" the woman said.

Catherine gave them the price.

The couple exchanged glances.

"That includes the chair," Catherine added, when she saw the tentative look on their faces. "I can provide you with a description of its historical background. It's one of my finest pieces."

"Let's get it." The woman turned toward her husband. Her eyes gleamed. "We've searched for so long. And we haven't seen anything this nice."

The husband paused.

Catherine held her breath. Had he heard the rumors?

"Can you ship it to our home in Texas?" the husband asked.

"Of course." Catherine's spirits buoyed, and she released the air that had built up in her lungs. She was glad she'd gone with her gut when she'd spotted the desk at a Cape Cod antique store. At the time, she'd wondered whether the price tag would allow her to make a reasonable profit or turn the piece into an expensive dust collector. She decided to go for it when the owners assured her that if she couldn't sell it, they would repurchase it at cost. She headed to the back counter to get a shipping form and bumped into Michael, who'd slipped in while she was busy.

"Good morning. Have I come at a bad time?"

Catherine's breath quickened. "Uh, good morning. Sorry, I'm working with customers."

"Go right ahead. I'm in no hurry."

His rugged good looks magnetized her, and she stole glimpses of him while completing the shipping form.

She finally wrapped up the paperwork and slipped it under the counter. "Thank you." She handed the couple responsible for her biggest sale to date her card. "Should you decide to shop online, this has my website address. If there's anything else I can help you with, please let me know."

The customers left, and Catherine walked over to where Michael inspected a miniature replica of Rhode Island's Point Judith Lighthouse.

A DISTANT LIGHT

"The detail on this is amazing." He turned it over in his hand. "I've spent my share of time looking at it, and I can vouch that whoever crafted this didn't miss much."

"Oh, that's right. You and Tina are from Rhode Island. I guess that makes you an expert."

"Well, I don't know about that. It appears *you* qualify as one, based on the merchandise you've selected. The couple that just left seemed excited about their purchase. And if I heard right, it wasn't cheap."

"It's a beautiful piece. I hope it brings them years of happiness."

Michael returned the lighthouse to the shelf. "On a separate note, has that guy next door stopped by?"

"No. I guess Jerry got the message."

The door chimed.

Michael jerked around to check out the store's latest visitor. His shoulders rolled when a woman walked in and pulled off her gloves.

Based on his reaction, Catherine suspected she knew why he'd stopped by, which warmed her heart. "I appreciate you coming by to check on me."

His face softened, and he fingered his beard. "Is that what you think I'm doing?"

A variety of emotions swirled inside her. She arched an eyebrow. "Isn't it?"

He blushed. "Can't kill a guy for caring." He paused. "By the way, what did you mean last night when you said Jerry had been spreading derogatory comments about your merchandise?"

Catherine had figured it would be either Helen or Tina who would grill her about what she'd said to Jerry, but Michael had beaten them to it.

"A customer came in the other day and said she'd heard that my inventory came from third world countries that employ child labor. I couldn't imagine who would say such a thing until last night, when Jerry flew off the handle. I decided to toss the accusation out there and gauge his response."

"So, you think it's him because he's angry that he didn't get this space?"

"I can't say for sure, but he's the only one who seems to have an ax to grind."

"Jerry didn't deny it."

Catherine nodded. "Right."

"Well, I sense another sale in your future, so I'll let you get on with your customer." He smiled, walked toward the door, and turned. "Funny, I have a sudden urge for an ice cream cone."

CHAPTER TWELVE

Christmas Eve

Michael rolled over, still sleepy, despite having gone to bed at his usual time. Even when exhausted, his mind wouldn't shut down. If his recent woes regarding his future hadn't been enough to haunt him, Tina had dropped a bomb, a week earlier, that their family were coming for Christmas. He hoped the rest of the family or the season's good tidings would keep the atmosphere from becoming icy.

He dragged himself out of bed, showered, and dressed. Then he palmed the doorknob at the connecting entrance to Tina's house, took a deep breath, and pushed open the door. "Good morning!" he called out. "You decent?"

She rushed into the living room. "Are you kidding? I'm on my third cup of coffee, and it's not even nine o'clock."

"I know why *I'm* jittery." Michael snorted. "But what's up with you?"

Tina swatted the air. "You know how Dad can be. I want everything to be perfect, so he can't find anything to complain about." She fluffed a throw pillow, gave it a light karate chop, then moved to a tabletop and wiped at invisible dust. She then glanced around the room. "Do you see anything that needs changing before they get here?"

He clasped her shoulders. "Calm down. You don't have to impress him. It's your home and it should please you, not anyone else."

She shook her head. "I know, but…"

Michael threw up his hands. "Hey, I'm no one to give advice. I've been talking myself down off the ceiling since you said they were coming. I don't get it. We're not kids. Why do we care what he thinks?"

Tina gave a half-hearted laugh. "Because we do." She sighed. "At least Mom and the others will be here. He tends not to be as much of a pain with them around."

"I wouldn't worry too much if I were you. Dad will be too busy lecturing me to have time to criticize you." Michael looked at his watch. "What time did Mom say they'd be here?"

Tina glanced at the nearby grandfather clock. "In about fifteen." She rolled her eyes. "Hopefully, everything went well with their trip."

"Leave it to Dad to charter a plane and hire a limo. Heaven forbid he'd ask us to pick them up." Michael laughed. "Can you imagine Dad climbing into my truck wearing one of his custom-made suits?"

Tina slapped his shoulder. "Or perish the thought, if one of the kids sat next to him with sticky fingers."

Michael looked away. When had his dad become an aberration of the man who used to play cowboys with him in the yard? Who was this man who'd become so judgmental?

Tina checked the warming trays overflowing with eggs benedict, crisp bacon, link sausage, fluffy Belgian waffles, and home fries.

A few minutes later, the crackle of tires against the crushed shell driveway brought Michael to the window. "They're here!" he called out. He wiped his sweaty palms on his pant legs, slipped his hands into his pockets, and fingered a few coins.

They went outside together to greet their family.

His father stepped out of the gun-colored limo and extended his hand to his wife.

Michael wrapped her in a tight hug. "Merry Christmas, Mom."

"Same to you, sweetheart." She stood back, her hands on his forearms. "You look wonderful, son."

He then leaned in to hug his father. His dad held out his hand and gave an abrupt nod. "Michael." He turned to his wife. "He *should* look wonderful. After all, he's a kept man."

Michael stiffened, and clenched his jaw. The chill emanating from his dad was palpable.

Tina placed a reassuring hand on his shoulder, halting the confrontation.

Michael moved on, welcoming his brother and his family after they stepped from the car. "Good to see you, David." Michael held out his hand to his older brother, too much like their dad in recent years, for him to hug, especially considering his father's cold reception and proximity.

David grasped Michael's hand and gave it a limp shake. He would never succeed as a fisherman. Michael's former crewmates' firm handshakes defined them. They symbolized trustworthiness, a trait David had locked away in the vault at their father's jewelry business years earlier.

Michael examined the older brother he'd once idolized and who'd always been his polar opposite. David, the straight-A student. The guy who never had to study to ace a test, while Michael had cracked books until the wee hours, only to garner grades barely acceptable to their father. David had had a stable of friends, while Michael had a few close ones.

While growing up, Michael had admired his brother's willingness to hear him out, advise him, and help him see both sides of the proverbial coin without advancing his views. It wasn't a one-way street, either. David had confided in Michael, too. He'd made Michael feel like his opinion mattered, and that alone had boosted Michael's confidence during his formative years.

"Denise." Michael gave her a broad grin. "You look amazing. My brother is one lucky man."

Denise, David's wife of ten years, was the personification of how

David used to be. Caring. Warm. Gracious. And if that weren't enough, she was gifted with shoulder-length natural blonde hair and a body that reflected how much time she spent in their in-home gym. What made her most attractive, however, was that she'd always been fiercely dedicated to her husband and their children.

She stepped up and threw her arms around Michael's neck. "Mick, you're not looking too shabby yourself. Island air must agree with you." She stepped back. "It's so good to see you! I can't wait to hear all you've been up to."

He smiled. Denise was the only person to call him Mick, and although he was not fond of the nickname, he'd never had the heart to call her out on it.

His niece and nephews squealed with delight when they saw him.

He crouched down and held open his arms. "Uncle needs a hug."

They nearly knocked him off his feet when they obliged with an array of hugs and sloppy kisses.

"Will you play with us later?" his youngest nephew asked.

"You bet."

The outpouring of unadulterated love warmed him, and he forgot for the moment about the stressful day that lay ahead. He stood and went to retrieve the luggage where the driver deposited it onto the driveway.

His mother pointed at two pieces of Louis Vuitton. "Those are ours."

Michael nodded and carried them upstairs to the room Tina had prepared for their parents. It was only a week. It was only a week.

"Who do you think will take the Super Bowl?" Michael asked David.

His brother leaned back, relaxed. For a split second, the David of years gone by smiled back at him.

"The Pats, of course. Who else is there?"

Michael laughed, glad to glimpse the brother he'd once idolized, even if only for a few seconds. "I'd like to see Seattle kick their—"

Abigail, Michael's five-year-old niece, suddenly ran over and tugged on the edge of his sweater. "Uncle Michael! Uncle Michael!"

He crouched down and smiled. The little girl, her mother's mirror image, was beyond cute with an explosion of blonde ringlets and shamrock-green eyes. *How nice it would be if she were* his *daughter*, he found himself thinking. "Yes, honey?"

She wiggled her finger, beckoned him closer, and whispered in his ear. "Will Santa know I'm here?"

He picked her up and gave her a squeeze. "Can you keep a secret?" he whispered back.

The little girl bobbed her head vigorously.

"Auntie Tina spoke with him."

The girl's eyes widened. "She did?"

"Uh-huh. Santa knows that you will all be here, and that you have been a very *good* girl."

David laughed. "Maybe Auntie should've checked with Mommy first."

The little girl slithered down, out of Michael's grasp, stomped down her black, patent leather Mary Janes, and jammed her fist against her hip. "Don't say that, Daddy! I *have* been good. And you know it." Then she looked up at her mother. "Right, Mommy?" Before Denise could respond, she turned and ran in search of her siblings.

"Come on, everyone." Tina motioned. "Breakfast is served."

Michael pushed himself to sidle up behind his parents. "I take it your trip was uneventful."

"The charter flight helped," his dad mumbled. "Can't imagine..."

"It was fine, dear," his mother said. "You know your father. Unless things are perfect..."

His dad mumbled again.

Michael knew only too well how his father could be. Pity the poor pilot or limo driver if things didn't go according to plan.

"Everything smells delicious," Mom said to Tina. "You've gone to too much trouble for us."

Dad eyed the table overflowing with everything from traditional breakfast fare to baskets of fragrant, fresh-baked muffins. "Should've had it catered."

Michael cringed. It was evident Tina had been slaving in the kitchen, yet the offhanded comment was the thanks she got.

Tina's smile disappeared. "No trouble at all." She shot her father a frosty stare.

After breakfast, the women congregated in the kitchen, helping Tina clean up. The children ran off their energies in the backyard. That left Michael, his brother, and their father in the living room.

Why did Michael envision his father as a hunter, ready to take aim?

"Tina should have a food show," he said. "No professional could do it better."

"You're right," David said. "When did she learn to cook like that?"

Their father swatted at the air. "When you live thirty miles off the coast, you have all the time in the world to perfect a skill."

Michael clenched his teeth.

"So, Michael, how's the world been treating you?" David asked in a blatant attempt to ignore their father's sarcasm.

"Can't complain. My carpentry business is putting food on the table and keeping a roof over my head."

"Give me a break," Dad huffed. "The roof is your sister's, and you can't possibly consider part-time carpentry the bedrock of your future."

David stepped up. "Dad, it's Christmas."

"It's okay." Michael directed his attention to his father. "As difficult as it may be for you to believe, I'm happy with the status quo."

"I'm sure you are. I keep hoping you'll come to your senses and ditch your sense of rebellion. You're not getting any younger, you know."

"Rebellion? That's why you think I'm not another mini-you?"

David closed his eyes, and his shoulders slumped.

Michael regretted his words as soon as they left his mouth. His brother shouldn't be a victim of the cross fire.

"Do yourself a favor and take a cue from your brother. Look at how successful David is. He and Denise and their family, they live a *very* comfortable life, one I might add that's completely self-supported." He shook his head. "Unlike you, who lives off your sister."

Michael stiffened and swallowed hard. "I'm not living off anyone. And your idea of success and mine are two different things. So let's drop it."

"I better check on the children." David said and rushed off, no longer comfortable with the role of peacemaker.

Michael wasn't surprised. His brother hadn't stood up to their father in years. In many ways, he struck Michael as a broken man despite his lovely wife and adorable children. "Can't we just agree to disagree?"

His father shook his finger at him. "No, we can't. That's your problem. You always refuse to acknowledge what's obvious to others."

Michael's heart pounded and his neck pulsated. "And that is what, exactly?"

"That you're nothing more than a vagabond, who, thanks to your sister, has a very nice place to live."

Michael wondered who might've overheard, and through the corner of his eye, saw Tina approach. "I have a house in Rhode Island in case you've forgotten," he hissed.

"That bachelor pad of yours? I'm surprised it's not in foreclosure."

He loved his father, but for the past twenty years, he hadn't liked him. If this were anyone else, Michael would've decked him by now. "Not that it's any of your business—the rental income it throws off is sizeable. It's proven to be a wise investment."

Tina stepped in.

Their father shot her a look telegraphing her to back off.

"I couldn't help but overhear." Tina glared at her father. "Let me make something crystal clear. Michael is not *living off me*, and for you to suggest otherwise is offensive not only to him, but to me as well. So, while you're in my home, I'd appreciate it if you'd keep your opinions to yourself, and if you can't, maybe you should find another place to stay. I've worked too hard to make you all comfortable to allow you to ruin Christmas for the rest of us."

Even for his strong-willed sister, standing up to their father was nothing short of a herculean feat. Michael wanted to hug her, but she turned on her heels and returned to the kitchen.

"While I'm here, I intend to map out a plan for you to join the company," his father said, as if Tina had not just given him a piece of her mind. "We're opening our third store. It'll be the perfect opportunity—"

How dare his father attempt to lasso him into a plan, one that he'd made clear wasn't on his radar? "Michael's cheeks burned and his hands trembled. "Not interested."

"That's it." His father threw his hands in the air. "I've had enough of your cavalier attitude. I'm offering you your only opportunity for any measure of success, and you turn it down. What's wrong with you?"

"Why can't *you* understand, I don't want or need your handouts? I'm happy with the way things are."

But was he? Lately, he'd been second-guessing his life's decisions. Yet the last thing he'd do was let his father in on that bit of information.

"I held out hope that we could make something out of you. And that finally, you'd make me proud."

Michael's head snapped back as if he'd been slapped.

His mother walked in. "Charles, what's going on? I thought we agreed to—"

His father held up his hand. "This is between me and my son."

"Dad's ashamed of me," Michael said, and his throat tightened.

"Oh, honey, that's not true." Her eyes darted to her husband and then back to her son. "You must've misunderstood. He couldn't possibly have meant that. He loves you."

His father waved her off. "Make no mistake, that's *precisely* what I meant."

CHAPTER THIRTEEN

Christmas Day

Ever since her break up with Jack, Catherine had spent her Christmas holidays ensconced on her sofa devouring comfort food while watching holiday-themed movies. It was a tradition she was not eager to continue. So, when Tina invited her to her home for Christmas dinner, she'd accepted, even though it might be awkward for her with Michael there. She'd told herself it was Christmas, so just deal with it.

Various outfits lay scattered across Catherine's bed. After several trips to the mirror, she decided on black velveteen slacks paired with a red top sprinkled with small, tasteful polka dots. She'd purchased the duo at a high-end boutique on Boston's Newberry Street two years earlier for a client holiday party, and had worn it only a few hours before sending it to the cleaners and hanging it in her closet.

When Tina offered to have Michael pick her up, Catherine assured her that the walk would do her good. She hadn't shared with anyone how much she still struggled with solo treks since her attack. She told herself it would be daylight, and as far as the trip home, Tina would likely offer up a ride. Catherine reached into her coat pocket and felt for the mace canister she'd purchased after her attack. She couldn't imagine having to use it in a place as idyllic as Nantucket, but as Michael said, one had to be careful even here.

Catherine stepped outside and raised her hood to the cold winter air. Clear of snow or ice, the walk would prove invigorating versus treacherous.

Despite the sunny day, she was relieved when Tina's gray-shingled Cape Cod home on West Chester Street came into view. It reminded her of Jack's grandparents' house, further down the same road. She remembered the flower boxes overflowing with brightly colored pansies and pocket gardens that encircled the house. Two rockers and a porch swing outside the blue-peacock-colored front door had always been welcoming. She smiled, shook off the pleasant yet melancholy thoughts, and stepped onto Tina's porch. Maybe she'd take a walk down there someday soon, and perhaps even catch a glimpse of Jack.

A posted sign on Tina's front door announced, "Merry Christmas! You've arrived. Come on in."

Catherine turned the knob, pushed open the door with decorative leaded glass insert, and stepped inside. The main living area's pale seafoam walls gave off a beachy vibe despite the harsh winter day. Large creamy overstuffed chairs, a sofa, a huge armoire, and a crackling fire in the white brick fireplace completed the room. The rustic, wooden planked dining table spilled into the living room from the open dining area directly behind it, the rich wood tone resembling the overhead beams and wide boarded floor.

The house was abuzz. Guests turned in Catherine's direction and then resumed what they were doing, as if it was no surprise that someone else had arrived.

Catherine's natural shyness kicked in. Maybe she should've declined, stayed home, and stuffed herself with a quart of Rocky Road. Other than Tina and Michael, no one looked remotely familiar.

Then, as if her thoughts had sent up a distress flare, Tina entered the room wearing a red-and-white apron with "The Elf Made Me Do It" inscribed on it with rhinestones. She wiped her hands on a dishtowel slung over her shoulder and hugged Catherine. "So glad you decided to come." She stepped back. "Thank you for the pastries from The Bean. It wasn't necessary, but who can say no to such deliciousness?"

Tina took Catherine's coat and hung it on a nearby hook. "Don't you look nice," she said. "Come. Let me introduce you to my family."

After meeting Tina's parents, her other brother, and his family, Tina motioned Catherine to a drink trolley set up in the corner of the dining room. "Help yourself," she said. "I'd join you, but I have a date with a turkey."

Catherine glanced at Tina's father, who struck her as aloof with a bit of a hard edge. His wife, on the other hand, appeared to be the yin to her husband's yang. She was warm and gracious, welcoming Catherine as if she were a long-lost friend. Opposites for sure.

Catherine turned her attention to the drink trolley and platters of assorted finger foods. She wondered if it was the pine-scented air from the massive tree in the corner of the living room or the aromas floating in from the kitchen that had her reminiscing about happier Christmases spent with Jack? Her eyes stung. She poured herself a glass of merlot to dash her thoughts and was about to put a few pieces of finger food on a small plate when she felt a hand on her shoulder.

She whirled around. The tiny hairs on her arms stood at attention. "Merry Christmas, Catherine." Michael's affectionate vibe gave her goose bumps.

"Merry Christmas."

"Tina said you were invited to Helen and Bill's, too. Glad we won the coin toss."

Catherine tamped down the stirring in the pit of her stomach that had become all too familiar. "I promised them I'd stop by on New Year's Eve." She glanced around. "I'm so glad I came. Tina's home is lovely."

Michael nodded. "It is, isn't it? Its warmth draws you in. Much like my sister is known to do."

Catherine glanced around the room. "Her decorations are amazing."

"Did you see the family of carolers lining the stairs?"

"No."

He extended an elbow. "Well, follow me. You're in for a treat."

The family of four dolls were resplendent in Victorian-era outfits. The young boy wore green, large-ribbed corduroy pants and a red-and-green plaid woolen vest under a burgundy velvet jacket trimmed with faux fur. His black, patent leather shoes and jaunty cap completed the look. And if that wasn't delightful enough, he held a golden songbook in one hand, as if he was about to belt out a tune. The father's outfit mimicked the son's. And the mother and daughter's ensembles, with matching textures and patterns, were equally impressive.

Catherine fingered the mother's coat. "These are exquisite."

"Tina bought them from Linda after she first opened. I believe the clothing is handmade," Michael said.

He motioned her to follow him. "Come on. As much as I'd like to keep you all to myself, Tina will kill me if I don't allow you to mingle."

Catherine wasn't fond of mingling. Snapshots of business functions she'd had to attend flitted across her mind. She recalled how she'd prepped for days to gather small-talk topics. Somehow, this felt different. Maybe it was Michael's presence that fortified her. It felt like they'd known each other for decades instead of a few short months.

"Well, if it isn't our newest neighbor," a fortyish man said when they stepped up to a small circle standing in front of the fireplace.

"That's me," she said, a little too perky.

The man extended his hand. "I've seen you around town but haven't had the opportunity to introduce myself. I'm Nat. I own Nat's hardware store, across the street from you." He tilted his head to the left. "And this is Carol. She owns This and That at the other end of Main Street."

Carol gave Catherine an obvious once-over.

Catherine was dying to ask if they'd heard the rumors about her merchandise, but that could potentially make a bad situation worse. If they hadn't, it would only serve to propagate the gossip. "Nice to meet both of you," she said. "I'm Catherine."

Carol's lips squeezed together. "I know who you are." She fixed her gaze on Nat. "She's the one with that *lighthouse* store."

"You obviously haven't visited A Distant Light," Michael interjected. "Because if you had, you'd know it's far more than that."

"Well, from what I've heard from Jerry..." Carol said.

Catherine bristled but kept her forced smile in place, putting Helen's advice into practice. *Don't let on how you feel.* "Oh, so you're a friend of Jerry's?" she said with an air of casualness, not close to what she felt.

Nat cackled. "Yeah, probably the only one he has left. Since it's Christmas, I'll be kind. Let's just say he's quite a character."

"Not your place to judge," Carol sniffed. "He's been justifiably upset lately. He wanted to expand into the space she now occupies."

"He had the same opportunity as anyone else." Catherine heard the clip of her words when Carol all but ignored her presence. So much for Helen's advice.

Carol huffed. "Hardly. As I hear it, you were afforded insider information and swooped in before anyone else had a chance to claim it."

"Really?" Michael said. "Who said that?"

"Who do you think?" Nat said. "Come on, Carol, you make this sound like some Wall Street transaction." He shook his head. "Insider information, hah. That's a good one."

"Well, you can't deny that you're friends with Helen from Sunny Skies." Carol inched forward. "Can you?"

"Helen's a friend. So what?"

"See." Carol wagged a finger. "That's how you found out."

Catherine couldn't deny that. "Well, maybe if Jerry had a better relationship with Linda, she would have told him first."

Nat raised his glass. "Touché." He leaned in. "Look, I'm not one to mince words." He looked at Carol, then at Catherine. "It's no secret that I've had my share of run-ins with the guy since I moved here to take over my late father's store. So, unlike some other people, I haven't put any stock in what Jerry has been spreading around town."

So, Jerry *was* behind the rumors. Was Carol his accomplice? Catherine rolled the disclosure around in her mind. Should she act surprised? Or simply take it all in and act on it later?

"Thank you for your support," Catherine said to Nat.

"From what I've heard, you've put him in his place. Good for you." Nat chuckled. "He's had it coming for a long time." He leaned in and lowered his voice. "He doesn't look kindly on that sort of thing. Especially from a woman."

Carol stiffened as if someone had stuck a rod down her back.

Catherine refrained from rolling her eyes. "Oh, so he's a chauvinist on top of being a jerk."

"Dinner's ready!" Tina called out, preventing any further conflict Catherine was sure would follow based on the dagger eyes coming from Carol.

Catherine welcomed a wave of relief when she realized that her designated seat was at the end of the long table, flanked by Michael to her right, and Tina at the head. Thank goodness Tina hadn't sat Catherine next to the witch who most likely had helped undermine her future!

After dinner, everyone left the table, rubbing their bellies and mumbling they were so full they couldn't take another bite. Even Tina's father, who struck Catherine as stodgy, cleaned his plate and gave a hint of a smile when he headed for the living room. Later, when the desserts were displayed, everyone came down with a case of selective amnesia about how full they'd been.

Catherine surveyed the table. A variety of pre-sliced pies followed by platters of luscious mini creations, cheesecake, banana cream pudding, chocolate tortes, and cookies adorned the center. In the middle, a gorgeous crystal platter featured the pastries Catherine had sent over.

Tina's guests eventually filtered out, leaving just Catherine, Tina, and Michael alone in the living room. The rest of the family were long since ensconced in their rooms.

Tina flopped onto one of the overstuffed chairs and kicked off her shoes. "What a day!"

"Everything was beyond wonderful," Catherine said. "Thank you for inviting me. I *so* enjoyed myself, except for meeting Carol."

"Sounds like Nat thought Jerry was behind the rumors," Michael said.

Tina frowned. "Nat came right out and said it was Jerry?"

"Yes, and after meeting Carol, I think she might be his accomplice." Catherine folded her arms across her chest.

"That's too bad." Tina sighed. "But I can't say I'm surprised. For some unknown reason, she and Jerry have bonded recently. She even asked if she could bring him along, but I shut that down."

Catherine stood. "I appreciate that." She looked around. "Is there anything I can help you with before I head out?"

"No. Once I put away what's left of the desserts, I'm heading upstairs to slip between the sheets. It's been a long day, and I'm exhausted."

"Then I'll call it a night," Catherine said.

Tina hoisted herself out of the chair and peered out the window. "Michael, be a dear and drive Catherine home. It's starting to snow, and I don't want her walking in the dark."

Before Catherine could offer up a phony protest, Michael grabbed his coat. "Give me five while I warm up the car."

CATHERINE UNBUCKLED HER SEAT BELT, craned her neck, and leaned forward when Michael pulled in front of her store. Four concrete-based reflective signs lined the sidewalk, declaring that parking was only for A Distant Light. "What the heck are those?"

She bound out of the truck before Michael could come around and open her door.

"You didn't have those put there?" he asked.

"No. Why would I do that? I bet this is Jerry's handiwork." Catherine stomped her foot. "What's wrong with that man?"

Michael shook his head. "Why would he do this?"

"I guess he can't let it go."

"Maybe I ticked him off when I visited his store."

Catherine shook her head. "That was weeks ago. And besides, you said Jerry wasn't even there."

"Right. I bought a cone and left."

CHAPTER FOURTEEN

The next day

"What I can't figure out is why Jerry would designate parking spots in front of my store?" Catherine said to Tina. "Makes no sense."

"If he's behind this, he knows full well that it's a violation of city ordinance to have those signs. He wanted the council to think you put them there, so you'd get levied a hefty fine, which might force you out of business."

"But I'm innocent."

"It'll be up to you to prove that." Tina pointed to a man taking pictures outside. "And if I'm not mistaken, you're about to find out how very much his stunt could cost you."

A few minutes later, the door chimes sounded. "Hello, Tina." The man tipped his cap. "Didn't expect to see you here." He looked at Catherine. "Are you the proprietor?"

She stepped forward. "Yes."

"Are you aware that you cannot put signs along the street?"

"I didn't put them there."

"Then who did?"

Tina put her hands on her hips. "Darren, who reported this violation?"

Darren scrutinized the paperwork in his hand. "The proprietor of the Double Scoop. Those signs limit his business."

Tina threw her hands in the air. "Just as we suspected. He put them there and wants it to look like Catherine did."

Darren furrowed his brow. "Why would he do that?"

"I heard him say he was interested in expanding and is upset that he didn't get a chance to lease this space for himself," Tina said.

"Oh, please. How would those signs further Jerry's cause? What would he have to gain?"

"He had to know that it would bring me a citation," Catherine said. "I believe he's determined to have me toss in the towel so he can have this place for himself."

The man scratched a spot above his ear and made a note on the paperwork on his clipboard. "Well, it will take some proof to support your allegations."

Catherine huffed. "But I told you—"

"What you've described is, at best, bizarre," Darren said.

Tina's eyes narrowed. "So, what do you expect her to do?"

"Remove the signs, and pay the fine."

"But I didn't put them there, and besides, they're too heavy to move," Catherine said.

"They weren't too heavy to put in. Shouldn't be any different to get out."

"Doesn't seem right. Catherine shouldn't have to pay to have them hauled away for something she didn't do," Tina said. "What other alternatives are there?"

Darren scratched his head. "Well, she could go before the committee and plead her case. It meets on the fourth Tuesday of every month. Keep in mind for every day these signs stay put the meter's running, though."

Catherine frowned. "What does that mean?"

"Means, one thousand dollars a day."

Catherine gasped and covered her mouth with her hand. It was the fourth Wednesday of the month, which translated to thirty thousand dollars until the committee met again. No way. Catherine's throat tightened. "That's crazy. I can't afford that."

"Don't have to," he said. "If you remove the violation."

"Hold on." Tina rubbed her forehead. "Let's be reasonable here, Darren. You have my word that she didn't do this. Doesn't that count for anything?"

He turned to face Tina. "This has nothing to do with you. Besides, it's not me that has to be convinced. The council will expect proof."

"But the meeting isn't for another month!" Tina yelled.

"Okay, listen." He leaned in. "I shouldn't say this, but since she's a friend of yours, here's my suggestion. Off the record, of course."

"Of course." Tina said.

"Pay someone to get those things out of here. Keep the receipt, and bring it to the council to plead your case."

"What does that get me?" Catherine said through clenched teeth.

"It keeps the fines at bay. Which, as you've already figured out, will be substantial."

"But if they don't believe me, I'll be stuck with the bill."

"I'd spend my time gathering documents, so they *do* believe you. Assuming they rule in your favor, they can issue Jerry a citation and order him to reimburse you."

"But how do I go about proving it?" Catherine asked.

"That's up to you to figure out. I've already said too much." He walked toward the door. "Don't forget. We never had this conversation."

CATHERINE HAD TEETERED on the edge of anger and despair ever since Darren had come by the store. She found it hard to fathom that the man who owned the quaint ice cream parlor next door was behind this stunt to drive her away. On the other hand, based on how he'd challenged her at *Stroll,* there had been times, after holding back her anger, she'd wanted to confront him in his own store. But her better judgement had prevailed.

Within an hour of Tina calling him, Michael pulled up with another man to help dump the signs.

Catherine rushed outside. "Thanks for coming."

"No problem." He tilted his head toward the man standing beside him. "My friend Al and I will have these out of here in no time."

"What are you going to do with them?"

"Well, my first thought was to bring them to the dump. Al suggested that maybe we should store them in Tina's garage."

"Why?" Catherine asked.

"Michael said that the guy's a real…" Al paused as if wracking his brain for a non-offensive term. "Pain. So, they could be used as evidence. Or," he winked, "maybe show up in front of their rightful owner's place if you know what I mean. Assuming, of course, you're able to prove who that is."

"Oh, she'll prove it all right. Not many places around here could provide and deliver these, especially on Christmas. And I'm sure with the right amount of coaxing, we'll find out who's behind this."

Catherine looked over her shoulder at the Double Scoop and frowned. "Not that we don't already have a good idea."

With considerable effort, the men launched the stone stanchions into the back of Michael's truck.

"How much do I owe you two?" Catherine asked.

"You don't owe me a dime," Al said. "I'm happy to help a friend, but it seems to me Michael could use a nice meal."

Michael blushed and elbowed Al. "Cut it out."

Now, what? She didn't want to embarrass Michael in front of his friend by blowing off the suggestion. If it weren't for him and Al, this would have cost her a bundle. Catherine wasn't ready to commit. Yet…

Michael waved his hand in the air. "Hey, ignore my friend. I'm glad to help."

Before she could respond, Jerry marched out of his store, sporting a fat grin. "Not surprising you're unaware of the city ordinance. Why would a wash-a-shore know about such things?"

Catherine had learned that a wash-a-shore was anyone not born on-island. Wasn't Jerry one, too? She put her hands on her hips. "You seem to know enough for both of us."

Jerry held up his hands and feigned innocence. "What are you implying?"

"I'm not *implying* anything." She pointed to the truck. "I'm saying you put those in front of my store. And if it's the last thing I do, I'll prove it."

Jerry threw back his head and laughed. "Good luck with that."

Catherine lowered her hand and clenched her fists. Oh, how she'd love to wipe that stupid grin off his face.

Michael glanced at the signs. "Uh, Jerry, just so you know, my fee for removing those is twenty-five hundred."

"And why do I care?" Jerry coughed out a laugh.

"Because when the town council learns the truth and orders you to reimburse Catherine, I'll be waiting for you right here with my hand out."

CHAPTER FIFTEEN

A month later

One by one, the council members entered the hearing room. They took their seats at the dais as if they were a jury. Catherine supposed that was a fair analogy since they would be deciding her fate. A few of them had made a point of stopping by her store to welcome Catherine and introduce themselves, while others had politely schooled her on council etiquette. Today, those same faces were stoic, masking any hint of a previous friendly encounter.

Shivers ran down Catherine's arms. She gripped the podium to calm her shaking hands. Would they side with Jerry? How would she come up with the money if they did? Or, what if it was a split decision? Then what?

She took a deep breath and turned her head to survey the audience. Had Jerry slipped in at the last minute? She scanned the room—no sign of her next-door neighbor. Catherine smiled at Michael, Tina, and Helen, who sat behind her in the front row. Then through the corner of her eye, she spotted Carol tucked in the back row, wearing black sunglasses and a scarf wrapped around her head, looking like a Jackie Onassis wannabe.

A DISTANT LIGHT

The chairman looked over his glasses. "First on the agenda is Catherine O'Malley, the proprietor of A Distant Light on Main Street, cited for illegal signage, is that correct?" he asked, looking at Catherine.

She bit her lower lip. "Yes."

The chairman rifled through some papers. "Since it appears you rectified the offense within twenty-four hours, your fine is one thousand dollars." He banged his gavel. "You can pay the clerk on your way out."

Catherine lifted her chin. "With all due respect, I have no intention of paying the fine. I didn't put the signs there, and I can prove it."

The chairman took off his reading glasses. "Is that so?"

Catherine inhaled a deep breath and gathered up the signed affidavits that Michael had provided from the company that had supplied the signs, and handed them to the chairman. "This will clearly show that the owner of the Double Scoop is responsible, not me."

She had been amazed that Michael had obtained the proof, recalling that when she'd asked him how he'd done it, he'd merely said, "What you don't know won't hurt you."

"Well, well," the man said, and passed the paperwork to the committee members seated to his left. "If these documents are legitimate, it looks like the wrong person has appeared before this council."

She shook her head in disbelief. Legitimate? Of course they were legitimate. Did they think she forged them?

"I'm sure you understand we have to confirm this. Assuming we find that this company did, in fact, deliver the signage to your store without your direction, then the next step will be to address the purchaser," the chairman said. "Based on that, I will place the fine in a pending status."

Tears blurred Catherine's vision, and she turned to Michael. How could she ever repay him for what he'd done?

He winked.

Carol rushed from the room.

The chairman raised his gavel. "Next agenda item."

~

CATHERINE'S EYES FLEW OPEN. What was that? In a half-awakened state, she looked at the clock on her bedside table. 3:06. The first thing that popped into her mind was that March 6th was her late mother's birthday. Was she sending Catherine another message? If yes, was she telling Catherine she should have taken Rusty's offer? Or had her decision to open a store been ill-advised? She listened, but there was only silence. Staring at the ceiling, she wondered if she'd been dreaming. Catherine pulled back the covers, went to the window, and craned her neck. The street was deserted. Again, she listened. It must've been the sign outside her store swinging in the wind that she'd heard. Yes, of course. Her shoulders relaxed. She climbed back into bed and pulled the covers up to her chin and promptly fell back to sleep.

~

CATHERINE WAKED INTO CONSCIOUSNESS, then padded to the kitchen for a cup of coffee to sweep away the cobwebs. After a few mouthfuls, she jogged downstairs to fetch the morning paper from the doorstep. Then she disengaged the alarm and opened the door. A putrid smell filled her nostrils. The night of the mugging, and being thrown against the dumpster, flashed across her mind. She slammed the door and gulped down breaths to calm her racing heart. Had the man who attacked her tracked her down, intent to finish what he'd started? No. He was in prison. She peeked around the shade that covered the glass insert. Garbage covered the steps. Maybe a trash can pushed along by the overnight wind was to blame. That's what she must've heard in the middle of the night. But wait—the garbage cans were stored *behind* the stores. Catherine's stomach tightened. This was intentional.

~

A DISTANT LIGHT

"What's wrong with that man? Why would he do this?" Catherine muttered, ridding the last of the garbage from her front steps. Should she confront Jerry? Share her suspicions with Helen or Tina? If she did the latter, they'd insist she stay with one of them for a while. As inviting as the room at the inn that Catherine considered hers was, she wouldn't let Jerry scare her away. Maybe, when the Double Scoop opened, she'd just march next door and give him a piece of her mind.

∼

A fresh-faced young woman, her blonde hair pulled up in a messy bun, approached the counter when Catherine entered the 1950s motif ice cream parlor. "May I help you?"

Catherine swallowed the anger that had built up all morning. "I'm here to see Jerry."

"Sorry, we don't expect him in today."

Catherine's brows drew closer together. "What? When will he be here?" She did her best to hide her shock that he was not there—and her disappointment at not being able to confront him.

The young woman shook her head. "Hard to say." She shrugged her shoulders. "Off-season, he pops in when the spirit moves him."

"Is he on-island?"

"Probably not. Jerry stays at his house on the Cape during this time of year."

"May I have his number so I can call him?"

"Sorry. I can't give it out."

Catherine's thoughts whirled around like a top. Should she leave without letting Jerry know she'd come to see him? No.

"Okay, please give him a message."

"Of course." The employee reached for a paper and pen. "What's your name—"

"Catherine O'Malley. I'm the owner of A Distant Light."

The woman snapped her fingers. "I thought you looked familiar."

"Please let Jerry know I stopped by to thank him."

The woman looked up. "Thank him?" A surprised look covered her face, as if anyone would have reason to thank her boss for anything. "Will he know what this about?"

Catherine gave her a sly smile. "Oh, he'll know. Trust me. He'll know."

∼

CATHERINE POURED Michael coffee and opened a folding chair for him at the rear of the store, after she'd called to fill him in.

"Wait." He sat down. "You think Jerry flung garbage all over your steps, and you thanked him?" He rubbed his forehead. "What am I missing?"

"I hoped to drive him crazy trying to figure out why on earth I'd want to do that. And that he'd stop by to find out."

"Did it work?"

"Not so far. What the employee said about him being off-island might be true. Emphasis on *might*."

"So, you still think it's him?"

"Yes. It would be easy for Jerry to make it look like he's not around. How do I, or anyone else, know for sure he's really off-island?"

Michael fingered his beard. "I heard he sold his house here a year ago and now uses the apartment above the store when he's in town. If he were here, I'd think his employee would hear him moving around."

Catherine's jaw fell open. "He lives upstairs over the store? I didn't realize there was another apartment over there."

"From what Tina said, it's a mirror image of yours."

Catherine opened another chair and plopped down. "Now *that's* scary. It was bad enough when I thought he lived somewhere on Nantucket. A stone's throw away puts a whole different slant on things."

Michael leaned forward and folded his hands. "When I went in search of information about the signs, I heard that he'd always been something of an odd duck. But lately, his actions have raised many eyebrows. Like selling the house, which he'd owned for decades, overnight. One guy speculated that dementia might be playing a role.

It's one thing to be upset that he missed out on renting the space, but to try pushing you out through intimidation is a whole different enchilada."

Catherine swallowed. "This morning, I was angry. Now that I know he could be so close to me overnight, it's unsettling." She rubbed her hands on her forearms. "It actually gives me chills."

"I didn't mean to alarm you," Michael said, putting a comforting hand on her shoulder. "I thought you knew about the apartment. If it makes you feel any better, from what I've heard, no one thinks he's capable of violence."

"I wish I could be as sure as you." Michael's mere touch sent a shotgun blast of tingles through her.

He removed his hand from her shoulder and folded his hands in his lap. "I'm truly sorry if I've rattled you."

Catherine shuddered when she thought how weak she must appear, and how Michael always made her hormones race. "You must think I'm such a baby." She shook her head. "This is so unlike me. I'm usually the strong one in the room. Jerry's latest attempt to bully me has shaken me to my core."

"Of course, who wouldn't feel that way after what you came upon when you opened your door?"

"I wish that's all it was. It's more than that." Catherine sighed. "A *lot* more."

Michael raised a brow.

She blew out a breath. "Shortly before I moved here, I was mugged on my way home from work one night. During the attack, he pulled me into an alley, threw me up against a dumpster, and stabbed me."

Michael's eyes widened, and then he slowly nodded. "Oh, boy. I get it now. A garbage dumpster."

Catherine nodded. "Uh-huh. I sometimes have flashbacks." She gazed into her lap. "I've fought hard to suppress those fears. But when I opened the door this morning, the horror of that night came roaring back." She raised her eyes to him. "I guess I haven't been as successful at purging those images as I thought."

Michael stood and opened his arms. "Come here. You need a hug."

She hesitated. As much as she'd love him to hold her, might it send the wrong signal? The opportunity to feel safe and secure in his arms was too good to pass up, however. She slowly got to her feet.

He wrapped her in a warm hug.

At first, Catherine flinched, but she told herself to relax, and then laid her head against his chest, letting the sound of his beating heart soothe her.

"I had no idea." Michael rubbed her back in small circles. "No wonder you're frightened."

The tears that Catherine had withheld flooded down her cheeks.

He patted her like he would a child. "It's okay. Let it out. You'll feel better."

It had been so long since a man had held her. Even though Catherine reveled in it, after a few minutes, she willed herself to pull back. "Forgive me." She wiped away the tears on her cheeks. "I didn't mean to dissolve into a blubbering mess."

He tilted her chin upward. "There's nothing to forgive."

Her breath caught. Was Michael going to kiss her? Did she want him to?

"You shouldn't be alone tonight, in case he tries something else."

Oh, brother, he *had* misread her willingness to be held.

He chuckled. "I know what you're thinking. Don't worry. I'm not suggesting I sleep here." He moved his hand away, stroked his chin, and broke into a wide smile. "Although…"

Catherine's shoulders relaxed. She laughed at his blatant attempt to lighten the moment.

"What if I call Tina and enlist her help?"

Catherine waved a dismissing hand. "I'll be fine. Besides, she'd probably want me to stay with her. And the last thing I want is for Jerry to think he's chased me away."

Catherine put down her dust wand and picked up her phone when she heard the familiar ringtone. "Hi, what's up?"

"Heard you've had a rough day," Tina said.

Catherine pictured herself wrapped in Michael's arms, and a shiver ran up and down her spine. "I take it you've spoken to your brother."

"It's not good for you to be alone tonight," Tina said. "But I understand not wanting to leave. So how about I pack my PJ's, grab a pizza, and head your way after work?"

"I'll be okay. You don't have to babysit me."

"It's not that. You'll actually be helping me out. I have a taste for pizza, and no one to share it with."

"What about Michael?"

"He's working on a project in his woodworking shop. He'll be burning the midnight oil. So we'd actually be doing each other a favor. You have wine?"

"Of course."

"Great. I'll see you around six," Tina said, before Catherine could argue. "Who knows, maybe we'll catch Jerry in the act."

"Do you really think he'll try something again so soon?"

"Beats me. I never saw the garbage thing coming."

A LITTLE AFTER SIX, Catherine prepared the sofa bed with fresh linens, a blanket, and two fluffy pillows for Tina's stay.

Later, after they devoured a good bit of the veggie pie Tina had brought with her, Catherine poured them a second glass of wine.

"I don't want to work up a case of indigestion, so let's not discuss Jerry." Catherine wrapped the remaining slices and put them in the fridge.

"Sounds good to me. What should we talk about, then?" Tina laughed. "We could discuss how our day went, but at this time of year, with things as slow as they are, that would take about three minutes."

Catherine put a finger to her chin. "Uh, let's see. Tell me what life was like for you before Nantucket."

Tina wiped her mouth with a napkin and tossed it in a nearby trash can. "Well, I married when I was twenty-one. Major mistake."

"Why?"

"I thought I loved him, and I suppose on some level I did, but in hindsight, it was raging hormones topped off with a dose of rebellion."

"Go on," Catherine said, her chin resting on her fist, interested to learn more about her friend.

"We met at Brown University and were consumed with all sorts of liberal ideas and opinions. My father epitomized the establishment, which at the time was the absolute worst. Tom and I planned to show the world how white-collar bigwigs were destroying the lives of everyday people. It all sounded romantic and exciting until we quit our studies without thinking of how we'd make a living. Let me tell you, reality set in real fast when we found ourselves homeless, dirty, and hungry." Tina shuddered. "A few months of that, and the established world my father had built looked pretty darned inviting. We divorced six months after we said "I do," and I moved back to the castle."

Catherine frowned. "The what?"

Tina smirked. "That's how Michael and I refer to our parents' house. Of course, it's not a *real* castle. It's just a huge house."

Catherine pictured the tenement in Boston's south end where she grew up and wondered what it must've been like to grow up in a mansion. "How long did you stay?"

"Ten years. During which, I finished school and fell head over heels for a local businessman." Tina laughed again. "Talk about the establishment. Ironic, huh?" She drained the remaining wine from her glass and put it down. "Anyway, I thought I'd finally found Mr. Right."

Catherine lifted the bottle and refilled their glasses. "Did you two marry?"

Tina rolled her eyes. "Hardly. Unbeknownst to me, he already had a wife." Her eyes narrowed. "He should've been an illusionist instead of a banker. I cried for weeks."

Catherine reached across the table and patted Tina's hand. "How did you find out?"

"Believe it or not, his wife called me. She found my name and address on a florist receipt in his jacket. It was the worst call of my life. Not only was I devastated, but I'd never felt so stupid in my life. I gave new meaning to the word *naïve*. His wife said it wasn't the first time she'd made a call like that."

Catherine shook her head. "Boy, imagine being her?"

"Can't. So, enough about me. You're pretty enough to have had the pick of the litter. Why aren't you hitched?"

Catherine sighed. "When I met Jack, I knew almost immediately he was the one."

"Where did you two meet?"

"Switzerland. I was there on business, and he was on vacation." Catherine chuckled. "He sent a waiter to my table to ask if he could join me for dinner. I guess you could say he picked me up."

Tina leaned forward. "I assume you let him?"

Catherine smiled. "Not right off the bat, but then I figured, why not? We were, after all, in a public place. Long story short, we found we had a lot in common, like living in Boston, for instance. We had dinner and spent the rest of our time hanging out and sightseeing whenever my schedule permitted."

"So, you picked up where you left off after you got home?"

"It took Jack several weeks to get in touch with me. By which point, I'd chalked it up to a vacation fling and tried to push him from my mind. Which, trust me, wasn't easy. Turns out, I'd only given him my business card, and being a commercial pilot, he was on the move during normal business hours. Once we reconnected..." Catherine gazed out the window into the night, and reminisced about walking hand in hand from the train station in Fribourg down steep cobblestone streets lined with wrought-iron lampposts and heavy, woodframed shop signs, leading to its center.

Tina waved her hand in front of Catherine's face. "Earth to Catherine."

She gave a weak smile. "Sorry. The memories are pretty intense."

"I see that. Which begs the question, why aren't you two still together?"

Catherine sighed. "Jack wanted marriage, followed quickly by children, which meant I'd have to quit my job. When he proposed, my career had just taken off, and I wanted to see where it would take me. I wasn't ready to walk away from everything I'd worked so hard for, and he didn't want to wait."

"Why did you have to give up your job? Sounds pretty chauvinistic."

Catherine shook her head. "It was a mutual decision. We wanted our children to have a stay-at-home parent, and since his salary far outpaced mine at the time, it seemed like a no-brainer."

"Couldn't you get married and put children on hold for a while?"

"I suggested that. All I wanted was two more years. He said by then he'd be forty, and what if we didn't get pregnant right away? He didn't want people thinking he was our children's grandfather when they were teenagers."

Tina leaned back in her chair. "Wow."

Catherine tilted her wineglass toward her mouth. "Ridiculous, right? It wasn't all his fault, though. There was plenty of blame to go around. Neither of us would bend. When I think back, I wonder how we could've been so dense."

"Sounds like you regret your decision."

Catherine nodded. "Every minute of every day. If only I hadn't let success blur what was truly important." She fiddled with the cork on the wine bottle. "I didn't want to leave my job without the brass ring. Silly me. I focused on the wrong ring."

Tina twirled her wine in her glass. "So, who pulled the plug?"

"I suppose I did." Catherine shrugged. "After I begged for time and he wouldn't hear of it, it not only hurt, but it made me mad. I never thought it'd be permanent, though. I figured he'd come around. In the end, I suppose we were both too strong-willed to turn the other cheek. I'd convinced myself that my career was enough. It's fair to say I became the poster child for 'live to work' instead of the other way around."

"Did you ever try to contact him?"

"No, although I've considered it several times."

"Maybe it's time to stop thinking and start doing."

"Part of me wants to, but another part is afraid I'll find out he's moved on. Made a life for himself. Unlike me."

"You have to do what makes you comfortable. If I were in your shoes, I'd try, rather than live with not knowing. You're too young to dwell in the past."

"It's hard. Right now, at least I have my fantasies. Once I call, those might be shattered, along with my heart."

Tina nodded, then squinted as if trying to focus. "So, let me get this straight while I'm still sober enough to try. What made you suddenly decide to move to Nantucket? Is it the wine, or am I missing something?"

Catherine giggled. "Probably a little of both. All roads lead back to Jack. He'd spent his childhood summers here at his grandparents' house. He returned whenever he could and introduced me to the other love of his life, as he often referred to the island. Before long, it had captured my heart, too."

"Where was their house?"

"Shell Road."

"That's not far from me."

"I thought so. When I came to your house at Christmas, your street looked familiar. I think that's the route we drove to get to their place."

"Probably. What's their name?"

"Chandler."

Tina nodded. "Lovely couple. They passed a couple of years ago."

Catherine briefly closed her eyes. "Yes. Helen mentioned that."

"Records show a trust owns it. I know because I thought of purchasing it and using it for rental income. But then Michael arrived and renovated my garage, so I lost interest."

Catherine's vision blurred. "I've tried to get up the courage to go by the house, but I'm afraid the memories will overwhelm me."

"Maybe with time it will be easier."

"Maybe." Catherine doubted there would ever be enough time to put the pain she felt over losing Jack behind her.

"I understand how you came to love our little slice of paradise, but why ditch your career and move here now?"

"Late one night on my way home from work, a man stabbed me, and I came close to bleeding out. Later, I learned that my heart stopped in the ambulance and I needed CPR."

"Holy smoke."

Fortified by the wine, Catherine said, "I saw the light people talk about."

Tina's eyes widened. "Really?"

Catherine nodded. "I heard my late mother tell me it wasn't my time. That our choices define us."

"Holy double smokes. I guess you took stock and decided a change was in order, so why not here?"

"Exactly."

Tina gave Catherine a sly smile. "Did the potential of bumping into Jack play a part in your decision?'

Catherine rolled the question around in her mind. If she admitted that it did, would Tina think she was pathetic for acting like a teenager, clinging to a relationship that ended so long ago? "In all honesty, I can't say it hasn't crossed my mind."

Tina stood. On her way around the table to give Catherine a hug, she stumbled and almost fell into her friend. "Whoops," she said with a broad grin. "No more wine for me."

"Whoops, is right." Catherine picked up the empty bottle. "We finished this off." She tossed it into the recycle bin. "Good thing you're spending the night."

Tina giggled. "Pity to Jerry if he tries anything tonight. I'm just drunk enough to let him have it."

∼

A DISTANT LIGHT

THE STREAMING sun felt like someone was sticking needles in Catherine's eyes the next morning when she rolled out of bed and shuffled across the room.

Tina sat on the edge of the sleeper sofa's mattress, rubbing the back of her neck. "Wow. I don't know about you, but it feels like a parade is marching inside my head. And someone's doing the rumba in my stomach."

"I hear ya. I'm about to take a couple aspirin," Catherine said. "You interested?"

Tina held out her hand. "Please."

"Coffee?"

"Another brilliant suggestion." Tina walked to the kitchen, filled a glass with water, and swallowed the pills.

Without so much as a second thought, Catherine loaded coffee beans into the grinder, a Christmas present to herself, and hit the button.

Both women then covered their ears with their hands as their faces contorted in agony.

Catherine slapped at the off button and leaned on the counter for support. "Next time we decide to have a chat fest, let's stick to coffee."

"Done."

For several minutes they sat at the kitchen table and nursed their hangovers in silence. Then Catherine pushed back her chair and stood. "As much as I'd love to crawl back into bed and pull the covers over my head, I have to get moving. My store needs me." She opened the refrigerator. "I'll make us scrambled eggs and toast. We'll feel better if we eat."

"Okay," Tina moaned. "I guess if you can soldier forward, so can I. I'll stop back after I shower."

Catherine smiled. "I appreciate that. You have to go to work. You got me over the hump last night. I'm a big girl. If Jerry comes by, I'll deal with him."

Tina grasped Catherine's shoulders. "Are you sure?"

"Of course. I won't let my imagination run wild." Catherine gave a nervous laugh. "The man isn't a serial killer, for goodness' sake."

CHAPTER SIXTEEN

Michael gazed out the window of his woodworking shop, watching blasts of white crystalline flakes whip around in a frenetic dance. He lowered his goggles and went to work on a hutch he planned to surprise Tina with for her birthday.

Not long after he'd arrived on-island, his sister had enlisted him to transform her attached garage into a guest suite that she could rent during the summer for extra income. This left her with a second detached three-car garage, now used in part for his woodworking shop and large enough to accommodate both of their vehicles. Michael later learned Tina had an ulterior motive. When he'd finished, she'd insisted he move out of her guest room and into the renovated space. Thus, handing him a permanent living solution.

"What are you up to?" Tina called out a few minutes later, brushing snowflakes off her coat as she rushed into the repurposed space, allowing in a big gust of wind.

Michael turned off the saw and pushed up his safety goggles.

"Thought you could use some hot chocolate," Tina said, putting down the cup and wrapping her arms around her middle. "You should turn the heat up in here. It's freezing." She eyed the sheets of lumber. "What're you making?"

"Nothing special," he lied. He patted the top of his table saw. "Just trying out my newest toy."

Michael took the steaming mug of cocoa topped with whipped cream and recalled the night of *Christmas Stroll* that he'd spent with Catherine. "Thanks." He wrapped his hands around the mug. "Great hand warmer."

Tina put her hand on his shoulder. "I stopped by for more than hot chocolate."

He raised his eyes over the top of his mug. "Why am I not surprised?"

"You haven't been yourself lately. What's going on?"

Michael thought he'd done a good job of masking his feelings. He should've known that his sister would see right through him. He lowered the mug. "You know me better than I know myself."

"It's my job," Tina said. "You're my baby brother. So, what's up?"

"Just a lot on my mind."

She winked. "Like Catherine?"

His face warmed. Was it that obvious? "Amongst other things." He slid over a beautiful rustic oaken bench complete with wooden pegs that he'd made, sat down, and patted the space next to him.

Tina joined him. "Care to share?"

Michael set his cup down, lowered his head, and raked his hands through his hair. "It's not just one thing."

"Never is. Maybe it'll help to talk about it."

His shoulders slumped. "It started with Dad."

She slapped the bench. "I knew it! I thought I put an end to his nonsense when I saw he had you cornered on Christmas Eve."

Michael smiled. "I wanted to hug you for trying."

"I guess you didn't blow him off like you usually do."

"I tried, but this time was harder."

"Anything I can do?"

"No." He turned to face his sister. "I'll deal with it."

"What did he say that has you so bothered?"

"He said I'm a loser because I'm not following in David's footsteps."

Tina patted Michael's knee. "That's nothing new. He's been

harping on that since you left college. So, that can't be *all* that's upset you."

Michael looked away. It was hard for him to repeat the words that had sent daggers to his heart. "He's ashamed of me."

Tina shifted in her seat to face him. "Oh, Michael, that's not true. He was just frustrated. He loves you," she said in a soothing tone. "Maybe you misunderstood."

"You sound like Mom. But he corrected her, and in no uncertain terms, told her that's exactly what he meant. And if that isn't bad enough, he reiterated for the umpteenth time that I'm loafing off of you." He pushed his thumb and forefinger together. "It made me feel this big."

Tina balled her fists and shook her head. "Arghh. You have every right to choose the way you want to live, and just because it's different from what he wants, doesn't make it wrong. And as far as living off me, like I told him, that's ludicrous. You pay your share, and if it weren't for you, I wouldn't even have a place to rent."

Sure, he paid her rent, but only a fraction of what she could get from anyone else. On the other hand, he had transformed the space, and he did help her out around the house, so that's not what was really bothering him. His father had always pushed him to join the family business, but this time, the elder Benton said Michael hadn't amounted to much. And since Michael had recently questioned how his life had evolved while trying to come to terms with the fear that he could die a lonely man, his father's words had cut deeper than usual.

"Besides," Tina said. "I'd be lost without you."

Michael gave her a weak smile. "We both know you'd get along fine without me. But thank you for saying that. I'm not getting any younger, though, and most men my age are married with children by now. Yet here I am, with no family of my own, and no prospects to start one."

Tina's eyes glistened.

It warmed his heart when he saw in her face a portrait of how much she loved him.

"I sense there's more that you're not saying."

Michael nodded. "I got a call from the captain of the fishing vessel where I worked. He wants me to come back temporarily. A crew member is injured and will take a month or so to recover."

Tina cocked her head. "Is that something you'd consider?"

"I don't know."

She stood. "Do you want to know what I think?"

"Somehow, I think I'm about to hear it, whether I want to or not."

"What you're going through is a classic mid-life crisis. And honestly, I think Catherine has a role in this."

"No, she—"

Tina held up her hand. "Let me finish. Dad's words are much the same as they've been in the past. The difference is this time *you've* been thinking about what he was obnoxious enough to say." She patted his hand. "You'll be forty soon, and you see that the years ahead could be less than the years that have preceded them. Trust me. I know. I've struggled with the same thing. It's not at all unnatural."

"So, let's say you're right. What does any of that have to do with Catherine?"

"Oh please, it's obvious you have feelings for her. I suspect you can even see yourself making a life with her. When you consider how you'd support her and the family you two might have, you hear Dad saying, 'get a real job,' and you think maybe he has a point."

"Trouble is, I can't figure out what else to do other than fishing and this," Michael replied, gesturing at the tools of his carpentry trade. "Although I could slip into Dad's world without much effort, that's the last thing that would make me happy. So, where does that leave me?"

Tina placed her hands on her brother's shoulders. "Here's my advice. As much as I'll miss you, take the captain's offer. Put some space between you and life as you've come to know it. Time alone with your thoughts will give you a chance to recharge. And what better place than the sea, where you've always said you find peace? Catherine isn't ready to move forward with a relationship anyway. So, nothing to lose from that standpoint." Tina laughed. "And who knows, maybe the old saying, 'absence makes the heart grow fonder,' might just end up applying. And if it doesn't, Catherine isn't the only woman who'd be lucky to have you by her side."

Michael wrapped his arms around his sister. "I love you."

"I love you too." She locked eyes with him. "And while you're considering your future, don't discount your carpentry talent. You may find that your forever job is right here under your nose."

MICHAEL PEERED through the plate-glass window of A Distant Light and saw the sole customer head for the door. He had replayed his discussion with Tina and the confrontation with his father in his mind more times than he could count. Maybe he did need a break. Hadn't he quit his fishing career to come to Nantucket for the same reason? To figure out his next steps?

What had that gotten him other than turning a woodworking hobby into a business that allowed him to eke out a living? On the other hand, his island stay had provided an opportunity to be close to his sister. That alone had made it worthwhile. But over time, the void he had felt deepened into a sinkhole, gaining depth and texture every day. And not in a good way.

Yet his love of the crescent-shaped spot of land thirty miles off the coast of Cape Cod was indisputable. Its quiet harbors, lighthouses, dramatic cliffs, quaint towns, and array of beaches felt more like home than Rhode Island ever did. As much as he loved Nantucket, there was no disputing that his career options here were limited, making his decision difficult. Leaving would be hard. He'd miss his sister and the comfortable routine he'd adopted. But he'd promised the captain an answer and he intended to keep his word.

Tina was right, though, his inability to decide on whether to leave, even temporarily, was due in large part to Catherine. He'd even fantasized about how a conversation with her regarding his departure might play out.

"It's temporary. Enough time to help out a friend."

Then while tears streaked down her cheeks, Catherine would declare, "Michael, please don't go. It'll break my heart."

As jaw-dropping as that would be, it would only complicate things. He couldn't expect her to spend the rest of her life with a man with no steady job or reliable way to put food on the table and provide for her in the way she deserved.

Besides, as Tina pointed out, Catherine wasn't really ready for a relationship. So why even tell her? Her cavalier reaction might make things clearer, and in the process, crush his feelings.

Michael went to the door, opened it, and stood aside for the customer to exit. "Hey, I happened to be nearby and thought I'd stop by and see how you're doing." He shut the door. "Is now a good time?"

"Sure. I was about to close," Catherine said from the back counter. "Flip the sign over if you don't mind. Coffee?"

"Sounds good."

She opened two folding chairs and headed to the refreshment table.

"Has Jerry shown himself?" Michael asked.

Catherine looked over her shoulder. "No, and no further incidents, thank goodness."

"He's trying to figure out why on earth you'd thank him for the stunt he pulled."

She carried over two steaming mugs, handed one to Michael, and sat down. "It made me crazy, trying to figure him out. So, I've tried my best to let it go."

"Speaking of driving one's self crazy, you're not alone." Michael tapped the side of his head with his forefinger. "And for me, it's proven to be a short trip."

Catherine sipped her coffee. "Cut it out. You're the most even-keeled person I know."

"Looks can be deceiving."

"Is there something I can do to help? You've been there when I've needed you. The least I can do is return the favor."

Even in the short time they'd known each other, he'd learned that he could trust her. How much would he be willing to divulge? Should he launch into his relationship with his father? The captain's offer? Or keep it neutral and talk about finding fulfillment? "I don't want to straddle you with my problems. You have enough on your mind."

Catherine reached out, touched Michael's arm, and smiled. "Don't be silly. Friendship is a two-way street, isn't it?"

He suppressed an urge to reach out and stroke the side of her face. Catherine was not only beautiful, she was also smart, and above all, kind. He closed his eyes to center himself and brushed away the thought of taking her into his arms. "I don't know how much Tina has shared about our family…"

"Not a whole lot, and nothing about you. All I know is that you grew up in Providence, and Tina has referred to your childhood home as the castle."

Michael bobbed his head and laughed. "That's how she and I have always thought of it. My father grew his business from the ground up and provided well for our family over the years."

Catherine nodded. "I overheard a conversation between him and your brother on Christmas. Sounds like he works for your dad."

"He does. And if dad had his way, so would I."

"That's not something you're interested in?"

"No way." Michael turned to look out the side window. "That's at the root of our friction."

"Sounds like he doesn't approve of what you're doing?"

"That's putting it mildly. I'm sure he was thrilled when I left commercial fishing a couple of years ago. He probably figured I'd come to my senses and would approach him looking to fill the executive-level position he's always pushed on me."

Catherine sipped her coffee. "But he must know how you feel about that."

"Oh, he knows, alright. I've always made it clear that it wasn't my bag. The nine-to-five grind, the suit and tie, and all that goes with a job like that, has zero appeal."

"What does interest you?"

You!

"I haven't come across my dream job yet." He gestured at the surrounding space. "Does this make you happy?"

Catherine sighed. "Happy is subjective. I thought I'd found my calling at the company I worked for in Boston. Unlike you, I was partial to that nine-to-five grind and all that went with it."

"Since you're here, I assume it didn't float your boat any longer."

"Ha, you sound like a fisherman."

He looked into her eyes. "Glad I could make you smile." His voice held that low sexy tone. "It becomes you."

"Thank you." She paused and peered into her cup. "If it hadn't been for the mugging, I'd probably still be there."

"You liked it that much?"

"I thought so. After the attack, I reconsidered some of my past choices." She lifted her eyes to him. "Sometimes, it takes an event of that magnitude to rocket ourselves out of the groove we find ourselves in."

"Were you badly hurt?"

She nodded. "Technically, I died in the ambulance and had to be resuscitated."

Michael fell back against his chair. "Wow, guess it wasn't your time."

"That's what my mother said."

"Does she live in Boston?"

Catherine's eyes misted. "She passed three years ago."

"Three years? Oh, I thought the mugging was more recent."

Catherine closed her eyes and drew in a deep breath. "The attack happened last year, not long before I came here."

Michael scratched his head. "But I thought you said—"

She looked up through moist eyelashes. "After my heart stopped, I saw the light many people mention. My mother came to me. She told me it wasn't my time to cross over, and that our choices define us. That I should go back and fix what was wrong."

Michael blinked. "Talk about heavenly intervention."

"I know, right? Shortly after, I took her advice."

"So why Nantucket?"

"The man I had fallen in love with once introduced me to it, and the island instantly captured my heart."

Michael's shoulders drooped. She was in love with another man. That's why she'd resisted him. What a fool he'd been. No wonder Tina had said she wasn't ready for a relationship. He swallowed hard. "Does your boyfriend visit you often? Or does he live here?"

"Neither. We broke up several years ago. It devastated me. Honestly, it's been hard to put it behind me."

Michael chastised himself for the sense of relief that rolled over him. Then he squeezed his lips together. "I know what you mean about this island. It has a way of pulling you in. I felt the tug the first time I visited Tina."

"So, I guess we can thank the island's magic for bringing us here."

Michael shifted in his seat. "I wish I had a crystal ball, or some insight into the future."

Catherine laughed. "Don't we all."

"Maybe. But you came here with a purpose, found your calling, and did something about it. I, on the other hand, am still trying to figure things out after two years."

"My best advice is to listen to your heart. As I've learned, our time on earth is too short not to live a life that makes it sing."

"How did you know this would do that?"

Catherine looked down at her hands. "Honestly, I didn't. Ever since my childhood, I've had a passion for the sea. I collected lighthouse miniatures during my teens, when most girls my age were accumulating shoes. I attached all sorts of romantic notions to them about sea captains guided home to their waiting wives and families by their beacons. So, after the attack, I asked myself what would make me professionally happy and content. I arrived at opening a store that would allow me to search the world for unique nautical items, and in the process, be my own boss. I thought maybe I might also find some inner peace and future happiness." Catherine cocked her head to the side. "So, what do you enjoy doing?"

"I, too, love anything that hints of the sea."

Catherine smacked her hands together. "There you go. Now you have to figure out how to make something out of it that will lift you, and in the process, provide a living."

Unknowingly Catherine had just given him a glimpse into her soul. She was romantic yet realistic. He loved that about her. Michael swallowed the final mouthful of coffee and slid his empty mug onto the counter.

Catherine touched his forearm. "Is something wrong? Something I said?"

"Funny you should mention sea captains returning from the sea. I'm not a captain, but I am going away for a while."

She blinked. "What? Where? When?" tumbled from her mouth so fast, her cheeks reddened from embarrassment.

"I've been asked by the man I worked for in Rhode Island to help him out. I think a little time at sea will help me sort out some things."

Were her eyes glistening?

"Is this permanent?"

"I don't think so. Like I said, just helping out for now. A crew member had a bad fall, and the captain, my best friend, asked if I would fill in until he returns."

Catherine blew out a stream of air. "Whew, for a minute, I thought I'd never see you again."

He leaned in and looked into her eyes. "Would that bother you?"

"Of course, silly. You've been a good friend."

He wanted much more than her friendship. But that would have to do for now.

"How long will you be away?"

"About a month. Who knows, maybe being out to sea will allow me to figure out how to make my heart sing like yours." He took her hand in his. "And like those sea captains you used to think about, I'll think of you as my shining beacon."

CHAPTER SEVENTEEN

Two Weeks later

Sunlight tugged at Catherine's eyelids. She stretched, rolled out of bed, and headed for the kitchen. She'd been feeling down, but couldn't put her finger on why. Maybe the clear sky, an unusual recent phenomenon, would help lift her spirits. Rays of buttery sunshine pierced the windows, instantly boosting her mood.

After breakfast, she pulled on a pair of sapphire-blue cords and a cream-colored turtleneck sweater. As usual, at ten, she opened the store and found herself filled with optimism that the sun-licked day would kick-start her outlook and maybe even attract some customers.

But despite the sunny skies, the day dragged on. Hadn't she shared with Michael that her store made her heart sing? So, what had changed? The previous two weeks hadn't been any different than their predecessors. And it's not as if she hadn't experienced her share of overcast winter days since coming to Nantucket. So, what was up with her mood? Maybe a walk to the inn would cheer her up. A visit with Helen would undoubtedly help shake off the doldrums.

After her only customer of the afternoon left, Catherine flipped over the door sign. She wrapped a scarf around her neck, bundled herself into her down parka, pulled on her hat, and slipped on a pair of gloves that matched her scarf. Then she set the alarm, stepped outside, and locked the door. The brisk air energized her. Fresh air. Sun on her face. Life was good.

Catherine passed The Book Corner, The Bean, and soon approached South Water Street, where This and That occupied the corner. She stopped and surveyed the store window. Should she stop in and gauge Carol's reaction? Maybe her attitude had softened. Catherine shook her head. Why chance what might be a nasty encounter, sabotaging her momentary good mood?

She gazed out at the calm harbor waters while waiting to cross the street. The white caps, a daily winter occurrence, had taken a break. She watched the returning fishing boats approach their docks and begin the task of unloading the day's catch. Squawking gulls zigzagged across the sky and swooped down in search of snacks.

Catherine sighed. Nantucket felt like home, so it couldn't be her decision to move here that had been bothering her. She couldn't blame the shortage of customers for her downheartedness, either. It's not as though the store had been a complete ghost town. Business had been decent, given the season. The locals had started dropping by, if only to escape the elements.

She was also sure it wasn't loneliness bothering her, since she could write a book about how that felt. Besides the occasional customers, Tina brought her lunch at least once a week and stayed to chat while they ate. Helen popped in, too, under the guise of saying hi, but she always slipped her a sweet treat.

Catherine smiled, thinking of how her friends conspired to make sure she ate enough. She loved them for that. On her last visit, Helen had purchased eight nautical-themed placemats saying she'd use them to enhance her dining room tablescape for a seafood extravaganza she planned for her guests. Catherine suspected Helen just wanted to stoke her store revenue.

So, why this sense of gloom? It engulfed her like a morning fog. Catherine stepped off the curb to the sound of a fishing trawler blasting its horn. Michael's face suddenly popped into her mind. She blinked. Could his absence be what was eating at her?

She pinched her lips together and continued walking. It wasn't like she was used to seeing him every day. Upon learning he'd planned to leave the island, she'd been relieved at not having to duck his invitations. But why was she feeling far from relieved now then? It was like the emptiness one sensed after the loss of a loved one. She mentally snapped her fingers. Of course. The recent dreary weather must have magnified the hole left in her heart by Jack.

She hurried up the stairs of the inn and headed inside.

"Catherine!" Helen rushed over with open arms. "What a surprise. Did you close early, or are you taking a late lunch?"

"Closed early. I haven't seen you in a few days, and I found I was missing you," Catherine said, thinking it wasn't that much of a stretch. Then she slipped out of her coat and hung it in the hallway closet.

"Well, the feeling's mutual. I hope you'll stay and share an early dinner with me."

"Love to."

Helen clapped her hands. "Good. I've made Yankee pot roast for our guests, and there will be plenty for us. Bill's off-island for a few days gathering essentials, and you can be my guinea pig."

"For what?"

"To try out my latest concoction before I feed it to our guests."

Catherine threw back her head and laughed. "Ha! As if that's necessary."

Even during the harsh winter months, the welcoming inn hosted a handful of repeat guests, thanks to the warm hospitality and tasty food. She recalled how Jack had often insisted he returned during frigid times to indulge in Helen's "concoctions", since that was the way she'd always referred to her meals.

"Remind me: What's the secret ingredient that makes your pot roast gravy so delicious?"

"Fresh cranberries," Helen whispered.

Catherine hadn't been with the woman, who was old enough to be her mother, more than five minutes, and already the cloak of gloom that had covered her in recent weeks completely lifted. She followed Helen to the private owners' quarters at the rear of the house and into the kitchen.

"Between you and me," Helen said. "I'm glad we'll have some quiet time to ourselves. It'll give us a chance to catch up."

Catherine hadn't realized how tense she'd been until the stress rolled off her shoulders as she stood next to Helen at the stove. "Is it okay if I make myself a cup of tea?"

"Of course. You know where I keep the tea bags."

Helen stirred the aromatic juices that bathed the roast, as well as baby carrots, pearl onions, celery, and sprigs of fresh herbs. She replaced the lid on the cobalt-blue enameled Dutch oven, but not before the spices, assorted vegetables, cranberries, and simmering beef created a collage of decadent fragrances in the air.

Catherine felt her stomach rumble.

"So." Helen pulled out a chair and sat. "How are things going at the store?"

"Mostly quiet." Catherine lifted her cup. "*Too* quiet. If it weren't for you and Tina stopping by, and a handful of regular customers, I'd be further down the stir-crazy path than I already am."

"Speaking of Tina, I saw her at Bartlett's Farm the other day. She said Michael's gone off to sea for a while. I got the sense she misses him like crazy."

"I'm sure she does. They're very close."

Helen nodded. "Now, what's this about you feeling stir-crazy?"

"Honestly, I'm not sure *what* I've been feeling. Maybe it's the weather."

Helen placed her hand atop Catherine's. "You should stop by more often. You know you're always welcome." Then she paused and took her hand away. "Maybe your mood is low because *you* miss Michael too."

Catherine couldn't deny she missed him. "I suppose I do. He's supported me a lot since I came here. It's selfish, I know, but I've grown accustomed to being able to call on him."

Helen winked. "Is that the only reason?"

Catherine's face warmed. "Of course. Why else?"

"Maybe it didn't sink in that you have feelings for him until after he left. I watched you two together at *Christmas Stroll*. You would make such a cute couple."

Catherine shook her head. "No, no. Nothing like that."

Helen cocked her head to the side. "Are you sure?"

"Absolutely. Michael and I are friends, besides I'm not ready for anything more."

"But if you *were* ready?" Helen pressed.

Catherine considered the snippets of Michael's actions and words that had invaded her thoughts in recent days, but she chalked them up to nothing more than missing a friend. "No sense discussing hypotheticals."

Helen reached across the table and patted Catherine's hand. "I get the sense you're *still* dealing with your breakup with Jack. You know as well as anyone that life comes with decisions we often regret. But as they say, life goes on. Or at least, it should. The last thing Jack would expect is for you to sabotage your future by reliving the past."

Catherine choked back her emotions. Leave it to Helen to push to the forefront of what she knew in her heart to be true. "I know. But I can't turn off how I feel."

CATHERINE STARED at the slice of freshly baked carrot cake Helen offered. "Are you kidding? I don't have an inch of room left. I'm stuffed."

"Nonsense. There's always room for dessert, especially one with such an assortment of healthy ingredients."

"I've eaten way too much already, including ladling on almost a bowl of your gravy."

"I'm glad you enjoyed it."

Catherine smiled and clasped Helen's hands. "There have been times when I've wished I still lived here."

Helen hugged her. "That would be fine with us. You're family, as far as we're concerned."

"Thank you." Catherine stepped back and checked the wall clock. "Time for me to get a move on."

"Well, if you're—"

Catherine crouched and put a finger across her lips. "Listen."

Helen frowned. Her eyes shifted left and right. "What? I don't hear anything."

Catherine giggled. "You mean you don't hear the cake nagging me to take it home?"

Helen laughed. "Well, let me wrap it up then, so it quiets down. Then I'll take you home."

"Thanks, but these legs need a good stretch. And a walk will help banish some of the calories I've inhaled." A few minutes later, Catherine left, armed with the wrapped paper plate, while Helen waved goodbye from the front door. After a few steps, Catherine paused. If she continued, she'd be back at her apartment very soon, stuffing her face with cake. And hadn't she said she should walk off some of the calories that threatened to go directly to her rear end?

She cut across to N. Water Street instead, then turned right onto Easton, where the Brandt Point Lighthouse stood tall at the end of the road. She made her way across the hard sand leading to the structure and headed for the boulders that encircled it. She put the wrapped paper plate on top of one of the stone surfaces flattened by years of pounding surf. As the sun neared the horizon, splashes of flamingo pink and lavender streaked across the sky. What a breathtaking final curtain call to a cold yet sunny winter day.

Catherine lifted her hood over her hat against the wind that picked up, dropping the temperature. Off in the distance, the Hy Line ferry motored toward the nearby steamship wharf. At this time of year, the passengers would be locals, who like Bill, left and returned to the island for various reasons.

The majestic sentry next to her began its nightly sweep of the water. Waves lapped the shoreline, illuminating fingers of white foam sinking into the sand and disappearing when the water retreated.

Only the sounds of the sea filled the air. Even the seagulls called it a night.

Catherine turned and looked down the street at the massive seaside compounds that lined Easton Street—dark and shuttered tight against the winter. Their inhabitants were not expected until the start of yet another vibrant summer season, when the island would come alive and visitors wished they lived there.

She shoved her gloved hands into her pockets, gazed at the dark carpet of water, and recalled Michael saying she'd be his shining beacon. She hadn't known how to respond at the time, not sure what he'd meant. She'd convinced herself that he'd played off her comment about lighthouse beacons and sailors. But was that really it? Could he have been sending a message that she'd been too dense to unravel?

When she raised her eyes to the sky, her thoughts shifted and her lips trembled. She couldn't look to the heavens and not think of her parents, especially her mother. "Mom, should I call Jack?" she whispered. Then, as if on cue, her mother's words reverberated in her mind.

More to do. Our choices define us.

"I know," Catherine said, as if her mom were standing right next to her. "But I'm afraid. What if I find I've been a fool for clinging to hopes of a reunion?"

She blinked away the tears that blurred her vision. Helen and Tina were right. She wouldn't know if she didn't try. Before she could change her mind, she reached into her purse, pulled out her phone, and dialed the number she'd never forgotten.

After three rings, a woman answered. "Hello?"

Catherine's stomach somersaulted. She felt nauseous, and her mind raced.

Should she hang up? Ask to speak to Jack? What good would that do?

She had her answer now. He'd moved on. It was time to spare herself any further embarrassment.

"Hello?" the woman said again.

Catherine disconnected the call. Now what? If she allowed herself to pursue a relationship with Michael, would she always compare him to a ghost's supposed perfection? On the flip side, what if she opened her heart to Michael and he realized that Nantucket was nothing more than a stopover in his life's journey? That being at sea for long stretches were what made *his* heart sing?

Then she'd be the one who got hurt, just like before.

She sighed, bent over, and picked up the plate.

"Opening your heart to love isn't always a piece of cake, is it, Mom?"

CHAPTER EIGHTEEN

Time away crystalized one inescapable truth for Michael. His feelings for Catherine were stronger than he'd imagined. He couldn't wait to get back to Nantucket and risk the consequences of admitting it to her. He'd felt like he'd won the lottery when Captain Drake announced that the crew would be heading back to port sooner than planned. Michael silently thanked the thousands of pounds of mackerel they'd snagged in their nets for the unexpected opportunity.

On his way to man the next wheelhouse shift, he pushed hard against the howling wind and drenching rain. Until sunset, the skies had been clear, now the FV Amelia lifted and bottomed out in twenty-foot swells as if it was a bathtub toy. Thunder boomed. Lightning bolts surrounded him. Menacing waves flooded the decks. For every step he forged forward, he took two back.

Michael braced himself against the railing that led to the safety of the bridge. Water streamed off his woolen skullcap and ran down his face and neck. Saltwater lashed him, and he wiped at his stinging eyes with his sleeve. Then the roaring wind slammed him against the starboard side. He made his way back to the stairs, reached again for the railing, and hung on. If he didn't maintain his hold, he'd wash overboard, lost forever, and Catherine would never know how he felt about her.

Breathless, he struggled to maintain his dual-handed death grip and propelled himself up the steps. He grabbed the doorknob with one hand, holding fast to the railing with the other. A gale-force gust joined forces with a wall of horizontal rain and suddenly crashed into his back like a battering ram. His grip on the doorknob slipped, and he hung, suspended in a swirl of air and sea. Then his head struck the deck, hushing his pleas for help.

THE SPACE around Michael slowly gained definition. Something cold pressed against his forehead.

While a crew member manned the helm, a second crew member knelt next to Michael, his face lined with worry.

"What happened?"

Before Michael could answer, the door to the bridge flew open and Captain Drake rushed in. Michael was sitting on the floor, his back against the wall.

"Hey, man, I hear you took quite a blow. You feeling okay? Not nauseous or anything, right?"

Michael blinked. "Nah. No big deal. I guess my sea legs finally gave out on me."

"Your sea legs had nothing to do with it. This is one brutal storm. At least we came up with a decent catch before Mother Nature unleashed her fury," Captain Drake said.

"Do you want me to take the next shift?" the crew member who came to Michael's rescue asked.

Drake studied the two men. "I've got this. You guys go below and grab yourself some grub while you can. If this storm doesn't calm, it'll be all hands on deck."

Michael shifted the ice pack, then reached out his hand to the man who saved his life. "Thanks, buddy."

"No problem, bro. Glad I decided to come up when I did to see if Ralphie needed help."

The two crew members shook Michael's hand and left.

When Michael attempted to get to his feet, the room spun, and he sat back down with a heavy thud.

"Give that ice a little time," Drake said. "And stay put for a while."

Michael knew that his friend wanting to hang around was his way of keeping an eye on him, to ensure the injury was nothing more than a bad rap to the head.

"Maybe it's good that you're at the helm. Not sure I could handle it during this storm," Michael admitted. "This weather is something else. Worse than I remember."

Drake swatted away his words. "You'd be fine. I wouldn't have given you the shift if I didn't think you were up for it. You're one of the best."

Michael repositioned the ice pack. "Thanks."

"Hey, I know I've said this before, but I appreciate you coming to my aid," Drake said. "You covered my butt, big-time. We needed this catch. Last trip out, we came up empty."

"No problem."

"For the record, if you decide you want back permanent, just say the word."

"Thanks, but this trip has made me see that my fishing days are probably behind me." Michael pursed his lips. "Especially after tonight. Problem is, I'm not sure what else I'll do."

"I thought you'd started a business on Nantucket?"

Michael moved the ice pack around again. "Ouch." He grimaced. "I did, but I'm not sure if I can make it into something it's not."

"Like what?"

"Enough to support a family."

Drake raised an eyebrow. "You got plans in that regard?"

"Not at the moment, but I hope one day to be married with kids."

Over the years, Drake had stepped into David's older-brother shoes. Drake listened, advised, and never judged him—just like

Michael's older brother had done before he'd fallen under their dad's spell.

"Your father isn't still trying to convince you to join the family business, is he?"

"Of course. He'll never give up."

"Well, as I've said before, it's your life, not his. Though, I'm surprised about you and fishing. You've always loved the sea. Why isn't this your thing anymore? It can't be the money. You know what that can be."

"I guess I've just fallen in love with Nantucket. It's where I want to settle down, start a family, live my life."

"Well, geez Louise, it's not like there aren't fishing boats over there."

"I know. And I've thought about it, but I don't want to be away from home for long stretches anymore."

Drake removed his baseball cap, which was inscribed with "Best Dad" in gold lettering across the front, and scratched his head. "I know what you mean."

MICHAEL SCANNED THE PT. Judith, Rhode Island dock. He hadn't hesitated when Drake had invited him to join the guys at The Pelican's Roost for dinner before heading home. A chance to say goodbye and wish him well, Drake had said. Michael considered the camaraderie of his crewmates a major perk of the job.

These were men you could trust. And Drake? Well, he was special. Michael had kept in touch with him after moving to Nantucket, but other than occasional visits to his Rhode Island house to make sure it was secure when not rented, he hadn't seen much of Drake. Still, he considered him his best friend. Whenever they talked or saw each other, it was as if time had stopped. If there was anyone he knew he could rely on besides Tina, it was Drake.

The restaurant, a former fishing shack, smelled of sawdust, peanuts, and stale beer. Long benches cozied up to picnic-style tables covered with newspaper. Meals were served on brightly colored paper plates, while utensils that were wrapped inside tightly rolled napkins stood stacked in the tables' middle. Red metal lanterns provided the lighting, and hung from hooks affixed to wooden posts that supported the roof. Fish of all kinds were mounted on wooden plaques around the interior, and served as the restaurant's only decoration. Except, that is, for the orange neon sign behind the bar that flashed "Bottoms Up."

Michael glanced around the table. He'd miss these men, who were always willing to put their lives on the line for each other at sea, sometimes even pulling a crewmate back from the brink of certain death—like what had been done for him. Or on land, they'd be at the home of one in need with only a moment's notice. These were men of character, whose handshakes were better than a written contract. He'd miss them deeply.

"I've got the first round." Michael held up his credit card for the waitress. "What's fish and chips without a cold brew?"

After a couple hours of lively discussion sprinkled with fish tales, Drake pulled Michael aside when he readied himself to call it a night and bid his friends goodbye.

"You got a few minutes?" Drake asked.

"Sure."

Drake tilted his head toward the door. "Let's step outside. I need a smoke."

Outside, Drake lit up and blew out a gray stream that curled toward the sky in the frosty air. "When you heading back?"

"Sometime tomorrow. I haven't had a renter at the house for about a month, so I want to check things out. Why? You need something?"

"No. I thought you might want to stop by and talk to Frank before you head back."

"The fleet owner?"

Drake flicked ash off his cigarette. "Uh-huh. I hear he's in negotiations to buy out the owner of a fleet on Nantucket. From what I've heard, the guy there is retiring, so I think Frank might need someone to run the business. I can let him know I suggested you stop by if you think you'd be interested."

"You think I'm qualified?"

"Absolutely. You know the business as good as most. And you've always had a good head on your shoulders. I'm sure the current owner could show you what needs doing before he walks away."

Michael smiled and looked out across the parking lot into the night. Maybe he wouldn't have to reinvent his woodworking business after all. If this worked out, and it sounded like it might, it could be the kind of job that Catherine said would make his heart sing.

CATHERINE GOT a sick feeling in her stomach when her phone dinged and she saw a message from Michael. He had never texted her before. Was he about to drop something on her, like he'd decided to stay in Rhode Island? If so, why did that prospect bother her? Her finger hovered over the message. She inhaled.

Click.

I'll be back around 5 tomorrow.

Pick you and Tina up at your place. 5:30.

Dinner on me. Big surprise!

Catherine rubbed her finger across her lips. Why would Michael include her in a dinner invitation with his sister? Could he miss her as much as she missed him?

Then the phone rang, startling her, and she fumbled to keep from dropping it.

"Michael's coming home!" Tina blurted when Catherine answered.

"I got a message, too. He's made dinner reservations for tomorrow. Not sure why he invited me, though. What do you think this is all about?" Catherine asked.

"Beats me. Whatever it is, I sure hope we'll think it's as good as he seems to."

Catherine paused. "You don't think he's decided to move back to Rhode Island, do you?"

"Gosh, I hope not." Tina sighed. "I'd miss him like crazy."

Catherine almost chimed in with "me too," but she swallowed her words. "I'm sure he feels the same. You're very important to him."

"I think you and I share that distinction."

Catherine's pulse quickened. "What?"

"I know my baby brother, and he's not one to share personal news with just anyone. I've suspected he had feelings for you before he left, and this seals it."

Catherine picked up a piece of paper and fanned her face. Thankfully, Tina couldn't see that her cheeks were on fire. "Don't read too much into it. I'm his friend. We talked about his finding purpose before he left. He probably just wants to bring me up to date."

Tina laughed. "Uh-huh. You keep thinking that."

"What am I supposed to think?"

"Come on, Catherine. You can't expect me to believe you haven't at least considered that maybe you two—"

"I think of him as I do you: a good friend. That's it."

Why couldn't she admit it? Since the night at the lighthouse, when she'd called Jack and a woman had answered, she'd toyed with the idea of pursuing a relationship with Michael.

"Well, brace yourself," Tina said. "Because I'm willing to bet that whatever his news is, it's not about his hope for a lingering friendship."

CHAPTER NINETEEN

A bubbling cocktail of excitement and nerves, Michael pulled up to A Distant Light and headed for the door. It was unlike him to be presumptuous and assume that Catherine would agree to dinner. But he feared, if he'd asked, instead of assumed, she'd just sidestep his invitation as she had in the past. Hopefully, having Tina along would ease her angst.

"I'm back!" Michael called out, and then closed the door behind him.

Tina ran to him, cradled his face in her hands, and kissed him on the cheek. "Boy, I've missed you, baby bro." She stepped back and gave him the once-over. "You look good."

"Hi, Michael," Catherine said. "Tina's right. The sea agrees with you."

His heart pounded at the sight of her. He smiled and checked his watch. "We better get going. I made reservations for five-thirty." He drew in a breath, hoping Catherine wouldn't volley up an excuse to cancel.

∼

AFTER BEING SHOWN to their table, Catherine stood off to the side while Michael pulled out a chair for his sister. The old-fashioned gesture was well ingrained as he stepped behind it and slid the chair under her as she sat.

Tina touched her brother's forearm and smiled. "Thank you."

Catherine moved to take her seat.

"I'll get that." He mimicked what he'd done for his sister.

She smiled. "Thank you."

Such a gentleman, she thought to herself.

Catherine stared out two large windows, one on either side of their corner table. "This is the best view I've seen of the harbor from any restaurant." The French doors that lined the rest of the wall were closed tight against the chilly temps. Candles flickered on the wood-top tables, and a faint vanilla aroma floated in the air.

She rested her chin on her hand and drank Michael in. She allowed herself to admit what a delicious mix of charming and handsome he was. The white of his teeth against his dark beard and tanned, rugged good looks sent a cavalcade of unexpected shivers through her.

Then the waiter arrived, took their drink orders, and left behind a basket of bread.

Tina reached for a slice. "Okay, we're dying to hear. How was your trip?"

Michael leaned in. "The first two weeks weren't bad, although I have to admit, I learned how out of shape I was." He grinned. "I'd be ready to crash at night when the rest of the crew were gearing up to play cards or watch movies."

"Was it a worthwhile trip?" Catherine asked.

"It was, thank goodness, or we'd still be out there. Mostly mackerel this time around. It helped compensate for the rigors of the trip."

The waiter delivered their drinks.

Catherine brought her wineglass to her lips. "Were the seas rough?"

"Just the last night. If it hadn't been for a crewmate coming to my aid during a violent storm, I would have been shark bait."

Catherine's breath caught. She covered her mouth with her hand. Then to quell her nerves, she lowered it and dipped her knife into a pat of raspberry and honey-infused butter fashioned in the shape of a rosette. She did her best to look calm as she spread the mix over her bread.

Tina's eyes widened. She reached out and touched Michael's forearm. "How awful. Thank goodness he was there."

Michael shifted his eyes from Tina to Catherine and back again. "It was an eye-opener, that's for sure. I'd already decided it would be my last trip, but that clinched it."

Tina picked up her wineglass. "I can see why."

Michael fixed his eyes on Catherine. "Someone once said that I'd know when I found something that made me happy. She said my heart would sing."

Heat crept into her face and neck. Sure that red splotches formed a patchwork design on her neck, she adjusted her collar and lowered her face.

The waiter returned. "Ready to order?"

"We'll need a few more minutes," Michael said. "I've managed to monopolize these ladies, and they haven't even had a chance to read over your menu."

"No problem." The waiter went to check on other diners.

"Michael, don't keep us in suspense," Tina said. "What's your big surprise?"

Catherine blinked and realized she was holding her breath.

Michael winked at her. "I'm happy to say that I have finally found what makes my heart sing."

At the prospect that he had made a decision that might take him away from Nantucket, Catherine's thoughts scattered like pollen on a spring day, and her heartbeat raced at the speed of a hummingbird.

"Do you both know what you want?" Michael asked, eyeing the menu.

"I'm ready," Tina said.

"Me too," Catherine echoed, anxious to hear his news.

Michael motioned the waiter, standing off to the side at a discreet distance. He approached, took their orders, and left.

"You have us on pins and needles," Tina said, and gave him a piercing stare. "Spit it out before we burst, will you?"

Catherine clasped her trembling hands in her lap.

Please don't say you're leaving Nantucket. Please don't say that.

"For starters, I'm staying put."

She let out a whoosh of air, somewhat surprised at the magnitude of her relief.

"Good," Tina said. "I was prepared to tie you down if you'd decided otherwise."

"So other than the obvious, what does that mean?" Catherine prompted.

Michael flashed that smile of his.

Inside, she swooned. He was so darn sexy that if she weren't careful, she'd melt away like a stick of butter.

"Well, as I've said in the past, fishing and carpentry are all I know."

Tina tore off a piece of bread. "So, if you've decided that fishing isn't in your future, then it sounds like you're going to grow your carpentry business."

"Nope."

Tina slumped back against her chair. "Why do I feel like I'm stuck in a game show?"

Catherine laughed. "Come on, Michael. You've got us on the edge of our seats."

He looked at her. "You may not be familiar with a fishing company on the docks here called Sea Fare, but Tina is."

Tina passed the breadbasket to Michael and looked at Catherine. "Garth Abernathy owns it. Been around for decades."

"Well, he's retiring, and Frank, the owner of Fresh Catch, the fleet I worked for, is buying it."

Catherine deflated like a balloon with a slow leak. So, Michael would return to the sea and be away from Nantucket for long stretches. But wait. Didn't he say that fishing wasn't in his future? She knit her brow. "I'm confused."

Tina laughed. "That makes two of us."

Michael stirred his drink. "Thanks to my friend Drake, I've stumbled onto something that I never thought possible. A way to stay in the fishing business but not have to ship out. The owner of Fresh Catch has offered me the position of manager at Sea Fare once the sale is complete. I'll be responsible for day-to-day operations, ensuring the boats are maintained, that we have sufficient staff, and negotiating contracts with vendors who buy our product. And in addition to my salary, I'll also get a percentage of the profit."

Tina pushed back her chair, walked over behind her brother, threw her arms around his shoulders, and planted a kiss on the top of his head. "I'm so proud of you." She wiped at a tear and smiled at Catherine. "Happy for all of us."

Catherine beamed and held up her wineglass. "I'd say that's definitely worthy of a toast."

CHAPTER TWENTY

Catherine picked at her cuticle and bit her lower lip. She'd piled so much pressure on herself to create her first warm-weather window display that she couldn't think straight. The upcoming season would be her only opportunity to garner the interest of thousands of visitors who flocked to the island after the winter chill departed. And if that wasn't enough to send her mind spiraling out of control, there was the fact that an eye-catching display might finally snuff out any lingering whispers—thanks to Jerry—of substandard merchandise. Another reason why it had to broadcast class.

Early on, Catherine had been confident that creative ideas would rain down like April showers. That imagining a distinctive, upscale look would come as easy as an afternoon stroll. But that hadn't been the case. Not even close.

During her career, she'd advised her staff to step away when they faced a mental block. Divert their focus. Clear their minds. But even when she employed a healthy dose of that advice, she came up empty.

She moved her phone from hand to hand. Maybe brainstorming with Tina, who'd seen her share of Nantucket Main Street displays, would help. She punched in her friend's number. "Hi. It's me," Catherine said, before Tina had a chance to say hello.

"It's not like you to call before lunch. Something wrong? It's not Jerry again, is it?"

Catherine heard the irritation rise in Tina's voice. "No, nothing like that."

"Good, because I was getting ready to read him the riot act."

Catherine smiled at her words. "I'm freaking out. I've been wracking my brain for days to come up with a spring and summer design for my front window, but the only thing I've developed is tension headaches."

"Take it easy. It's only February. You have loads of time."

"Not really. The April Daffodil Festival is just around the corner. And it'll take time to purchase what I need and find someone to pull it together for me."

"Is there something I can do to help?"

Catherine paused. "I thought maybe if we put our heads together, it might help me unlock some ideas."

"Sure. When?"

Catherine squeezed her eyes shut and winced. "Today?"

"Noon?" Tina asked without hesitation. "I'll bring sandwiches."

Catherine exhaled a breath of relief. "Perfect on both counts."

CATHERINE WATCHED her cross the street and opened the shop door.

"Hi, hi." Tina chirped, holding up a brown paper bag. "I ran home and threw together some leftovers."

Tina's idea of leftovers were much the same as when Helen referred to her culinary delights as "concoctions." One thing was for sure. Whatever was in that sack would make for a mouthwatering lunch regardless of their collective creative outcome.

"Smells delicious."

"Eggplant parm on Italian bread. I made so much last night, there's enough left over for Michael to have for dinner."

Catherine went to the back counter and unfolded two chairs. She motioned Tina to have a seat and did the same. Then she unwrapped the wax paper from her sandwich. "Speaking of Michael, how's his new job working out?"

Tina sighed. "My brother is a perfectionist. He thinks that because he's worked in the fishing business, he should be able to stroll in, review the tasks at hand with the previous owner, and get everything right the first time."

Catherine bit into her sandwich. "Sounds more like confidence to me."

Tina chuckled. "Call it what you will. But he's putting undue stress on himself by setting unrealistic expectations. He's only been on the job a week, for goodness' sake, and he thinks he should be performing as well as the guy who did it for thirty years."

Since Michael's return, Catherine had been unable to deny her attraction to him. The mere mention of his name now released a swarm of butterflies in the pit of her stomach.

"Catherine?"

She waved her hand as if shooing a fly. "Don't mind me. This window thing has my mind racing."

"Calm down. You're just like my brother. You both need to take a break."

Catherine shook her head. "Without a killer display, A Distant Light could fail, and that would mean back to Boston to get a real job."

"It won't fail, and you're not going anywhere. So get that out of your head right now. We'll figure this out." Tina finished her sandwich and balled up the wrapper. "What message do you want your display to send?"

"I want to showcase my merchandise in such a way that will be obvious that A Distant Light doesn't carry mass-produced items. I plan to squash any lingering rumors to that effect. Aside from silencing the whispers, I want it crystal clear that my inventory is worthy of its price tags." She looked Tina in the eyes. "If this venture of mine is going to work, I need stellar summer sales to roll me into the winter months." Catherine's shoulders slumped. "I only have one shot at making a stunning first impression for the summer tourist season, though, and up until now, I haven't been able to come up with anything."

"What has you stumped?"

"The backdrop. The setup. It has to be rich. Imaginative." Catherine sighed. "Too bad A Distant Light isn't a boutique, because then I'd know precisely what to do."

"Go on," Tina prompted. "Tell me."

"Why?" Catherine motioned at the surrounding space. "This is far from an apparel store."

"Humor me."

Catherine shrugged. "Well, I'd fill the window with imported outfits from Europe and across the United States, and accent them with scarfs, brightly colored beaded necklaces, pairs of espadrilles, and straw hats with long flowing ribbons."

"Keep going."

"I'd place Lightship Basket purses atop gauzy-wrapped pedestals of varying heights, and slingback sand chairs would serve as bookends. Then I'd drape beach towels over the tops of the chairs and scatter around a few pairs of flip-flops."

Tina nodded. "Keep going."

"Why? We're wasting time."

"You wanted my help, didn't you?"

Not sure where Tina was going with this, Catherine still appreciated her volunteering to help, so she went with the flow, suppressing an urge to roll her eyes. "I'd have bursts of oatmeal cremes, pink-and-white stripes, and lime greens coloring the space, beckoning customers to take a look inside."

Tina rubbed her hands together. "Okay, now that we've got your creative juices flowing, try to think of displays you've seen that were equally captivating." She snapped her fingers. "Like at the stores on the Cape, where you shopped for some of your merchandise."

Catherine squinted, her lips thinning. "I don't recall... Wait, now that I think about it, I'd have to give one store owner props for their creativity. But it had nothing to do with anything nautical. So what's the point?" She tossed the waxed paper and brown bag in the trash with force and gritted her teeth. "This is so frustrating."

"What was it that intrigued you?" Tina pressed.

Catherine exhaled, raised and lowered a shoulder. "I suppose the whimsical nature of the shop. It carried, amongst other things, carved wooden horses from antique carousels."

"So, you found the horses interesting?"

"Yes. What I found ingenious was that they thought to use a scaled-down version of an old-fashioned merry-go-round, complete with lights and music in the center of the store."

"What made it so special? The craftsmanship?"

"Well, that was good, but I thought it was brilliant that they used it as a stage to display other merchandise unrelated to carousels. It tied everything in the store together. Provided a theme."

Catherine paused. An idea edged into the crevices of her mind. She smiled and hurried behind a standing privacy screen where she kept a microwave and her coffee supplies.

"What are you doing?" Tina called out.

Catherine returned with a pad and pencil. "I need to get this down before I lose it." She feverishly sketched while Tina stood and glanced over her shoulder. When Catherine finished, she let out a stream of air and put down her pencil. "What do you think of something like this?"

Tina furrowed her brow.

Catherine pointed at the drawing. "This is a planked ship deck. It could be the stage, like the carousel." She traced the sketch with her finger. "Oval, with a low bow and stern to add definition, but no starboard or port sides. That way, I could place my merchandise on it and not block it from view."

Tina bobbed her head. "Something like that would have to be constructed. I doubt you'd find anywhere to purchase it."

"Right, I would have to enlist a carpenter."

"Like Michael."

Catherine shook her head. "Absolutely not. He has his new job to consider. The last thing he needs is a side project. Especially one that'll require this level of time and effort."

"You won't find anyone else to match his skill level."

"That's not the point. I don't want to burden him. Besides, you said he's already frustrated."

"He'll be upset if you contract with someone else." Tina picked up Catherine's phone. "Here. Call him."

Catherine hesitated. There was no doubt Michael could turn her idea into something spectacular. After all, look what he had done with her sign. The last thing she wanted was to jeopardize his job by piling on additional stress, however. On the other hand, she'd certainly welcome his opinion.

"All he can say is no, and that's as apt to happen as me winning the lottery," Tina said.

Catherine stared at the phone. "That's what concerns me. He's too nice to say no."

"Call already, will you? I have to get going."

"He's probably busy."

"You won't know if you don't try."

"Okay. Okay." Catherine punched in Michael's number.

Tina gave Catherine a thumbs-up and headed for the door.

"Thank you," Catherine said as the phone rang in her ear. "And thanks for lunch."

Tina waved her hand in the air.

"Hi, Michael. It's me, Catherine. Sorry to bother you, but—"

"You can thank me later, little brother!" Tina called out, laughing, and walked out the door.

"Hey, Catherine," Michael said, "What a nice surprise."

Hearing his warm and sexy voice, her face grew hot. Her knees felt like Silly Putty. "There's something I'd like to discuss with you. Can you stop by after work?"

MICHAEL CALLED his sister right after he'd hung up with Catherine. "What does Catherine want to talk to me about? I know you know."

"I take it you'll be seeing her," Tina said.

"Right after work."

"Well, then, you'll find out soon enough." Tina hung up.

He should've known that his sister wouldn't spill the details. Throughout the afternoon, he checked his watch often, willing the hands to move faster. Thankfully, his new job made it easy for him to stay busy, though no matter how hard he tried to keep his curiosity at bay, negative thoughts kept creeping into his mind. Had Catherine confided to Tina that she'd met someone? Had his sister suggested she tell him, rather than lead him on?

Or maybe she'd thrown in the towel and was returning to Boston.

Michael squeezed his eyes shut to block out the unthinkable.

He leaned back in his chair, releasing the tightness across his shoulders. Could it be that Catherine just wanted him to know she'd loosened her grip on what might've been with Jack and was ready to move on?

He chuckled. *Wishful thinking, Buddy. Wishful thinking.*

JITTERY, Catherine was bouncing on the balls of her feet by the time Michael pulled up. She rushed to the door and opened it. "I'm sorry to have bothered you. I know you're busy with your new job, but Tina insisted and dialed your number for me."

He flashed a wide grin. "That's my sister for you. So, what has you looking like a kid on Christmas morning?"

Catherine wasn't sure if the electrical bolts shooting through her were due to her joy over what she thought would be a dynamite display, or from being within a whisper length of Michael. She pulled the sketch from her pocket and spread it open on the counter. "What do you think? And don't worry about hurting my feelings. I want your honest opinion. This is too important."

He studied the drawing. "I take it this is for your front window?"

"Sorry, I'm so excited that I forgot to mention that." Catherine glowed with enthusiasm. In her eagerness to explain, she brushed against him when she pointed at the drawing. "I'd like the display to be the deck of a ship." She felt her cheeks grow hot again.

"Uh-huh. I see that."

Catherine swallowed, struggling to maintain focus. Her hormones telegraphed messages to her brain that she wasn't prepared to deal with. "I want to use it to stage my merchandise." She looked at him. "You don't think it's too much, or that it'll overwhelm the space, do you?"

He locked eyes with her. "No. And maybe."

She pulled herself back from losing herself in the lure of his hazel eyes. "What do you mean?"

"It could overpower the window if it's not the right size. Do you have a tape measure?"

Catherine pushed her lips together. "This is why I didn't want to call you. You have enough going on. I'll find someone else to construct it. I only want your opinion."

Not true, Catherine thought to herself as soon as she said it. She would love nothing more than to have Michael turn her rendering into a head-turning 3D display. And in the process, it would also give her an excuse to spend more time with him.

He held out his hand. "Measuring tape, please."

"But—"

"Do I have to go to the truck and get mine?"

Catherine let out a rush of air, reached under the counter, and handed it to him.

"Thanks," Michael said, and jotted down the dimensions of the space that would house her creation. "Six feet by three feet should be about right. Considering the size, it'll need a base to steady it, and maybe a couple of oars crisscrossed in front would be a nice touch."

"You'll have time for this?"

"Of course. It'll be fun."

"What about your job?"

"I don't work twenty-four seven. And besides, you don't seriously think I'd want you to work with anyone else on something that will require a lot of collaboration?"

Catherine's heart pounded, and she looked up at him through her eyelashes.

As if he'd done it a million times, his arms slipped around her waist.

She sucked in a breath. Should she push herself out of Michael's embrace? She couldn't do it. It had been so long since a man held her, Catherine had forgotten how good it felt. In the past, memories of Jack would be the strength she needed to keep her feelings for Michael at bay, but she told herself now to listen to her heart. She grew lightheaded, and her calves vibrated. Michael held her upright.

Then he leaned forward. His gaze was so intense, she blinked. He placed a gentle kiss on her lips, then pulled away, asking if he should continue. She put a hand behind his head, pulled him toward her, and pressed her lips against his.

CHAPTER TWENTY-ONE

Catherine's alarm jolted her awake. She opened her eyes to the sun streaming in the double front windows of her apartment. She sat up and stretched her arms over her head. The light made her feel like she could float. Giddy over the memory of Michael's kiss, she scrambled out of bed and went straight to the kitchen to brew her morning coffee.

He had called her after his visit the night before, and they'd talked for an hour. She recalled him saying he'd see her today. While she stood at the coffeemaker, she began counting the hours until she'd be with Michael again. Watching the piping-hot liquid drip into her mug, she visualized the moment that had changed everything.

Catherine had considered stepping away from Michael's embrace, but when the time came, she'd tossed away her doubts. Like a long-lost friend, she'd welcomed his arms around her, and his touch had invoked sensations she hadn't enjoyed in years.

Armed with a new spring in her step, she pulled her robe tight around her and jogged downstairs to pick up the morning paper from the front steps. The paper was a relic, she knew, but she preferred to turn the pages and not drag her finger across a screen.

"About time," a man said when she opened the door.

Catherine gasped and drew her robe closer. She didn't see anyone. Was her mind playing tricks on her? She grabbed the paper, stepped back, and pushed on the door.

Jerry came around the edge of the steps.

Catherine clutched her chest. "You startled me."

"Did I?" He gave her a sly smile, walked up the steps, and leaned in too close. "I'm sorry." His smirk belied his apology.

"What do you want?" Catherine asked, her patience wearing thin.

"For starters, you can take your pretty little self back to wherever it is you come from."

"Dream on." She tried pushing the door closed. "If you don't mind—"

He held tight to the outside handle. "But you see, that's the problem. I *do* mind."

Catherine tried again to close the door.

Jerry jammed his foot against it. "I'm not finished."

In the past, his actions, like the garbage episode, had unleashed the PTSD she'd worked hard to suppress. This time, he'd frightened her.

Catherine slid her hand onto the alarm pad inside the doorjamb. If she activated the silent distress button, the local police would swarm in within minutes. "If you don't let me close this door, I'll call the police."

He shook his head. "See, that's what happens when someone like you moves here. The overall balance of things gets turned upside down."

"What?"

Jerry pinched his lips together like he'd eaten a lemon. "Why would you want to involve the police? We're having a friendly conversation, is all." He wrinkled his nose in disgust. "Wash-ashore, that's why. It's all you are, all you'll ever be."

"And what makes you exempt? You're as much one as I am."

He glared at her. Catherine squeezed her lips together. Her finger hovered over the panic button. "Say what you came for." She held tight to her grip on the door. "I don't have time for your nonsense."

Although it didn't seem possible, Jerry stepped even closer.

"Seems your boyfriend went and dug up some dirt that could cause me problems." He shook his finger at her. "And let me say, I'm none too happy about it." He peered around her. "Is he here?"

She wasn't about to disclose that she was alone. Who knew what he might try? "He's busy. I'll give him a message."

"It's for his ears only." He let out a breath tinged with what? Garlic? Alcohol?

Catherine jerked her head back, reminded of the man who mugged her. Her pulse quickened. *Calm down*, she told herself. *Breathe.*

"Long night for you two, I guess." He cocked an eyebrow and gave her a wicked smile. "Ah yes, I remember what young love was like."

How would Jerry know about the change in her relationship with Michael unless he'd been stalking her? They'd only shared their first kiss last night. Catherine huffed and pushed her shoulder against the door.

Jerry's face hardened. "Not so fast. You need to hear me out." He stepped back a little. "You've caused me nothing but grief since you got here. Because of you and that boyfriend of yours, I've been summoned to appear before the town council, where they'll probably try to hit me with a hefty fine. Even though we both know the so-called information you've supplied is all a bunch of garbage. You know as well as I do that your boyfriend paid someone to lie and incriminate me. And I intend to see to it that he gets what's coming to him."

Catherine clenched her teeth. "Quit trying to intimidate me," she said. "And don't you dare threaten Michael. You should've considered the consequences of your actions before you put those parking signs out front. And speaking of garbage, you're the one who went in search of it so you could toss it all over my front steps. Which I might add, you should thank me for not reporting." She shook her finger at him. "I'm giving you fair warning. Back off. Or else."

"What? You'll rat me out again?" He held out his hand and faked a tremor. "I'm shaking."

Catherine's eyes narrowed. "Don't push me, Jerry. You may think you know who you're dealing with, but trust me, you don't have a clue." She kicked at his foot still lodged in her door, gathered all her strength, slammed the door in his face, and ran upstairs to her phone.

"Michael!" she said, breathless, when he answered. "Jerry was outside my door when I picked up the paper just now."

"Are you okay? He didn't hurt you, did he?"

"No, but I think he's been watching me," she panted. "Watching us."

"Keep the door locked. I'm on my way."

CATHERINE WASHED her face and changed out of her pajamas. She hadn't yet slipped into her shoes when she heard the squeal of tires. She slid her slippers back on, hurried downstairs, and opened the door.

Michael rushed in, locked the door behind him, and took her in his arms.

Her eyes burned. "Oh Michael, I'm sorry I called you, but he really scared me. I wasn't thinking straight."

Michael leaned away, and with his thumb, wiped away a tear running down her cheek. "I wouldn't want it any other way." He pulled her to him. "Tell me what happened." His tone was soothing.

Catherine hated how weak and frightened she appeared. How many times had she flown the globe alone and never felt the least bit uncomfortable, even in some countries where it had been warranted?

"He waited for me, so he knows what time I pick up the paper. That means he's been watching me."

Michael stiffened.

"He refused to let me close the door. He also got in my face. He called you my boyfriend, and he seemed to know that we're more than friends now."

"You didn't let on you were alone, right?"

Catherine shook her head. "No."

"That's good."

"I'm terrified that he's stalking me."

Michael released his hold on her. "I doubt it. He thinks he's clever to scare you. Regardless, he's frightened you, and I'll set him straight."

Catherine pulled back. "No. Please don't. It'll only make things worse. Maybe he wanted me to know that he's back on-island, and took the opportunity to get his kicks by taunting me."

Michael frowned. "I've worried he might pull something else. I'm sure this has to do with him wanting you to withdraw your evidence at the council hearing in two weeks."

Catherine paused. "Now that you mention it, he did say he's upset about what you've uncovered." She put her hands on her hips. "Well, he's in for a surprise if he thinks I'll back down." She gave a weak smile. "He got a good glimpse of my Irish temper when I kicked his foot and slammed the door in his face."

Michael gave her a gentle squeeze. "That's my girl."

OUTSIDE, Michael ignored Catherine's pleas for him not to get involved and gathered his thoughts. How should he handle Jerry so he wouldn't retaliate?

He walked into the Double Scoop.

A teenager behind the counter was leafing through a magazine when Michael entered. He looked up. "Can I help you?'

"Jerry around?"

The young man nodded. "Yes, I'll get him for you. What's your name?"

"Michael."

The boy dipped his chin. "May I let him know what this is about?" He leaned forward and lowered his voice. "You'd think he's a celebrity by the way he wants me to screen visitors."

Michael forced a smile into place. "He'll know why I'm here."

The boy went through a door behind the counter and returned with Jerry on his heels.

The old guy crossed his arms over his chest. "Figured it was a matter of time before you stopped by."

"Really? Why is that?"

"So you could apologize for the trouble you've caused me."

Michael stepped away from the counter. "Yeah, right. I understand you wanted to see *me*." Michael threw out his hands. "Well, I'm here and listening."

Jerry scratched his head. "Sounds like someone's playing you for a fool."

Michael stepped closer.

The store owner stepped back.

"What are you afraid of?"

Jerry huffed. "Afraid? Give me a break. Why would I be afraid?"

"Maybe because you know what you did this morning. Talking trash, asking to see me as if we have a score to settle." Michael chuckled. "Just as I've thought all along, you're nothing but a coward."

Jerry recoiled. "What the hell are you talking about?" He turned to the store clerk. "Have I left the store since you arrived?"

The young man looked at Jerry and then at Michael. "Not since I got here. We came in together."

"Did you see which direction he came from?" Michael asked.

The boy glanced at Jerry and lowered his gaze. "I didn't, sir. Sorry."

Jerry wagged his finger at Michael. "Tell that liar that if she ever accuses me of anything again, I'll…"

Michael crossed his arms over his chest and smiled.

The color drained from Jerry's face. "What?"

"Finish your sentence. You'll what?" Michael dropped his arms and leaned forward. "Go ahead. Spit it out."

"He's threatening me," Jerry said to his employee. "You're my witness."

Michael threw back his head and laughed.

"What's so funny?"

"Trust me, if I were threatening you, you'd *know* it."

Jerry stepped back again. "Do you see what the joke is?" he asked the young man.

The boy's gaze darted between Jerry and Michael. "Sir, I think he's laughing because he never said who sent him here, but you said *she* was a liar."

Michael slapped the boy on the shoulder, winked, then headed for the door. Halfway there, he turned and shot Jerry a menacing look. "Leave her alone." His face softened. "For goodness' sake, she nearly died after an attack on her life. The last thing she deserves is you bullying her." Then he frowned. "If you try anything else, you'll have to deal with me. And that's not a threat. It's a promise."

∽

"I'M GOING to the council meeting." Catherine announced during dinner with Michael the next night.

He nearly choked on his wine. "Why do you want to subject yourself to that?"

"I can't afford to have him spread more lies, or worse, convince the council that I'm at fault."

Michael waved his hand. "You don't have to worry about that. He's lost a lot of credibility. Besides, the proof you provided is undeniable. Nothing he says will change that."

"I don't trust him."

"That's no reason to subject yourself to his craziness."

He was right, of course, but Catherine couldn't chance Jerry tossing around more untruths about her store. If she was in attendance, she could defend herself.

Michael raised an eyebrow. "What are you thinking?"

"Ah, don't mind me, just woolgathering." She half smiled. "And the sheep are a pretty dull herd."

Michael rubbed the center of his chest with his fingers. "Somehow, I doubt that."

Catherine wrinkled her brow. "Are you okay?"

"Just a little heartburn. Must be the onion rings."

"Do you take something for it?"

"Never had to. It started while I was at sea. Probably due to the food onboard. Tina spoiled me with her healthy cooking, and I guess my body isn't yet ready to let me forget that I strayed."

"But it's continued?" Catherine pressed. "Maybe you should have it checked out."

Michael reached over and placed his hand on top of hers. "It's nothing. A few more weeks of my sister's food, and I'll be as good as new. Now can we please talk about something important? Like us?"

CHAPTER TWENTY-TWO

A week later

On the few occasions when Jerry had surfaced, Catherine had noticed that he hadn't so much as nodded in her direction. Still, she harbored a nagging sense that someone *was* watching her. She chalked it up to a witch's cauldron of PTSD boiling beneath the surface, ready to spill over at any moment. The slightest noise rattled her. She'd not slept well and had reverted to a childhood habit of biting her nails. Maybe she should listen to Michael and not attend the upcoming council meeting.

Why rip off the scab on a festering feud? Maybe she should leave well enough alone.

With a coffee mug in one hand, Catherine pulled back the curtain on the upstairs windows and glanced at the street below. All quiet. The surrounding stores, much like her own, were hours away from unlatching their doors.

She loved Nantucket. It was a picture-postcard of how life should be. The cobblestone streets lined with majestic oak trees would soon don a crown of green and provide a leafy canopy over the streets.

Residents would stop to exchange pleasantries with one another while giving a playful pat to the neighbor's dog and calling it by name.

Yes, she loved every bit of her new life, except, of course, for her encounters with Jerry. As much as Catherine hated to extend him any level of credit, she had to admit that even though his actions had given her angst, unleashed her PTSD, and sparked fear, in a lopsided way, he'd forced her to face certain undeniable truths. They had clarified how fragile her recovery from her near-death attack truly was.

She let the curtain fall from her hand and headed to the kitchen.

Thud.

Her grasp on her coffee cup suddenly loosened, and sent it crashing to the floor. She grabbed hold of the kitchen table to steady herself.

Calm down. Breathe. It's your imagination.

Thud.

The room closed in on her. She gasped for air, fumbled in a drawer, yanked out a brown paper bag, opened it, grasped the top like a bottle, and held the opening to her face.

Breathe.

~

Michael climbed the outdoor back stairs that lead to Catherine's apartment two at a time. He knocked twice, which was the signal they'd agreed on when she'd called him in a panic.

She instantly opened the door.

Once inside, he put his arm around her shoulders and guided her to the couch. "Sit down. You're shaking. Tell me what happened."

"I heard a noise," she choked out. "Sounded like a thud or a bang. I thought it was my mind playing tricks on me, but then I heard it again."

"Has it happened again since you called me?"

"No. I've been too afraid to go downstairs and check it out."

"Stay here. I'll have a look around."

Catherine grabbed at his arm. "What if someone's down there?"

"I doubt that. Your alarm would've sounded."

She closed her eyes. Why hadn't she thought of that? She opened her eyes and found Michael staring into hers.

He kissed her forehead. "Stay here. I'll be right back."

NOTHING SEEMED out of place or broken when Michael entered the store. He scanned the surrounding space. He picked up a golf-sized wood-handled umbrella next to the door. Raised in mid-air, he moved toward the privacy screen and checked behind it. Clear. Making his way to the front door, he saw the alarm light flashing red. He breathed a sigh of relief. The system was armed. Probably a pesky cat had toppled over a trash can in search of food or a bird that had flown into the plate-glass window.

"Catherine!" he called out, lowering the umbrella and putting it back where he'd found it. "All clear. Come on down."

She rushed down the stairs. "Did you find anything?"

"No, but the alarm's activated. I'll check outside once you turn it off."

Michael opened the door after Catherine keyed in the code.

Then she shrieked.

A knife, its blade catching the morning sun, stuck into the wooden door frame, held a white business-sized envelope with her name scrawled in large blood-red block printing.

Catherine stumbled back, squeezed her eyes shut, and put her hand on the wall for support. "What's happening?"

Michael rushed to her side.

She shook her head. "I can't believe Jerry would stoop so low."

Michael pulled the knife from the door, removed the envelope, and put the knife down. He tore open the envelope, pulled out a sheet of paper, and read it. His heart raced.

What the heck? He fought to hide his horror. Catherine didn't need him adding to her fears.

"What does it say?"

"Looks like you've been right about someone watching you. But I don't think it's Jerry."

⁓

Michael directed her to the chair behind the counter. "Have a seat."

When he handed her the letter, Catherine swore his hand trembled. She recoiled, afraid to touch it, as if whatever it said would permeate her skin, travel to her heart, and kill her. "Read it to me, please."

Michael swallowed. "You can run, but you can't hide. You thought I wouldn't find you? Well, guess again."

The room spun. Catherine's eyes searched for the brown bag, then realized she'd left it upstairs. "I can't breathe." She reached out for Michael's hand, grabbed it, and gasped for air.

He tugged her up from the chair, pulled his hand out of hers, and wrapped his arm around her shoulder. "Take it easy. I'm here. No one's going to hurt you."

She pulled out of the embrace after a few moments. "This has been my biggest fear ever since the night of the attack. The man who nearly killed me has come to finish what he started."

Michael furrowed his brow. "That was my first thought, too, but isn't he locked up?"

"Yes, I think so. The guy was a repeat offender. After I identified him and gave my statement, he pleaded guilty, and a victim's advocate told me he'd go away for life."

"So, it can't be him."

Catherine threw her hands out in obvious frustration. "Maybe he's escaped. Or paid someone to do this."

Michael ran his hands through his hair. "We have to call the police."

She grasped his arm. "No. The last thing I need is negative press. Jerry's already done enough damage. I can't risk more."

"What you can't risk is another attempt like this one. Sitting around and waiting for this maniac to try again isn't an option."

Catherine made small circles on her temples with her forefingers. "I need to think."

"Listen." Michael paced. "I understand your concern for your business. If the guy who attacked you *is* behind this note, we have more to worry about than Jerry. Your attacker is a dangerous man. He's already tried to kill you once."

Maybe she should take this as a sign to cut her losses, leave the island, and start over. Somewhere far away. The Caribbean? But hadn't she already fled to an island? And still, he'd tracked her down.

"You don't have to remind me what he's capable of," Catherine said with edge in her voice. She exhaled and put her hands atop Michael's shoulders. "Forgive me. I'm scared and frustrated. I didn't mean to jump down your throat." Tears filled her eyes. "Why is all this happening? First Jerry, now this. Maybe it's a way of punishing me for my past deeds."

Michael pulled her to him and rubbed her back. "You're not being punished," he whispered close to her ear. "But now we really do need to call the police."

CATHERINE OPENED the door when the police cruiser pulled up.

"I'm Officer Dinkins." A young man in uniform climbed the steps, wiped his feet on the mat, and entered the store. "You called in a report?"

Judging from his looks, Catherine supposed he'd just graduated from the police academy. Someone had seriously threatened her, and they'd sent someone with little experience?

"*I* called," Michael said.

"What's your name?"

"Michael Benton."

"Which of you is the proprietor?" he asked

His brusque tone of voice annoyed Catherine. Was he drunk on the power his uniform afforded, or compensating for his youth?

"I am," Catherine said.

Dinkins pulled a small notepad and pen from his breast pocket and focused his attention on her. "The report indicates you've received a threatening note." He looked around. "Is that correct?"

The smell of peppermint distracted Catherine. Was Dinkins sucking on a mint? He seemed put off. Had the call interrupted a breakfast stop at The Corner Kitchen? She shook off the momentary derailment.

"Yes. I heard a noise earlier this morning and called Michael. When he arrived, he checked the store to see if anyone had broken in. When we didn't find any evidence of that, we opened the front door and found an envelope pinned to the door." Unable to bring herself to reference the weapon, Catherine pointed at the knife laying on the counter. "With that."

Officer Dinkins stepped toward the counter, slipped on a pair of gloves, and read the letter. "How did it get inside?"

Michael stepped forward. "I removed the knife and the envelope from the door. Then I opened it and read it to Catherine."

Dinkins huffed and extracted a small evidence bag from his pants pocket. "You shouldn't have touched it." He slipped the knife and letter into separate bags.

The officer plucked at Catherine's last nerve. Her face grew hot. "Excuse me. A *knife* held the note in place. Who in their right mind wouldn't want to know what the thing said?"

Michael placed his hand on her forearm.

She took a deep breath, calming herself.

The officer ignored her sarcasm. "Do you have any idea who would do this?"

"My initial thought was the store owner next door."

"Next door, as in the Double Scoop? Jerry?" He feverously jotted a few notes. "Why do you suspect him?"

"He's been harassing me ever since I assumed the lease on this space."

"Have you reported that?"

Catherine shook her head. "I've only reported him to the town council because of a stunt he pulled that could've resulted in a hefty fine for me. As far as anything else, I've been hoping he'd come to his senses. Even though I have to admit, my last encounter with him was, at best, disturbing."

Officer Dinkins hesitated, appearing to summon from some invisible source what he should do next. "Tell me what has occurred with the proprietor of the Double Scoop. Start from the beginning, please." He flipped to a new page and wrote copious notes as Catherine explained what had been going on, including the upcoming scheduled council meeting hearing.

"From what Jerry said, he wanted to expand into this space," Michael interjected. "And when he didn't get the chance, he decided to intimidate Catherine in hopes that she'd relinquish her lease and go running back to where she came. Then he'd be able to take over." He glanced at the bagged letter and knife. "But this…"

Dinkins shifted his attention to Catherine. "You said your initial thought was the owner of the ice cream parlor. Does that mean you think that someone else might be responsible?"

Catherine side-eyed Michael.

"Go ahead," he said.

"Before I moved here last year, I was mugged on my way home from work." Was it her imagination, or did Dinkins' face light up as if he'd won a raffle prize? As unseasoned as she suspected he was, a case like hers could propel him to new heights at the police station. Maybe a promotion, if he solved the case.

"Where did that occur?" he continued.

"Boston." She shivered at the memory. "I nearly bled to death and had to be resuscitated. The man responsible was apprehended a short distance away, and after I identified him, he pled guilty. As a habitual offender, it was my understanding that he'd spend the rest of his life in prison."

Officer Dinkins nodded and continued his note-taking. "So, as far as you know, he's still incarcerated?"

"Yes. But I've always been fearful that he'd figure out a way to seek revenge. With a life sentence hanging over him, what does he have to lose?"

Officer Dinkins closed his notepad and slipped it and the pen back into his pocket. "Do you have a copy of the police report taken at the time? If not, I can look it up."

"It's upstairs. I'll get it for you."

Catherine returned a few minutes later and handed Dinkins the report, giving herself a silent thanks for packing it when she'd returned to Boston.

He folded it and slipped it into his other breast pocket. "We'll need to dust for prints," he announced with authority. "And whatever you do, don't touch anything. Your store is now an active crime scene." He headed for the door, then turned. "And for your safety, I suggest you make arrangements to stay elsewhere until we figure this out."

∽

"I AGREE WITH THE OFFICER," Michael said. "You shouldn't be here by yourself."

He and Catherine removed the lingering traces of the criminal investigation the police left behind. "Why not close the store for at least a few days, until we know it's safe for you to return? You can stay at my place, and I'll move next door with Tina."

Catherine let his words percolate in her mind. He was right. What if the perpetrator came into the store posing as a customer? It would be near empty since the summer season hadn't started. And then he'd have the perfect opportunity to carry out his plan. But Catherine didn't want to push Michael out of his house. And she didn't want to be a burden. Even though sales at this time of year were weak, a handful was better than nothing. Yet sales were the least of her worries.

What should she do? If she closed the store, she'd flee the island. Yes. That's what she'd do. But where? Not Boston. Maybe she could stay at Michael's Rhode Island house. No. He wouldn't allow her to stay there alone, either. She'd figure it out. She couldn't—wouldn't—put him or Tina in danger by involving them any further.

CHAPTER TWENTY-THREE

Catherine mindlessly tossed clothes and other essentials she'd take with her onto her bed.

"Please, reconsider my offer," Michael said, wringing his hands. "Stay at my place. It's no big deal. That way I'll know you're safe."

She gazed at him. He was such a gentle, caring man, making the notion of leaving him all the more difficult. "I appreciate your offer. I do. But being alone at your house all day with nothing to do but look over my shoulder would be as bad as staying here. Much as I hate running off like a scared rabbit, I have no other choice."

He stepped toward her. "You can't board the ferry and plan your future as it motors to Hyannis. You need a plan." He glanced at the bed jumbled with her clothes. "And at the moment, mine makes the most sense."

Catherine blew out a stream of air and flopped onto the small corner of open real estate left on her bed. "I know you're right. I'm having trouble focusing."

"Of course, you are. So, stay where I can keep an eye on you."

Downstairs someone pounded on the shop door. Catherine jumped.

What now?

She scanned the kitchen counter for the brown paper bag. Who was she kidding? She couldn't possibly go away by herself when a mere knock at her door nearly catapulted her into a panic attack.

Michael pulled back the curtain on the front window. His shoulders relaxed. "It's Helen."

Thank goodness. Helen had a knack for getting Catherine to see reason. Her older friend had somehow morphed into a mother figure. She'd help put things in perspective. Even if she couldn't, no one's hugs were better than Helen's.

Catherine flew down the stairs and opened the door to her friend.

Helen rushed in and opened her arms. "Come here. I came as soon as I heard."

Catherine relished Helen's hold on her while she fought back tears.

Michael walked up behind them and bolted the door.

Catherine stepped back. "How did you find out?" she asked, her voice quivering.

Helen gave her a gentle smile. "This is Nantucket. News of a police cruiser on Main Street travels fast." She pulled back and gave Catherine an appraising glance. "Are you okay?"

Catherine nodded. "Physically, yes. Mentally, I'm a mess."

Helen looked at a nearby folding chair, put her arm around Catherine's shoulders, and guided her to it. "Here. Sit down."

Catherine did as she was told and looked up at her friend. "I heard a thud this morning and called Michael. After he arrived and checked to make sure no one had broken in, he found an envelope containing a letter stuck to the door with a knife."

"What?" Helen's hand flew to her chest, and her eyes widened. "A knife? Who on earth would do such a thing?"

"At first, I thought Jerry was up to his tricks again, but the letter made me think otherwise."

Helen's gaze ping-ponged between Michael and Catherine. Her face was one giant question mark.

"The letter said, 'I can run, but I can't hide.'" Catherine shivered. "I've been afraid that the person who attacked me last year might track me down, and I think maybe he finally has."

Helen shook her head. "Wait, I thought you said he's in prison."

"He was. Or maybe he still is, and hired someone."

"What are the police doing about it?"

"They dusted for prints," Michael said. "Took a copy of the police report Catherine filed at the time and confiscated the letter and knife. We're hoping they get to the bottom of this fast."

"Well, you can't stay here," Helen said.

"Right," Michael agreed, relief written across his face. "The officer recommended she close the store and move to another location until they get a handle on it. I suggested she come to my house, and I'd stay with Tina, but I can't convince her."

Helen's expression was a mix of compassion and conviction. "Catherine, this is not the time to put on a brave front. Or a stubborn one, either. You must follow the advice of the police. You have no choice."

"I intend to, but I won't involve Michael any more than he already is. I don't want to uproot him. He should be concentrating on his new job, not me." Catherine stood. "Putting that aside, even if I were to take him up on his offer, I'd still be alone. So, what have I accomplished? If this guy found me thirty miles off the coast, he can locate me a short distance away. I'd never forgive myself if anything happened to Michael, or any of you, because of me. This maniac has his sights set on me, and collateral damage won't bother him one bit."

Catherine reached for Michael's hand and gave it a gentle squeeze. "The only option I see is to leave Nantucket. First, I have to figure out where to go."

"I understand all that, but being alone in a strange place is not a good idea," Helen said.

Catherine hesitated and thought about her friend's statement. She was right. Catherine needed to make wise decisions now. Following her attack, she'd pledged to take her mother's advice to heart. So, she'd dumped her job and moved to Nantucket. Had that been smart? She'd thought so at the time. Questioning it now wouldn't help.

Catherine looked at Helen and Michael's faces, which were laced with concern. She knew they wanted what was best for her. Helen had become a dear friend and confidant in a short time. Michael was in another league—not only was he a great friend, but she'd fallen in love with him, too. How could she leave? The thought of being alone in a strange place scared her. But what other choice did she have?

Helen laid her hand on Catherine's forearm. "I have a suggestion."

Catherine's eyes welled, and she shook her head. "I appreciate how much you both care about me. But whatever your idea is, it will place you in potential danger. I can't risk that. If something happened to either you or Bill, I don't—"

"Nothing's going to happen to any of us," Michael said. "The police will see to that."

"They can't watch us every minute of the day." Catherine put her hand up, stopping his next words.

"Listen to me." Helen's stern look gave her words authority. "You can't leave the island. Do you hear me? *You can't.* At least here, we can keep an eye on you and make sure you're safe. And Michael's right. The police will be extra vigilant."

"Hear her out, Catherine, please," Michael said.

"Take a room at the inn," Helen suggested.

Catherine shook her head. "Absolutely not, I—"

"You know how well we screen our guests. It's doubtful this lunatic could register without us suspecting something odd. Especially at this time of year, when guests are typically repeaters. Besides, the inn is under the watchful eyes of our police. This way, you won't be alone. Either Bill, or I, or both, will be there around the clock." She glanced at Michael, then Catherine. "You know we love having you, and Michael can visit after work and on his days off." Helen gave a firm nod of her head. "If I do say so myself, it's the perfect solution."

Catherine tried her best to put on a stoic face. Inside, she quivered like a bowl of Jell-O. True, staying with Helen and Bill would ease her nerves. But what if this guy got past their reliable screening, invaded the inn, and cut everyone down to get to her?

Catherine took Helen's hand. "That's very generous of you, but just like I don't want Michael and Tina in harm's way, the same holds true for you and Bill."

"Do you think I'd endanger the few guests we have scheduled for the next few weeks, or us?" Helen patted Catherine's hand. "You know better than that. Let's not forget, Bill is a close friend of Police Chief Anderson, who comes by to play chess with Bill every Wednesday night. So, one night a week, we'll have on-site protection. I'm sure when Bill relays the fact that you're a guest of ours, the chief will step up patrols. So, it's a win-win for everyone."

Catherine couldn't argue the logic. But if she stayed at the inn, she'd have to insist on paying her room and board, and that was an expense she couldn't afford.

Helen narrowed her eyes. "I can read that mind of yours. No, we will not accept payment from you. At least not in the form of money."

"But—"

"No buts. You can help me with the spring cleaning." Helen put her hands up to her heart in a prayer position. "As much as I hate to admit it, this old girl isn't capable of what she used to be. Besides, it gets lonely at the inn during the winter, so Bill and I would welcome the company."

Catherine's vision blurred.

"It's not like we have guests lined up at the door this time of year. So, as the saying goes, there's room at the inn." Helen let out a long breath and made a mock wipe of her brow, as if she'd just completed the Boston Marathon.

"Sounds good to me," Michael said.

"Don't you have to run this by Bill?" Catherine asked, feeling her resolve crumble.

Helen waved a hand in the air. "No worries. I know my husband of fifty-years pretty well. He'll be more than fine."

CHAPTER TWENTY-FOUR

A week later

When Catherine glanced in the bathroom mirror, the woman she saw staring back at her bore little resemblance to her former self. Dark circles had formed under her eyes. Her face was pale as chalk. "Why haven't the police come up with anything yet?" she said, slamming her hand on the rim of the sink. "I can't continue to keep my store closed. It's not like I have an endless supply of money."

As much as she appreciated Helen and Bill's generosity, she wanted to return to her cozy apartment that she'd come to think of as home. But how could she live there without fear? She closed her eyes, filled her lungs with air, and exhaled.

Then Catherine left the bathroom and looked around at the space dubbed "the penthouse" by the inn's proprietors. It mimicked the size of her apartment, sans a kitchen. The walls were bathed in pearl gray, while the king-sized, white wooden-framed bed with plump airy coverings gave the impression of a room featured in a coastal home magazine.

She headed to one of the windows wedged between dual dormers,

A DISTANT LIGHT

featuring a cushioned window seat covered in a bright floral print. She sat and hugged her knees to her chest in what had become her favorite place. It offered a clear view of the street below, and on days when the weather was less than inviting, raindrops pattered against the windowpanes, providing a hum of comfort.

The spot pleased her, but it also frazzled her. Its unobstructed view allowed her to scrutinize every person who passed by or lingered nearby for too long. Like the man the night before, who'd had his jacket collar up around his ears, wearing a baseball cap, and standing by the lamppost across the street. Was he scoping out the inn? Waiting for a chance to pounce?

No matter how antsy she was, Catherine smiled when she recalled how Helen and Bill welcomed her into their home, insisting she occupy the sizeable, converted attic space during her stay.

"You'll have more room," they'd said. "And the utmost privacy."

Although grateful for their generosity, she suspected that room to stretch out and the added privacy had little to do with allowing her to stay in their most pricey guest suite. Instead, her panicky state of mind surmised that it translated into the safest place in the house, since it was furthest from the lobby. And that meant Helen and Bill had agreed that the danger surrounding her was equivalent to a potential pending terrorist attack.

Catherine leaned her head back against the wall. She'd always prided herself on being independent, someone capable of handling whatever came her way. How pathetic she must seem now. As hard as she'd fought off the moniker of victim, that's exactly how she felt.

Determined to shake off the gloominess, she headed for the door to help Helen with her spring cleaning, a task she'd learned was of epic proportions, and sure to keep her mind occupied. All the windows required washing, the curtains needed to be steam cleaned, and the winter bed coverings exchanged for lighter versions. And if that weren't enough, all the wood in the common areas also had to be wiped down with Murphy's Oil soap and polished to a satiny sheen. And there was a lot of wood!

Catherine locked the door to her room, double-checked to make sure it was secure, and went downstairs. Before she traversed the last flight, however, she peeked over the railing into the lobby.

Empty. She exhaled.

Helen was wiping her hands on her apron. "You're down early," she said, from the dining room.

"I couldn't sleep. Thought I'd grab a cup of coffee, force down a muffin, then help you with your chores."

Helen slipped an arm around Catherine's shoulders and ushered her into the room. "I have a better idea. You're too wired for coffee. I've made some calming tea from fresh herbs. It'll help take the edge off. Instead of a muffin, I was about to scramble myself some eggs. The protein will do you good."

Catherine's eyes filled with tears. "You're so good to me. How will I ever repay you?"

"Oh, please. Having you here is a blessing. We've come to think of you as the daughter we were never fortunate to have."

Tears spilled down Catherine's face.

"Come here. You need a hug."

Catherine allowed herself to be held. "I'm more anxious now than after the attack. I thought I was doing the right thing, moving to Nantucket. But between Jerry and now this, I'm starting to wonder."

Helen released her and held her at arm's length. "There's no doubt you did the right thing. Think of how much you're loved." She stepped back and waved her hand, as if clearing the air. "So, did you hear from Officer Dinkins last night after we left you and Michael to watch television?"

"No. And that has me amped up, too. I've tried calling several times. All I get is—

'We're working on it. These things take time.'" Catherine lowered her head. "As much as I appreciate all that you and Bill are doing for me, I can't stay here forever. I have my business to consider. I don't know what I'm going to do."

"If it's any consolation, when the police chief was here the other night to play chess with Bill, he said Officer Dinkins has been working hard to get to the bottom of this. Even spending his own time on the case."

Catherine mentally chastised herself for rushing to judgment about Dinkins.

"So why can't I get an update then?"

Helen tilted her head toward the front door. "I think you're about to have your questions answered."

Catherine turned.

Officer Dinkins walked into the lobby.

She scurried over to him. "I hope you have news."

He tipped his hat toward Helen, then returned his attention to Catherine. "Some. We've confirmed that the man who attacked you is behind bars at the Massachusetts Correctional Institution Cedar Junction."

Catherine's shoulders unwound. "Well, that's a relief."

"It's better than if we'd learned he'd escaped," Dinkins said. "Still, you can't let your guard down."

"But if he's behind bars…"

"There are things we need to verify before we exclude him. And if we do, we're still left with the question of who threatened you."

Catherine tried slowing her breathing. Where was Helen's tea when she needed it? "What's to verify?"

"Well, for one thing, we have to ensure he has no reach to the outside. And for another, we have to determine what type of prisoner he's been."

"Why does that matter?"

Helen appeared with a piping cup of aromatic tea and handed it to Catherine. "Why don't you two go into the parlor, where you'll be comfortable?" She looked at the officer. "What can I get for you? Coffee? Pastry?"

"Coffee, black, will be fine. Thank you."

"Oh, mercy me. You must have something more than that. How about one of my mixed berry muffins?" She gave him a sly smile. "Just took them from the oven a little while ago."

Dinkins smiled. "Thank you. Sounds delicious."

Shortly after Dinkins and Catherine settled onto the couch, Helen came back with a tray of mini-muffins and a mug of steaming coffee. "Let me know if there's anything else I can get either of you."

"So why does it matter what kind of prisoner he's been?" Catherine asked again, after Helen left.

Dinkins swallowed a mouthful of coffee, broke off a piece of muffin, and raised it to his lips. "If he's been on his best behavior, it's unlikely he'd try anything to jeopardize the perks he may be getting for being a good boy."

Catherine nodded and sipped her tea. The mild blend hinted of peppermint, chamomile, rose petals, and a twist of citrus.

"And we also need to examine his circle of friends, or enemies, for that matter, both inside and out. A friend might want to show that he's willing to do what it takes to remain on his good side. Or an enemy might seek revenge by harming you to set him up." Dinkins popped another piece of muffin into his mouth and took a moment to savor it before swallowing and continuing. "We'll be reviewing visitor logs, security camera footage, and arranging for the local authorities to question the guy. We can't rule him out until we've done all our homework."

"So, although he's confined, he could still be playing a part in this?" Catherine asked.

"Unfortunate, but true." He finished his muffin and washed it down with the last of his coffee. "This isn't the time to let your defenses down." Dinkins stood. "So, for now, my advice is to remain here, where you're safe. I'll be in touch as soon as I have something to report."

Catherine walked the officer to the door. As soon as she closed it behind him, she hurried to the kitchen.

"The guy who attacked me is still in prison," she told Helen.

Helen's face lit up. "Thank heavens." Then she frowned. "But if he's in prison, then who do they think…"

"They haven't eliminated him completely. Maybe someone is extending a favor, or an enemy wants to shine a suspicious light on him."

"Does Officer Dinkins have any idea how much longer it'll be before he can put that to bed?"

"No. From what he said, there's still a lot of work to be done."

"Well, at least you've heard something." Helen went to the oven and slid out a plate with a gloved hand. "Here, I've been keeping your eggs warm."

CHAPTER TWENTY-FIVE

"I'd love to," Catherine said, giddy over the prospect of venturing out with Michael midway through week two of confinement. "The walls feel like they are closing in," she whispered. "But do you think it's safe?"

He wrapped his arm around her shoulder. "Are you serious?" He chuckled. "You're better off with me than inside a Brink's truck."

Although she'd been plagued with doubts in recent days about the turn her life had taken, she had no doubt that Michael would put himself in danger before he'd let anything happen to her. As comforting as that was, it also scared her beyond measure. "Sorry, Dinkins has made me such a fraidy-cat." She pulled her coat from a nearby hall closet and slipped it on with Michael's help.

"He only wants to keep you safe. We all do."

After letting Helen know that Michael had invited her out, Catherine climbed into the front passenger seat of his car. "Not that it matters, but where are we going?"

"My place."

Catherine side-eyed him. *What would she do if he—*

As if reading her mind, Michael said, "My woodworking shop, to be exact." He turned the key in the ignition, and the engine roared to life. "If I don't get started on your window display, it'll never be ready for the Daffodil Festival in a few weeks."

Catherine closed her eyes and leaned her head back against the headrest. "I can't believe I'd forgotten all about that. It goes to show where my mind's been."

"Don't beat yourself up. You've had a lot to deal with recently."

"But the store's my baby." She sighed. "Some mother I've turned out to be."

"Hey, speaking of the store, why don't I swing by so you can check it out? Maybe there's something there, or from the apartment, that you'd like to take back to the inn."

"Oh, Michael, I'd like that if you're sure it's not too much of an inconvenience. But you must be tired after working all day, and then there's my project. So, if—"

He pulled up to a light, flipped on his right signal before venturing onto Main Street, and smiled. "No prob."

Her heart melted, and she fought an urge to cup his face in her hands and smother him with kisses.

"Besides, I have an ulterior motive."

Catherine laughed for the first time in quite a while, surprised at how liberating it felt. "And what's that?"

"The longer I keep you out, the longer I have you all to myself."

AT MICHAEL'S DIRECTION, Catherine stayed put in the truck while he scoped out the building's front, sides, and the back stairs leading up to her apartment.

A few minutes later, he opened the passenger door. "All clear."

He shadowed Catherine to the front door.

She unlocked it and disengaged the alarm.

"Are you okay?" he asked.

The lump growing in her throat blocked her words. A tear rolled down her cheek. She swallowed as she looked around. "I've missed this place so much."

Catherine ran her hand along a nearby display case topped with a nautical-themed Irish linen runner. Oh, how she adored what she'd built here. Everywhere she looked, she unpacked a memory. Like talks with Helen long into the night about how she'd get her venture off the ground. And Tina's help, which had made for such a smooth transition. Her treasure finds on Cape Cod.

Yes, it was all spelled out, right here. Right now. She belonged here.

Michael touched her shoulder.

She turned, facing him with tears in her eyes. "What if I can never come back?"

He took her in his arms and rubbed her back. "Don't think like that. I promise that won't happen."

"I pray you're right."

"Trust me." He released her. "Do you want to check upstairs—see if there's anything you'd like to take back to the inn?"

Fear gripped Catherine, throwing her off-center.

What if someone was waiting, hiding upstairs?

"I'll go first," Michael said, soothing her nerves.

Catherine exhaled. She grabbed his hand as he turned to walk away and lowered her voice. "I know it's silly, but I can't shake the sense someone is watching us. He could've broken in upstairs and be living up there, just waiting for us to return. The alarm doesn't cover up there."

Michael headed up. "Wait here."

Catherine panicked. If something happened to Michael…

She ran to the back counter, reached below for a paper bag, and brought it to her face.

Breathe.

AFTER MICHAEL ASSURED her all was safe, Catherine stuffed a couple of sweaters into a shopping bag, and then they went downstairs. On their way to the door, she stopped at a display of lighthouse replicas.

She picked up a miniature of The Pt. Judith Lighthouse and pulled it to her chest. "This is one of my favorites. My parents took me on a boat tour years ago so we could see it up close. Even as a teenager, I remember the sense of calm it evoked."

Michael smiled. "I think I've mentioned it's one of mine, too. When I lived in Rhode Island, I'd sometimes drive to a nearby parking lot, take in the view, and listen to the surf, using the time to think." He eyed the replica in her hand. "Bring it with you. When you're anxious, it'll help you relax."

Catherine shoved it into her bag, set the alarm, and locked the door. Halfway to the truck, she heard a scuffling sound and froze.

Michael must have heard it too, since he tucked her behind him. "Who's there?" he called out.

Quiet.

"Show yourself!" he demanded.

A figure in an overcoat moved around the corner. Catherine fixed her gaze on the man's hand, which was shoved inside his right coat pocket.

Michael took a step backward, forcing Catherine to do the same.

Jerry strolled from the shadows, pulling his hand from his pocket.

Catherine flinched and grabbed Michael's arm.

Then he passed by, giving them a half-salute and a thin smile, but he didn't say a word.

Catherine released the breath stuffed inside her lungs, lowered her hand, and tried to step forward.

Michael remained planted in place.

Jerry unlocked the door to his store and went inside.

Only then did Michael motion for Catherine to get into the truck. He shadowed her until she was seated inside. Then he went around and got into his seat, hitting the button to lock all the doors. He looked at Catherine. "Something's not right with that man."

~

CATHERINE WATCHED Michael work his magic to bring her display to life. After about an hour, she stood. "Time to call it a night. How about we have a glass of wine before you take me back to the inn?"

Michael pushed up his goggles and turned off his equipment. "Sounds good." He grasped her hand and led her into what had been Tina's attached garage before he'd transformed it into a comfortable living space.

Once again, Catherine saw proof of his awesome talent. She loved the creamy shiplap covering the walls, reflective of the island's beachy theme. A big-screen television hung on the front wall before a reclining burgundy leather couch and a sand-colored overstuffed chair with a matching ottoman. A black pot-bellied stove hugged the far corner. It was so cozy.

A galley kitchen opened to the adjoining area. The white kitchen cabinets, marble-like quartz countertops, and a gray-and-white swirled tile floor were what she would've chosen. Catherine's eyes traveled to the staircase, which she supposed led to the bedroom and bath. "This is so nice, Michael. Hard to believe it was ever a garage."

He raised his chin with a gleam in his eye. "A lot of blood, sweat, and tears went into it, but I have to admit, I'm happy with how it turned out."

Catherine nodded her approval. "You should be."

He went to the kitchen, opened a bottle, filled two glasses with a sparkling liquid, and handed one to Catherine.

"Champagne?"

"Prosecco."

She took a sip. "Delicious."

He motioned to the sofa. "Have a seat."

She did, and in one smooth movement, he slid down beside her, draping his arm on the top of the sofa.

She snuggled into his warmth and sighed. "There have been days I've thought I must've been an ax murderer in a previous life to deserve all this."

Michael gave her shoulder a gentle squeeze. "You've done nothing to prompt Jerry's oddball behavior. And certainly nothing to deserve being threatened."

Catherine turned to him. "At first, I chalked Jerry's actions up to him being a sore loser, but over time, that's changed. He scares me now. Like tonight, for instance. I don't think it's a coincidence that he happened to be nearby when we were leaving the store."

"I agree. The guy is definitely creepy. I think we should let the police know how he's been skulking around. I'm sure they will figure out who's responsible for the knife incident, and then we can turn up the heat on Jerry."

Catherine slapped her forehead with the heel of her hand and scooted around to fully face Michael. "I don't know where my mind is these days. I was so excited about getting out tonight, and then a wreck after the Jerry thing, that I forgot to mention that Dinkins stopped by this morning. The guy who nearly killed me is still in jail."

"Wow." Michael sat up straighter. "That's good news." Then he paused. "Is he working any other leads?"

"He didn't say. But according to Dinkins, being locked up doesn't rule him out."

"What?" Michael arched an eyebrow. "Why not?"

"He needs to investigate things like who the guy hangs with on the inside, and who his visitors are. That'll give them insight into whether he's been calling in favors to get at me." Catherine blew out a long stream of air. "Dinkins still has to review reams of prison logs and hours of security camera footage, which translates to a boatload of time. Time I *don't* have."

Michael gave her a gentle squeeze. "It won't be much longer."

"I hope not. If the police don't come up with something soon, I'll have to return to Boston and get a real job."

He gazed at her. "That's not going to happen. Besides, I wouldn't know what to do without you."

To further reassure her, he took her in his arms, kissed her, and all thoughts of Jerry and her attacker floated away.

CHAPTER TWENTY-SIX

A week later

From her window seat at the inn, Catherine watched a patrol car pull up. Next, Michael's truck rumbled down the street and parked behind it. She'd anticipated his visit all day, but Dinkins came as a surprise. She observed as the officer approached Michael's truck.

Catherine craned her neck. Dinkins nodded, and Michael pointed at the inn. Then she scrambled off the seat, grabbed her room key, hurried out the door, locked it, and rushed downstairs. When she reached the bottom step, the men were entering the lobby.

Dinkins raised his nose in the air. "Something smells mighty good. Hope I'm not interrupting dinner."

"That's Helen's famous chicken cordon bleu," Catherine said. "And no, you're not interrupting. We wait for Michael."

"Good. I'll try not to take too much of your time."

"Do you mind if Michael joins us?" Catherine asked.

"Not at all. As a matter of fact, I have a few questions for him, too."

Catherine motioned. "Let's go into the parlor."

Dinkins and Michael followed.

Once inside, Catherine slid the tall mahogany pocket doors closed and headed for the couch.

Michael settled in next to her, and Dinkins sat across from them in a leather wing chair.

Dinkins leaned forward, resting his forearms on his knees. "I have some news."

Michael reached over and took Catherine's hand.

"The laborious task of reviewing logs and security camera footage is complete. Although we had to do a lot to rule him out, with the help of our Boston counterparts, I've determined that the man who attacked you is not our guy. Nor is anyone he associates with now, or in the recent past."

Catherine breathed a sigh of relief and fell back against the couch. Officer Dinkins, she realized, had worked hard on her behalf. She felt ashamed for once thinking otherwise. "I'm glad to hear that. But are we now back to square one?"

"Not really." Michael squeezed her hand with affection. "At least he's off the list."

Catherine straightened. "True. If it's not him, or any of his friends or enemies, then who do we look at next?"

"That's why I'm here. I have a few questions." Dinkins shifted his gaze to Michael. "And please, feel free to add anything you think might be helpful."

Michael nodded. "Of course."

Dinkins whipped out a pad and pen from his pocket and returned his attention to Catherine. "Besides Michael, are any of the locals aware of your attack?"

"Well, yes. My friends."

Dinkins poised his pen over the pad. "And they are?"

Catherine shifted in her seat. Why did it matter? Certainly, none of them were involved. "I can assure you that my friends play no part in this."

"It's routine. We have to rule everyone out."

"I think it's a waste, but if you insist, Helen and Bill, the inn's proprietors. And Michael's sister, Tina Benton."

Dinkins looked up from his pad. "That's it?"

Catherine thought how sad it was that she could only count four people as her current friends. "I've only been here a few months."

"Okay. Do you know of anyone who would want to harm you?"

Catherine shook her head. "As I've said before, no."

"During the initial report, you mentioned that you had a run-in with the owner of the Double Scoop."

"Yes. Several."

Michael piped up. "As a matter of fact, about a week ago, Catherine and I were leaving her store, and it seemed to us that he'd been hiding in the shadows."

"Initially, I just considered him a bully," Catherine said. "Someone accustomed to getting his way. Now I find it alarming, and his behavior has gotten worse."

Dinkins flipped back through his pad and read. "He wanted the space you rented, correct?"

"Yes, which resulted in Jerry trying to strong-arm me. Then his threatening words turned into action when he put 'no parking' signs outside my store. He knew it would result in having a fine levied against me."

"When was that?" Dinkins asked.

"On Christmas Day. That's why I went to the council. Recently, he's turned things up several notches. Like when I found trash covering my steps, and then again when he'd waited outside the store early one morning. As Michael said, it appeared as though he'd been stalking us last week. It's probably paranoia, but I've seriously felt as if someone was watching me."

"Okay, so are your friends the only locals who know of the attack?"

Catherine nodded.

Michael winced. "Wait. Jerry knows." He stood and began pacing. "How did I forget that?" He slapped his palm against his forehead. "I told him that Catherine survived an attack on her life."

His words surprised her. "When was that?"

"Right after he'd waited for you outside your store. I thought maybe if he knew, it'd evoke some compassion in him, and he'd lay off."

Dinkins made a note.

"We did mention that he's expected to appear before the town council because of the stanchion stunt, right?" Michael asked.

"Yes. I've determined that's scheduled for next week to address your allegations."

Michael gave Dinkins a look. "It's more than allegations. Catherine provided proof to back up her claims."

Dinkins nodded. "So, the only people who know about your attack are your friends and the owner of the Double Scoop. Is that correct?"

"Yes, here on Nantucket," Catherine responded.

Dinkins raised an eyebrow. "So, people off-island know about it?"

"Yes, my former colleagues."

"I'll need their names too."

Catherine swallowed. She doubted someone from her former workplace would be involved. Could they? Of course not. What motive would they have? Rusty's face flashed before her eyes. He'd wanted her back. Said her clients were up in arms. He'd pressured her, hadn't he? And Rusty, like Jerry, was a man accustomed to getting what he wanted.

Dinkins cleared his throat.

"Sorry." She rubbed her lips with her forefinger. "It's hard to believe that anyone there could have a hand in this." She exhaled. "But my former boss *was* pretty upset after I left. He's called numerous times, trying to convince me to return." Catherine looked at Michael. "Maybe they've lost clients, and he holds me accountable. Or maybe he's trying to scare me into coming back." She waved her hand, as if dismissing the thought. "No, the notion he could be involved is ridiculous. Even as Napoleonic as he can be, I can't imagine he has any part in this."

"If clients you were responsible for left the company, would that have negatively affected him?" Michael asked.

Catherine's brows furrowed. "Well, yes. My clients were some of the largest sources of company revenue. If they went elsewhere, his bonus and stock options would be slashed. And although I doubt it would end in termination, I can see how it could affect him in other ways."

"Any of that could result in a major lifestyle shift," Dinkins said. "Correct?'

She squeezed her lips together. "Yes. He wouldn't deal well with it. Who would? If there's one thing I know for certain about my former boss, it's the size of his ego."

~

Catherine ran a brush through her hair and then went downstairs to join Helen and Bill for a trip to Bartlett's Farm. It was a favorite of Helen's, and an excellent way to sideline Catherine's worries.

She found her friends waiting in the lobby. "Would you rather I stay here and cover the phones?"

"No. Getting out will do you good." Helen pulled on her coat. "The answering machine is on, and we have no guests."

Catherine released a breath. Thank goodness they had declined her offer. She'd only extended it out of a sense of obligation for all they'd done for her. The truth was, she'd have been a wreck being alone in the big old house.

"Okay, if you're sure."

"We are," Helen said. "Come along."

Moments later, they climbed into Lexi, the SUV Catherine had used to transport a good deal of her personal belongings to the island.

Lexi sputtered and coughed at Bill's first attempts to start the engine. Soon, however, she purred in response to his cooing and coaxing. Bill tapped the top of the dashboard. "That's my girl."

Even the beauty of mixed orange wood lilies, buttery-yellow bushy rockrose, and wild amethyst iris lining the road on the way to the farm couldn't quiet the thoughts racing around Catherine's mind in a loop of unthinkable scenarios. If only she'd had another update. It had been a week since Dinkins had stopped by, and she had yet to hear anything else.

How would she deal with it if Rusty *was* involved? Catherine took a deep breath and slowly released it. *Calm down.* she told herself. Although her former boss was self-absorbed, the idea of him threatening her or anyone else was impossible to fathom. He might be a jerk, but jerks didn't make the long trek to an island to plant a knife in a former colleague's door.

Did they?

Catherine turned her thoughts back to the present when Bill pulled into Bartlett's Farm.

"Before I pick up my order, let's have a nice lunch over there," Helen said, pointing to a restaurant on the edge of the lot.

"Sounds good. But only if you'll let me buy," Catherine replied.

Helen and Bill objected, but she dug her heels in.

Before long, they were seated around a small table overlooking the farm.

Helen raised a spoonful of tomato basil soup to her lips. "Have you heard anything from Officer Dinkins?"

"No, and it's driving me crazy."

"Well, the chief is coming by tonight for our weekly chess game," Bill said. "You can ask him then for an update."

Catherine picked up half her crusty baguette filled with curried chicken salad, mixed with raisins and chopped walnuts. "I will. I'm anxious to hear if they've spoken to my former boss."

Bill shifted his gaze from Catherine to Helen and back again. "They think he might be involved?"

"Officer Dinkins wanted the names of anyone who knew of my attack." Catherine wiped her lips with her napkin. "I gave him the names of my close friends here, and my boss and workmates from Boston. And Michael told him that Jerry also knows about it."

"Wait a minute, Jerry knows?" Helen asked.

"Michael mentioned it to him after one of Jerry's episodes. He thought it might draw out some compassion in him."

Helen put down her spoon. "Well, that's interesting."

"Very," Bill said. "I hope they don't uncover anything with regards to your former boss. It's bad enough you're going through this, but to think that someone from your past, someone you've known for many years, and maybe even trusted, could be involved? Now, *that* would be a hard pill to swallow."

Before Catherine could respond, her cell phone rang. She pulled it from her purse. "Officer Dinkins," she mouthed to Helen and Bill, and stepped outside.

∿

A FEW MINUTES LATER, Catherine returned to the table and flopped into her chair. "Dinkins wanted to make sure I attend the council meeting tomorrow." She paused. "I'm not sure why he thinks it's so important, and he didn't seem inclined to elaborate. So, I told him that's my intention."

Bill wiped his hands on his napkin and set it on his empty plate. "Maybe he simply wants to make sure you bring proof about the signs and be there to counter anything Jerry has to say."

"That's what I thought, so I reminded him that I'd provided receipts to the council. He grunted and said it'd be helpful for me to be there anyway."

∿

CATHERINE RUSHED to Helen's side when she saw her heading toward Lexi, holding two shopping bags in her hands. "Here, let me get those." Catherine took the bags and deposited them into Lexi's cargo area.

"Thank you, sweetheart," Helen said. "While I waited for the clerk to ring up my order, I gave some thought to Officer Dinkins' request. Keep in mind that he's put a lot of work into your case."

Bill opened the door, and Helen slid into the passenger seat while Catherine climbed in behind her.

"He probably also spoke to Jerry." Helen rolled her eyes. "And we know how Jerry can be. I think he wants to be sure that if there's any question about what you provided, you'll be there to defend yourself."

"Even though I'd planned on going, I have to admit, facing Jerry won't be easy. I'm afraid how he'll react when he's the recipient of a hefty fine. What if he becomes more unhinged than he already is?"

Bill peered in his rearview mirror at Catherine. "Don't you worry. You won't be alone. We'll be right there to support you."

The tension in her shoulder blades subsided. "Are you sure? I hate to impose, but I'd appreciate not being alone. And Michael will be working, so that rules him out."

Helen turned in her seat. "Consider it done. Did you ask if he's spoken to your former boss yet?"

"He said he'd called the Boston detective he'd dealt with regarding the inmate and asked him to question Rusty."

"And?"

"That's it. Nothing else."

CHAPTER TWENTY-SEVEN

At the hearing, Catherine sat flanked by Helen and Bill on one side, and Michael and Tina on the other. Michael had insisted on being there, and had arranged time off to be by her side. Then, when Tina had heard that the police had requested Catherine's presence, she'd rearranged her calendar, too.

Onlookers sat shoulder to shoulder in the small hearing room. A low din filled the air.

Jerry sat in front of where the council would preside over the proceedings. He turned toward Catherine at one point, his expression smug, then returned his gaze to the front of the room.

Her insides churned. What a jerk. How had Linda put up with him?

Michael squeezed her hand, leaned over, and whispered in her ear. "This will all be over soon. Then we'll go out to celebrate another chapter closed."

She didn't feel like celebrating. Of course, it would be good to see Jerry get his comeuppance, and put an end to his nonsense. But what about the person behind the knife incident? Could he still be out there, waiting to strike?

The council members soon entered and took their seats.

Then the door at the rear of the room opened. People turned and craned their necks to see who had entered the already packed space.

Catherine's gaze traveled toward the door, as well. Carol had stepped into the courtroom, her expression as negative as Jerry's. The women briefly made eye contact. Next, officer Dinkins entered and stood in front of the door.

Jerry turned and saw Dinkins. His expression of cockiness instantly diminished.

Did Dinkins make him nervous? If so, why? Was Dinkins holding something back from her?

The chairman banged his gavel, then shuffled through some papers. "Our first agenda item today is a dispute between the proprietors of the Double Scoop on Main Street and A Distant Light." He nodded at Jerry, then turned his attention to the audience. "Is Catherine O'Malley in attendance?"

Catherine stood. "Yes."

"Do you wish to withdraw your complaint?"

Withdraw? Had they already determined they'd rule in Jerry's favor and were offering up an opportunity for her to do what, exactly? Save face? Accept the fine, rightfully his?

"No."

"Please state your name for the record, and recite the basis for your complaint."

This was ridiculous. She'd already covered this at the first meeting. "Catherine O'Malley." Her voice came out stronger than she felt. "As I've said before, the proprietor of the Double Scoop had "no parking" signs placed outside my store, which, as you know, is a violation of city ordinance. I've provided proof to this council that he purchased these items, not me." Catherine then sat down.

The chairman looked at Jerry. "What do you have to say to that?"

Jerry stood, turned, glared at Catherine, and returned his attention to the chairman. His voice was conciliatory. "I wish to apologize for my neighbor, who has chosen to waste your valuable time with these baseless allegations."

Catherine stiffened.

He chuckled. "I would, however, be interested in seeing this so-called evidence."

The chairman extended a copy to Jerry.

The purchase receipt shook in his hand. "This is a forgery. There's no way... How did she get this?"

Michael stood. "May I say something?"

"And you are?" the chairman asked.

"Michael Benton, a friend of Miss O'Malley's."

The chairman scrutinized Catherine.

She nodded.

"Proceed," the chairman said.

"I obtained that document from the company that delivered the signs. And since I thought Catherine's *neighbor* might try something like this, I have a notarized statement from the company's owner indicating the validity of the receipt."

Oh, how she loved this man. Almost from the very first day they'd met, he'd had her back.

"Do you have that statement with you?" the chairman asked.

"I do." Michael pulled it from his pocket, walked to the dais, handed it to the chairman, and returned to his seat.

Catherine watched Jerry shift in his seat and shoot Michael a menacing look.

The door opened again, and as before, all the attendees turned to look. A second police officer entered, this one quite a bit older than Dinkins. He gave his colleague a nod and stood next to him, his hands clasped in front.

Jerry turned and saw the officers blocking the doors.

Catherine observed the look of worry erupt on Jerry's face. "What's going on?" she whispered to Michael.

He shrugged.

The chairman examined the document. "This is compelling."

Jerry, no longer smug, jumped to his feet. "This is absurd! I've been a member of this community for many years, and you're going to take the word of a couple of wash-a-shores?" he yelled.

The chairman banged his gavel. "Please sit down."

Jerry slammed his hand on the table in front of him. "I will not be a party to this kangaroo court!" Then he directed his anger at Catherine. "And you! You'll be sorry you ever moved here." He lunged toward her.

Michael jumped up and stepped between Catherine and Jerry. "*Sit down,* man."

But Jerry didn't back off. He looked around Michael at Catherine. "If it's the last thing I do, I'll make you regret…"

The chairman banged his gavel several more times. "Order! Order!"

Dinkins and the other officer moved in. They grasped Jerry's arms, pulled them behind him, and placed him in handcuffs.

Jerry's face turned the color of dark cherries. "Have you all lost your minds? I haven't done anything to warrant this!"

Dinkins looked at Catherine, and she swore she saw him puff out his chest.

"You're under arrest for malicious harassment." Dinkins looked at the other officer. "Read him his rights."

CATHERINE AND MICHAEL entered the station and approached the desk.

"Officer Dinkins, please," Catherine said.

"Your name?"

"Catherine O'Malley. He's expecting me."

A few minutes later, Dinkins ushered them into a dimly lit room. He motioned to two worn ladderback wooden chairs at a table. "Have a seat."

"What's going on?" Catherine asked. "You arrested Jerry because of his outburst at the council meeting?"

"I figured he might try something, and if he did, I wanted to witness what went down. If it went the way I thought it would, it'd give me a reason to take him in."

"So, you *used* Catherine to get at Jerry?" Michael spat out.

Dinkins focused his attention on her. "Look, I'm sorry for not letting you in on the reason I wanted you there, but it was in your best interest not to know. You were never in any danger with me and my partner in attendance. When he threatened you, he gave me what I needed to arrest him."

Dinkins settled into a similar chair across from Catherine and Michael. He folded his hands on the table. "All I had was probable cause to haul him in and question him about the knife. I didn't think he'd give anything up."

"Wait," Catherine said. "Are you saying you've ruled out my former boss?"

"I am. He was in California meeting with clients on the day of the incident. He's clean. The detective also questioned the rest of your colleagues and concluded we were barking up the wrong tree."

The anger that had built up in Catherine at being made a pawn disintegrated into disbelief. "So, you think *Jerry's* behind the knife incident?"

"Yes. We had questioned him, and during the interrogation, he let on that he knew of your attack. When I pressed him on it, he said he knew because Michael told him. I could tell he thought he was smarter than us. Thought I'd believe him. And since Michael said he'd spoken to him, I almost did. But then he added that the perp was behind bars, and that piqued my interest."

"I never said that," Michael said.

"Exactly. So, I obtained a search warrant, and while he was off-island, my partner and I went to his apartment, found some incriminating evidence, and confiscated his laptop. Amongst other things, we found he'd done numerous searches regarding the attack."

"But searching the internet doesn't prove he's behind the knife incident," Michael reasoned.

"That's what he said, which is why I wanted Catherine to attend the meeting today. I had a sense that he might threaten her when the meeting didn't go his way." Dinkins gave a bit of a smile. "Guess my hunch was right."

"But he didn't hurt me, so how were you able to arrest him?"

"A threat isn't based solely on a physical altercation. If you were scared, and it was obvious you were, intent to cause harm is all that's required."

"So, what happens now?" Catherine asked.

"We turn up the heat."

"And if he confesses?" Michael asked.

"Then we bring it to the prosecutor and go from there."

"And if he doesn't?"

"Then we still have him on harassment."

CATHERINE AND MICHAEL returned to the precinct for the second time that day following a call from Dinkins.

"Just like I thought. He crumbled like a stale cookie," Dinkins said, after he'd ushered them into a room.

Catherine stared at him. "Jerry confessed?"

"Yes. One of the pieces of evidence I was waiting on involved the knife. We had it traced, and with the help of the manufacturer, determined the point of sale. So, when I showed Jerry a photo of him standing at the register, he knew we had him dead to rights. He'll appear in court tomorrow."

Catherine's heart beat so fast it could've given a cheetah a run for its money. She felt light-headed. *Jerry?* He was the one who'd uprooted her life? Cost her money that she couldn't afford to lose? And for what? So, he could enlarge his ice cream shop. It was mind-boggling.

"I need a moment." She got to her feet, pressed her hands on the table for support, and took a deep breath to steady herself.

"Can I get you some water?" Dinkins asked.

"No. I'm okay. I just need a minute to think." After a brief pause, she headed for the door. "I want to talk to him."

Michael pushed his chair back and stood. "That's not a good idea. He might try something."

"I'll be safe. Officer Dinkins will see to that."

"Why do you want to talk to him?" Dinkins asked.

"I want him to know the effect this has had on me. Maybe I'll at least get an apology."

"Good luck with that," Michael huffed.

She took his hands in hers. "Talking to him is the only way I'll be able to process this. If nothing else, I want to look him in the eye and see what I see."

CHAPTER TWENTY-EIGHT

Catherine followed Officer Dinkins down a narrow hall to Jerry's cell. The walls were a drab shade of green, the harsh florescent lights casting fingerlike shadows across the cells. The smell of stale coffee and perspiration confirmed her feelings that this was not a place anyone in their right mind would choose to be.

Halfway there, Dinkins turned to her. "He's unstable. Hard to say what he might do. You'll have to communicate with him from outside the cell."

When they approached, the man who had shoveled so much anxiety and fear her way sat on the edge of the bed, his elbows embedded into his knees, his hands covering his face while he rocked back and forth.

A few hours earlier, he'd been smug and defiant. Now he was only an empty shell of the man she'd once feared. In spite of everything, Catherine felt sorry for him.

"You have a visitor," Officer Dinkins announced in a booming voice. "Ten minutes," he said to Catherine, and walked away.

Jerry jumped to his feet and glared at her. "What are you doing here? Come to gloat?"

She caught her breath and stepped back. "Hardly."

"So, why then?"

He didn't understand what he'd done to her. How she might have fled the island and everything she'd worked so hard to create. All because of him. "I take it you've never been the victim of a crime."

He gripped the bars and sneered. "What does that have to do with anything?"

As arrogant as he sounded, the look in his eyes and the set of his chin telegraphed a different story. His face read like that of a tired old man.

"If you'd ever experienced what I have, you never would've considered sinking a knife into my door. No less do it." Catherine wouldn't cry. She wouldn't give him the satisfaction of seeing how fragile she was. She swallowed instead. "Do you have any idea what it's like to look over your shoulder constantly? To stare at the ceiling for hours because you can't sleep? To be yanked from the place you call home?"

"I—"

She held up her hand. Anger shoved aside what had previously been fear and a degree of sorrow. She would not identify as this man's victim. She wouldn't allow him to control her actions or reactions any longer. "I'm not finished." Her voice raised several decibels, and neighboring cellmates peered through their bars to watch the goings-on. "You almost destroyed everything I've built here. What I want to know is, why?"

"You weaseled your way into the space that should've been mine. Who are you to interfere with my livelihood?" he snarled. "You had no right. You're not even from here."

Catherine stepped back. "I didn't weasel anything. But even if I did, are you saying that you were willing to put your future in jeopardy for something so ridiculous? Do you hear how pathetic that is? What did it get you?" She gestured to the surrounding space. "This. This is what it got you. So, I ask, was it worth it?"

He exhaled a long breath. "What do you want from me? I'm caged like an animal. You won. It's over."

"Won?" She stepped closer to the bars and narrowed her eyes. "You think this is a game?" she said through clenched teeth.

His shoulders slumped. "All I wanted was for you to go back to Boston. It's your fault that I had to take things to the level I did." He shook his head. "Never thought you'd hang on so long."

Catherine couldn't believe it. "How dare you blame me for your lunacy!"

Jerry leaned against the bars and gripped them. "Who do you think—"

She shook her head. "You were almost successful in your attempt to scare me away. But unfortunately for you, I have a wonderful support team here who convinced me to stick it out."

He gave a half-chuckle. "Remind me to thank them."

Catherine shooed off his sarcasm. "I'm sorry I've wasted my time." She turned to the sound of jingling keys announcing Dinkins' pending arrival. "I'd hoped that you'd be remorseful and apologize. Maybe then I could start to heal. But I guess that was naïve of me."

MICHAEL STOPPED by the police station the next morning on his way to work.

The woman sitting behind the desk, eyes glued to a computer screen, shifted her attention to him when he walked up. "Can I help you?"

"Is Officer Dinkins available?"

"No, he's on patrol. Can someone else help you?"

"I'm here to see one of the prisoners."

After Michael gave the woman Jerry's name, she made a quick call to obtain approval and then led him to Jerry's cell.

Jerry laid on his bed, hands clasped behind his head, staring at the underside of the empty upper bunk.

"You have a visitor," the woman announced, and then turned to Michael. "Ten minutes."

Jerry scrambled to his feet and bolted toward the cell door. "Now what? First, your girlfriend, now you. What is it with you people? I have nothing to say." He turned his back on Michael. "Leave me alone."

"I've spoken to some people who knew you when your wife was alive."

Jerry spun around. "Leave her out of this. She has nothing to do with any of it."

"What I'd like to know is how would you feel if someone treated her the way you have Catherine?"

Jerry glared at him. "My wife is dead. What don't you understand? *Dead.*"

"I know, and I'm sorry for your loss. So, if you can't make things right with Catherine for your own sake, do it in memory of your wife."

Jerry paced.

"All I want is for you to give Catherine the same respect you'd want for your wife if she were in Catherine's shoes."

Jerry turned to Michael. His face was devoid of emotion.

Michael shook his head. "I'm done. What's the use? I said what I came for."

"Which is what? Sully my wife's memory to make yourself feel better?" Jerry barked.

"I haven't sullied anyone, least of all your wife. I understand she was a wonderful woman. I'd hoped to help you see what you've done to an innocent woman in our community. Catherine deserves an apology for what you've put her through. I'd hoped to appeal to the man you used to be. Apparently, he died along with his wife."

Michael turned and walked away. He'd almost made it to the end of the hallway when Jerry called out.

"Wait! Come back."

Michael stopped and considered his next move. Should he waste any more of his time?

Jerry white-knuckled the bars, craning his neck in Michael's direction. "Do you think she'd revisit me?"

"Maybe if you put some effort into letting her know you want to talk to her."

"Can't you tell her?"

"Nope, it's your job to figure out how to get her back here," Michael said, and then he walked away.

CHAPTER TWENTY-NINE

Catherine peered out the front store window. Despite everything, she was thankful she hadn't fled the island during her ordeal. Grateful she didn't let Jerry scare her away from all that she held precious. Then she blinked in amazement. Carol, the proprietor of This and That, was hurrying toward A Distant Light. What could Jerry's friend want from her? Catherine went to the door and raised her hand to flip the door sign to "closed." Then she paused. What was she doing? She stepped away. She would not allow this woman to intimidate her.

Carol entered the store.

The mere sight of the woman slammed Catherine with angst. The air was so thick it felt like it could crack and shatter at any time. Her breathing quickened.

Might Carol be there to perpetrate an act of revenge on behalf of her friend?

Catherine slipped her hand into her pocket and felt for her phone. "Didn't expect to see you here."

Carol's hand trembled. She cleared her throat. "First and foremost, I want to apologize. I never thought Jerry could do what they've accused him of." She gazed at the floor. "I'm so sorry for standing by him and spreading malicious untruths about you and your store. I only hope you can find a way to forgive me." She lowered her head. "I thought I was helping a friend."

Catherine relaxed. It had to take a lot for Carol to face her and offer up an apology. "Thank you."

Carol lifted her head. "I'm also here because Jerry asked me to let you know he wants to see you." She put a hand on her hip. "I made it clear I'd no longer be a party to any of his nonsense, but he assured me that his request is nothing more than a follow-up to a visit you paid him." She sighed and lowered her hand. "I don't think he harbors any more bad intentions towards you, but I'm looking for you to confirm that he's not lying about you having visited him, and I suppose, to prove that he's not still using me."

"I did visit him. I was hoping at the time that he'd apologize, but he didn't."

Carol's face brightened a tad. "Maybe he's changed his mind."

CATHERINE FOLLOWED Officer Dinkins down the hall for the second time in as many days.

Jerry moved to the door of his cell.

"Ten minutes," Dinkins said to Catherine, then disappeared down the hall.

The man who stood before her no longer exhibited the belligerent vibes he'd used the other day. He hadn't shaved, and his shoulders hunched over, giving him the look of a broken spirit.

Catherine crossed her arms over her chest. "Carol said you wanted to see me."

"Thank you for coming. I...want you to know...I'm sorry for all the trouble I've caused you. Mind you, I'm not offering an excuse, but I haven't been myself since my wife passed. I see that now. I'm not saying that makes what I did right, but I want you to know, I haven't always been this poor excuse for a human being. You may not believe it, but once, I too, had good friends." His chest caved, and he lowered his head and shook it. "During the last year or so, most of them have faded away, except for Carol. And I did her wrong, too."

Catherine wanted to believe him. "I appreciate your apology. And I'm sorry for your loss."

Jerry zoned out for a moment, as if he'd gone back in time. He smiled. "Thank you. My wife was my rock. I've been so lost…"

Catherine surprised herself when she reached out her hand and gave Jerry's a gentle squeeze through the bars.

He gave her a genuine smile. "Maybe now we can both start to heal."

Instead of speaking, Catherine just nodded, lest her stinging eyes erupted with full-blown tears.

"Before you go, there's one more thing."

She stiffened. Was he about to pull the rug out from under her? Laugh in her face and tell her what a fool she'd been to believe him? That his actions were all a charade? Another ploy to undermine her confidence?

"Because of me, you lost potential sales, so if you give me an estimate as to what you think that represents, I'll make sure to reimburse you. It won't come close to paying you back for all I've done, but it's something."

CHAPTER THIRTY

*A*fter Catherine and Michael finished masking the inside of the store's front window with brown paper, Michael slid the new display into place.

Catherine stepped back, admiring the polished oaken ship deck. "It's magnificent." She rose on the balls of her feet and gave him a kiss.

"Glad you like it."

"Oh, it's more than that. I love it. If this doesn't help make my store a success, I don't know what will."

"Nice to see you happy." He wrapped his arms around her and pulled her close. "How about giving me another sign of your appreciation?"

Catherine gazed into his eyes, slipped her arms around his neck, and kissed him again, this time long and slow.

At the sound of someone clearing their throat, they broke apart like two teenagers.

"Guess you didn't hear the door chimes," the man said with the hint of a smile.

Catherine took a deep breath to calm her wildly beating heart. "May I help you?"

He extended his hand. "Miss O'Malley?"

"Yes."

He handed Catherine his card. "Bryan Monahan, District Attorney for the Cape and Islands."

Michael extended his hand to the DA. "Michael Benton."

Monahan laughed. "Three Irishmen. Well, fancy that."

Michael smiled. "Sounds like the start of a bad joke, and my cue to get a move on." He turned to Catherine. "Is it okay if I leave?"

She nodded. "Yes. Thanks again. See you tonight?"

"Absolutely." Michael kissed her cheek and left.

"I'll try not to take too much of your time," The DA said, and laid his attaché on a nearby counter. His green eyes were reminiscent of one of Catherine's long-ago cats.

"Coffee? It's fresh."

"Yes. Thank you."

She pulled up two folding chairs, then went to the refreshment table, poured them each a cup, and gestured for him to sit.

Monahan took a long sip of the coffee and swallowed. "Let me cut to the chase. First and foremost, I want you to know that we're prepared to prosecute your case to the fullest extent of the law, which means you may be required to testify."

Catherine's throat tightened. She did not want to relive the horror of the past several months, especially in public.

He removed a recording device from his attaché and placed it between them. "Are you okay if I use this, versus taking notes?"

"Of course."

He turned on the device. "Catherine O'Malley, case number 57634. I've spoken to local officials and plan to meet with them after I leave here. For the record, I want your perspective on what occurred. How the accused made you feel." He glanced at the door. "We can take a break if a customer comes in."

"How I feel plays a part in this?"

"Yes. Harm is not only physical. Intent that results in mental anguish weighs as heavily. It's not what he did. It's what you *thought* he'd do."

"What will he be charged with?"

"Malicious harassment."

Catherine drank some coffee to quench the dryness spreading down her throat. She spoke of all the incidents, from the first confrontation at *Christmas Stroll* to the parking signs, to the trash episode, to Jerry lying in wait for her early one morning, and concluding with the knife and note.

"Thank you. Very thorough." Monahan pulled a paper from his briefcase. "I understand you vacated your home and business for safety reasons, is that correct?"

"Yes. I almost fled the island until my friends stepped in and convinced me to stay." She gave him a small smile. "They made sure I was safe."

"Sounds like good friends."

"The best." Catherine stared into her lap.

"It's still raw, though, isn't it?" Monahan asked.

"Yes. But I've spoken with Jerry, and he's apologized. So, maybe now I can begin to heal."

"It's a start."

"What I want most is to put all this behind me so I can move on."

"And once we get justice for you, that will help, too."

Catherine wondered if she should say what was on her mind. "I'd prefer that he not be charged."

Monahan shook his head. "Sorry, but that's not your call."

"I'm the victim. Doesn't that count for anything?"

"Of course, but he's committed a crime, and he'll have to face the punishment dealt him if he's convicted."

"Does that mean jail time?"

Monahan nodded. "Could. And he'll be expected to pay the town back for the expense they incurred during this investigation, which is sizable."

"For what it's worth, I think he's truly sorry and regrets what he did. Of course, I'm not suggesting he shouldn't be held financially responsible, but jail time… Doesn't remorse play into your decision?"

"That's mainly something for the judge to consider at sentencing. As well as any previous charges, his standing in the community, things that might provide insight into whether he poses any further risk."

Catherine recalled Jerry's apology. The sight of the broken man etched in her mind. "I don't think he does."

"Why? Because he apologized? Unfortunately, it isn't beyond someone like him to try and manipulate the situation to ensure things go his way."

CATHERINE bent over and carefully lifted one of her newest finds, a standing antique brass compass, and placed it onto the ship deck replica.

Bryan Monahan must've seriously considered her comments, because he'd offered Jerry a plea deal, which she'd heard Jerry had agreed to. The deal didn't come without its share of ramifications, however. He'd have to plead guilty, have that forever reflected on his record, reimburse the police for expenses incurred during the investigation, and pay the fine levied by the town council for the unlawful signs. In exchange, he'd forego additional jail time and serve two years of probation.

The door chimes startled her, and she almost knocked over the compass. She hadn't seen anyone approach because of the brown paper that covered the front window.

To her surprise, Jerry walked in.

She put down the compass and turned to face him. Why was he here? Had Monahan been right? Had Jerry manipulated her to get a lighter sentence? Was he here now to have the last laugh? To taunt her for being duped? She tapped her back pocket for her phone.

He stared at her.

She willed herself not to flinch.

He stepped forward.

She stepped back.

"I came to thank you," Jerry offered. "The DA said that if it weren't for you speaking up for me, I'd be looking at two-and-a-half years in a six by eight."

Catherine released the breath she'd been holding. "You're welcome."

"The other reason I stopped by is to give you first dibs on the space next door. I have six months left on my lease, but I'll absorb that if you'd like to assume it and enlarge your business."

"Are you leaving Nantucket?" She hoped he'd say yes. Even an occasional sighting of him would serve as a constant reminder of all that'd happened.

He shrugged. "I think so. Thanks to the mess I've made, people I once considered friends here have turned their backs on me. But who can blame them? I figure it's best for everyone concerned if I return to life on the Cape. They're able to assign a probation officer to me there, so it's not an issue. And I won't have to face all the sideways glances and whispers of the island residents."

Catherine's shoulder muscles relaxed. "Thank you for your offer, but I have enough on my plate to get ready for the season. The last thing I need is to pile on renovations. And besides, who knows if I'll even turn a profit."

Jerry scanned the store and smiled. "You'll do fine. But I understand your apprehension." He paused. "Since you're not interested in expanding, and for the sake of transparency, I want you to know I have a backup plan for my space. A couple from New York who will be moving to the island are interested in buying me out. I think you'll like them."

Catherine felt like hugging him. This man had changed, not at all like the one who had caused her such grief. Instead, she reached out her hand. "I wish nothing but the best for both of us."

He shook her hand and thanked her again. Then he disappeared so fast, she wondered if the entire exchange had been a figment of her imagination.

CHAPTER THIRTY-ONE

Catherine stepped from the shower, wrapped herself in a towel, and reached for her ringing phone.
Michael.

"Aren't you the early bird?" she chirped. "You usually call on your way to work. Are you going in early?"

"Couldn't sleep. I didn't wake you, did I?"

"Heck no. I have a bunch of stockpiled deliveries, which means I'll be unpacking and setting up most of the day. So I want to get an early start." Catherine paused. "Are you okay?"

Silence.

"Michael?"

"There's something we need to discuss," he said. "I've made dinner reservations in 'Sconset tonight at six. Hope that's okay." His voice seemed off.

"Sure. But did you say 'Sconset?"

"Yes."

Up until now, their dinners had been casual fare, consisting of margarita pizza, lobster rolls, burgers, and craft beers. The only restaurant she knew of in the hamlet he'd mentioned, twenty minutes away, overlooked the Atlantic and would provide a perfect setting for a serious conversation.

"Sure, but can you give me a hint about what—"

"Sorry. I have to get going. See you tonight."

SEVERAL TIMES throughout the day while Catherine tried to busy herself with unpacking, she'd found herself staring off into space. What in the world could have Michael so anxious? She lifted a golden charger plate engraved with a tall ship from one of the boxes. Maybe he wanted to talk about Jerry. Not likely. Jerry had said his goodbyes and sailed away on the fast ferry a week earlier. She removed the last of six plates, grabbed the empty box, flattened it, and stored it in the back hallway.

Over the last several months, their relationship had blossomed from friendship into something more. And although neither of them had confessed to loving the other, she knew how she felt, and suspected Michael felt the same. Might he want to discuss next steps? Tell her he'd love to spend the rest of his life with her? The thought made her giddy.

She checked her watch. Five o'clock. Catherine flipped the sign to "closed" and went upstairs to take her second shower of the day. As she opened the door to the apartment, she froze and her knees weakened. What if Michael had decided to return to Rhode Island and had just waited until her situation resolved itself before dropping the news? Could his job managing the fishing company's day-to-day operations not be what he thought it would be? How on earth would she deal with that bit of news?

WHEN CATHERINE OPENED the door that night, she felt a wave of relief wash over her when Michael seemed more upbeat than when he had called earlier. Maybe he had been running late and that's why he hadn't seemed like himself. Yet later, as they drove past miles of conservation areas on their way to 'Sconset, she sensed that he couldn't wait to get to the restaurant.

Once there, Catherine swore Michael breathed a sigh of relief when the hostess approached, as if the woman had thrown him a life preserver.

"Benton, reservations for two," he said.

The woman checked her book and grabbed two menus. "Right this way." She led them to a corner table with a panoramic view of the ocean. "Is this all right?"

"Perfect." Michael pulled out Catherine's chair.

The hostess gave them the menus and left behind a wine list.

Catherine glanced around. Quintessential Nantucket. Pale splashes of blue covered the walls, and the slanted ceiling donned white wooden planks. Crisp bisque-colored linen covered the tables. Flickering candles in small, amber-colored glass globes set the cozy mood. Gentle waves of music drifted into the area from the piano bar. If she wasn't so curious, she'd be enamored with the romance of the space.

"This is lovely, Michael, but I've been wracking my brain all day about what's going on."

He let out an audible breath. "I have something to tell you, and I wanted a place where we could talk without having to raise our voices and strain to hear."

"Okay." A quiver crept into her voice.

Their waiter approached and took their drink orders.

After he left, Catherine reached for Michael's hand. "You look so serious. It's not at all like you." Butterflies set up camp in her stomach. "Please, tell me what's on your mind."

"I hope you know how very important you are to me."

Catherine flinched. She felt a *but* coming. "Of course. And I feel the same about you." She gazed into his eyes. She loved him and scolded herself for not telling him so.

He reached for her other hand. "I've been reluctant to share what's kept me up at night."

"Why?"

"You've been so fragile."

Catherine gulped. Just like Michael to want to protect her. She withdrew her hands. It sounded like whatever was coming would have nothing to do with expressing his love for her.

"What you've gone through made me realize I can't hold off any longer. When I thought your life was in danger, I better understood what you meant when you said life is too short not to let your heart sing."

She struggled to catch a breath. "You know you can tell me anything."

He stroked her face. "Catherine, you're the total package. Smart, beautiful. Any man would kill to have you by his side."

She swallowed.

"I've done a lot of thinking. And I remembered your mother's words the night of your attack."

The night of the attack? Catherine, confused, rewound her thoughts. "Our choices define us?"

"Yes." Michael removed his hand from her face, and released the other. Then he reached into his pocket and placed a blue velvet box on the table in front of her.

Catherine's hand flew to her mouth. Her eyes shifted from the box to Michael and back to the box. *Was this really happening?*

He grabbed the box and got down on bended knee. "I love you, Catherine. Marry me. Unlike Jack, I won't ask you to give up what you love doing, or in any way change who you are for me."

With tears streaming down her cheeks, she shook her head.

Michael scrambled to get up. "I'm sorry. It's too soon. I shouldn't have…"

She put a hand on Michael's shoulder to hold him in place and summoned a half-laugh. "I'm not saying no, silly. I signaled the waiter not to interrupt us."

His face broke into a collage of relief and joy. He opened the box. "I want to spend the rest of my life with you. Make a family with you. Catherine O'Malley, will you do me the honor of becoming my wife?"

Catherine placed her hands on the sides of his face. "I love you. too. Of course, I'll marry you!"

"You will?"

"Yes!"

He slipped the stunning solitaire on her finger, jumped to his feet, and pulled her up into his arms.

The surrounding patrons hooted and clapped.

The waiter re-approached with two flutes of champagne along with their wine. "On the house." He placed all four glasses on the table. "Congratulations," he said, and left the table.

Michael grinned. "Well, now that we've settled that, let's eat! I'm starving."

CHAPTER THIRTY-TWO

Two weeks later

Catherine raised her frosted glass of iced tea to Michael. "To us and all we've accomplished in such a short time."

He clinked his glass to hers. "I'm sorry I turned up the pressure by wanting a short engagement, but I've waited so long to be happy, *truly* happy in every sense, that I want us to get on with building our future as soon as possible."

"I do, too."

They lowered their glasses.

"May 17th is just around the corner," Catherine said. "There's tons of stuff that still needs doing."

Michael squeezed his eyes together. "Like finalizing the wedding party."

Catherine beamed. "Not for me. I checked that off my list this morning. I've asked Tina to be my maid of honor, and this afternoon I ran over to the inn on my lunch break and asked Helen and Bill to walk me down the aisle."

Michael smiled. "I bet they were all thrilled."

"Yes. Especially Helen and Bill. They're over the moon. And when I said I considered them surrogate parents, I thought we'd run out of tissues."

Michael twirled the stirrer in his iced tea. "I hope my discussion with my brother regarding my choice for best man goes as well."

"Your brother? I thought you had already asked Drake?"

"I did. But now I have to deal with the fallout."

Catherine reached for his hand and gave it a gentle squeeze, her diamond catching the table's candlelight. "Fallout?"

"My father will expect me to ask David."

"But Drake's your best friend." Catherine smiled. "A friend, I might add, to whom I'll be eternally grateful. If it weren't for him arranging an interview here for you, who knows…"

Michael nodded. "I owe the man a lot."

"Your brother loves you. He'll understand."

"I'm not worried about David. I'm pretty sure he'll take it in stride. Dad is another story." Michael sighed. "Thankfully, Drake has been around long enough that he understands our family dynamics. He'd be good if things change, which is a great example of why I chose him. He always has my best interest in mind."

"Definitely a good friend."

"I've assured him that no matter the outcome with David, he'll be the guy standing by my side at the altar, so he'd better be sure he has a suit."

"When do you plan to tell your brother?"

"Day after tomorrow. As much as I hate leaving you, this is something I need to do in person. The last thing I want is for our wedding day to be fraught with drama, and that could easily be the case if I don't handle this right. Besides, I've decided to put my house there on the market so I can buy something here once it sells. I want us to find our forever home as soon as possible."

"You're not going to keep it as a rental?"

Michael shook his head. "The house has served its purpose. And since the market is hot, now's the time to squeeze out as much profit as possible."

Catherine gazed out the window. "I've held onto my condo in case things didn't work out here. Since that's no longer the case, I too should sell. The only problem is finding the time."

"If you want, I can take a ride up and help with that once I finish in Rhode Island." He gazed into her eyes. "At least I'll feel like I'm doing something, since you won't let me help you with anything else for the wedding."

She could get the ball rolling on selling her condo by calling the agent she'd used when she'd purchased the unit. And when it sold, the realtor could overnight the paperwork.

"Hey, where'd you go?"

"Just thinking that I'll call the agent I've dealt with and have her list my unit. Then with our combined proceeds, we'll be able to find something we like."

"Is there anything from there you want me to bring back? I could arrange for the movers while I'm there, too."

"I took what I wanted when I went there last year. I've never felt a connection to the furniture. A designer picked it out for me, and it's her style, not mine. Though there are two rockers that belonged to my parents that I'd like to have. As for the rest, I'll ask the agent to coordinate selling it unless the buyer wants it. And as far as personal items, other than a few kitchen things and a storage bin of photos, there isn't much else that I want."

"I could bring all that back in my truck. Set it up with the agent, give me the keys, and I'll handle the rest."

"Are you sure?"

"It'll be a good way to help me settle down after meeting with my brother."

"Maybe it won't be as bad as you think." Catherine gave him an encouraging nod. "Afterward, if Drake's in port, you can swing by and make it official with him."

Michael's face softened. "I'm happy that the wheels of our future are turning. The only problem is, I'm going to miss you like crazy."

"I'll miss you more," Catherine proclaimed, and meant it with all her heart. "If I could, I'd be boarding the ferry with you."

He flashed her a smile. "I'm so glad that the Daffodil Festival has breathed life into your business."

Thanks to his caring spirit and killer smile, she melted into a hormonal puddle. "Me too. Oh, what I wouldn't give for a day or so of those old boring times. Not that I'm not grateful for the business, mind you, but there's so much left to do for the wedding that you *can't* help with."

"Such as?"

She sipped her tea. "I have to find a dress and help Tina and Helen do the same, hire a photographer, and order the flowers."

"I'll help with whatever I can when I get back."

"Helping me move my remaining stuff from Boston is huge. The rest will be fine. At least we don't have to look for a venue since Helen and Bill offered up the inn." She scanned her to-do list. "Tina has also volunteered to handle the menu, which is fine with me. And if they're not already doing enough, Helen and Tina volunteered to do the legwork for the food and decorations, including ordering tables, chairs, and a food tent for the garden." Catherine frowned. "I hope I can afford their taste."

"I wish you'd let me contribute."

"Absolutely not. You're paying for the pre-wedding dinner at Tina's. I'm the bride. The rest is my responsibility."

"It doesn't have to be. I want our day to be the wedding of your dreams. And if that means I can help make it so, I'm all-in."

"I'll be fine." Having to close the store had proven challenging to Catherine. If she kept with the budget she'd prepared, though, she'd be okay.

"Oh, before I forget," Michael said. "I've lined up a couple of groups for us to listen to when I return."

She leaned back against her chair. "I forgot all about hiring a band. It's exhausting trying to remember everything."

Michael kissed her palm. "But oh, so worth it."

CATHERINE MISSED Michael from the moment he drove his truck into the hull of the ferry the next morning. When he'd made it up to one of the decks, she'd waved until she thought her arm would fall off. Shoulders slumped, she made her way back to her store, fighting off tears along the way.

She was grateful that Tina had helped fill the void of her missing Michael by arranging a private showing at a consignment shop, owned by a friend of hers, for Catherine, Helen, and herself to look at dresses for the wedding.

Later that day, Catherine settled into the backseat of Tina's car. "I hope we all find something."

Tina glanced into her rearview mirror. "According to Jennifer, a bridal gown came in that she's anxious to show you. And she has dresses she thinks appropriate for the two of us, as well. Her taste is extraordinary, so I suspect we'll find something that suits us."

Catherine cringed. *Extraordinary taste.* She pictured her latest bank statement. Her savings had dwindled at an alarming rate.

"I hope so, because we don't have much time," Helen said. "And I want to look spectacular, so you don't regret your choice."

"You could wear a brown paper sack, and I wouldn't rethink my decision," Catherine said, giggling.

"Bill and I are so excited." Helen's eyes sparkled with glee. "We've never had the honor of walking someone down the aisle. No less, someone as special to us as you."

"Aw." Catherine's cheeks warmed.

"Have you heard from Michael?" Tina asked.

"Several times. Most recently, after he'd gotten to his house, waiting for the real estate agent. After he sees your brother and stops to chat with Drake, he's heading to Boston to schlep back a few items from my condo before it sells. I've called the agent who sold it to me, and she says it'll get scooped up faster than lemonade on a summer day, since I'm willing to sell it furnished."

"His house should sell fast, too. He's kept it maintained, and it's in a desirable area." Tina sighed. "If I could've swung it, I'd have tagged along with him."

Catherine's heart pinged. Maybe Tina thought she'd asked too much of Michael? "To help with hauling back my stuff?"

"No, to help deal with our family. That won't be easy."

Catherine leaned forward in her seat and craned her neck toward Tina. "Do you think it'll be that difficult?"

"What am I missing?" Helen said. "Or shouldn't I ask?"

Tina pulled to a stop at a traffic light and turned to face Helen. "Michael has to tell our brother that he's chosen the captain of the fishing vessel he worked with to be his best man."

"And why is that a problem?" Helen asked. "Are Michael and your other brother close?"

Tina shook her head. "Not in recent years. It's not David's reaction that concerns me. He'll be disappointed, but he'll roll with it. Our father, on the other hand, will take it as a personal insult."

"Oh, that's too bad," Helen said. "Maybe he should've called him on the phone."

"According to Michael, that wasn't an option," Catherine said. "He wants to be sure to clear the air of any lingering hostility before the wedding."

"He did the right thing." Tina pulled into the parking lot. "But sometimes the right thing isn't always pleasant." She pushed the gear shift into park. "Time to go shopping, ladies!"

A GOWN HANGING inside a glassed front antique armoire captured Catherine's interest as soon as she entered the shabby chic store.

Jennifer, the owner of Jennifer's Closet, followed Catherine to the oversized piece of furniture. "That came in yesterday. And it comes with a story." She lowered her voice. "The mother of the bride told me her daughter couldn't decide after narrowing down the choices to this dress and another one. So, she purchased both, knowing she couldn't return the one that didn't make the cut."

Helen rubbed her fingers together. "Sounds like a family with more money than they know what to do with."

Jennifer smirked. "They recently purchased two homes on the north shore, bulldozed both, and built a mega-mansion complete with guest quarters, a tennis court, an Olympic-size pool, the works. Unlike some other ultra-rich residents, the bride's mother is down-to-earth and *very* nice. She hoped that her daughter's inability to decide at the time of purchase would result in the find of the century for some other lucky bride." Jennifer opened the glass door. "Here. Let me take this out, and you can have a better look."

The sleeveless ivory satin gown, complete with a matching bolero-style jacket, scoop neck, a short train, and a bodice covered with hand-sewn pearls, was what Catherine had always envisioned for her wedding day.

Jennifer looked at her. "It should fit. Would you like to try it on?"

"Yes."

Jennifer took the custom-made dress to the fitting room. "Take your time. And let me know if you need any help."

Catherine pulled off her clothes, slipped into the dress, and stared at herself in the mirror, mesmerized. How well it fit, not to mention its sheer beauty. When she turned over the price tag, tears welled in her eyes. She couldn't afford it. She wiped her eyes and wrestled with whether to take it off versus prancing out to show her friends.

Minutes later, she emerged from the dressing room.

Helen covered her mouth with her hand. Her eyes glistened. "Oh, Catherine. It's so you."

"Stunning," Tina said. "Do you like it?"

Catherine ran her hand down the front of the dress and spun around. "I love it." Her brow wrinkled, and she lowered her voice. "But the price—"

Jennifer, standing nearby, waved a hand in the air. "Ignore the tag. I left it on to show its worth. The mother is willing to let it go for as low as twenty-five percent of that. She left it to my discretion. Since you're a friend of Tina's, and based on what I've heard you've been through with the owner of the Double Scoop, you *deserve* a designer dress for your special day."

"How do you know about what happened with Jerry?" Catherine asked.

Jennifer gave a knowing smile. "It's a small island. News travels fast. Your friends can attest to that. Not much happens here without folks knowing. Now—" She directed her attention to Helen and Tina, and waved her hands in the air with a flurry. "Let me show you ladies what I think will be perfect for each of *you*."

In little over an hour, the three women had their dresses and were carting them to Tina's car.

Tina started the engine. "Well, I'd say that we all had a worthwhile trip!"

"I can't believe I came away with such a beautiful dress," Catherine said, her voice soft. "I was so depressed when I saw the tag that I almost took it off. And then, the deal she gave me! I'm humbled by everyone's generosity toward me and our big day."

Helen half-turned in her seat toward her. "You're going to knock Michael's socks off when you walk down the aisle."

Catherine grinned. "I hope so."

"Hey, since we've broken the all-time record shopping for three dresses, how about we go back to the inn?" Helen asked. "I'll rustle up some leftovers, and it'll give me a chance to go over some things with you."

"Sounds good," Catherine said. "I'm starving."

"I have a couple things to run by both of you, too," Tina said.

Later, after the three women polished off shrimp fajitas accompanied by a large platter heaped high with warm tortillas, shredded lettuce, Pico de Gallo, shredded cheddar cheese, and sour cream, Helen pulled a folder from the sideboard and spread the contents on the table.

She pointed at a picture. "*This* is what I'm thinking would be nice for centerpieces."

A miniature lighthouse sat atop a blue base, intended to mimic the sea. Inside the tower, a candle created a flickering light. It's what Catherine would've chosen herself. But could she afford it? She discreetly checked for a price. There would be up to five tables in addition to the head table, which would require two centerpieces. Nothing native to Nantucket was inexpensive.

"How appropriate, based on Catherine's love of lighthouses and Michael's passion for the sea," Tina said.

"That's what I thought." Helen cocked her head to the side. "Catherine?"

Catherine didn't have the heart to burst Helen's bubble of enthusiasm. "Sorry. I was thinking how lovely they'll look." She hoped Helen couldn't sense her distress.

Helen rubbed her hands together. "Good. Since that's decided, have you and Michael come up with a guest list? I need a head count so I can order the tables, chairs, and centerpieces."

"We're thinking thirty people, not counting the wedding party. We want to keep it intimate."

"That'll work," Helen said. "In the event Mother Nature doesn't cooperate and we have to bring everything inside, we'll still have plenty of room."

"I've come up with a suggested menu." Tina reached into her purse and pulled out her phone. "Here, I took a picture of it to take to the caterers. Since the plan is to have the reception outside, we'll need a tent large enough to cover the tables, chairs, and food. I'll take care of ordering that."

"Are you thinking of a sit-down dinner?" Helen asked.

Tina eyed Catherine. "If it's okay with you, I thought buffet-style would lend itself nicely to the casual atmosphere you're looking for."

"That's what we were thinking," Catherine said.

Catherine and Helen previewed the menu. Lobster cocktail, crab cakes, bacon-wrapped scallops, New England clam chowder, bread, assorted rolls, mixed greens, roasted asparagus, Chicken marsala, and beef Wellington.

"Couldn't have done it better myself," Helen said.

Catherine's stomach did jumping jacks. The seafood and beef alone would add up to a hefty sum. She did the math in her head, adding up what everything would cost. Her breath caught. She wanted their wedding to be perfect. Nothing that reeked of bargain basement, but the winter sales drought and having to close the store while the police handled their investigation had cast a severe blow to her finances.

Helen and Tina turned towards her. "What is it?" they asked in unison.

"If you don't like something, just say so," Tina said. "You won't hurt our feelings." She gently elbowed Catherine. "We just want you to be happy."

"That's right," Helen soothed. "It's *your* wedding."

Catherine swiped at her eyes. "It's not that. I love it all. But I'm not sure I can afford it."

Helen gave Tina a sideways glance.

Tina nodded.

"We planned on surprising you," Helen said. "But the last thing we want is you carting around a boulder of worry."

Tina wrapped an arm around Catherine's shoulders. "Consider what Helen and I are doing as wedding presents. We want your day to be something you'll remember for the rest of your life. We've already agreed that we're willing to do whatever it takes to make it so."

"I can't let you do that." Catherine fought to hold back her tears. *Strength* was what she needed. "Do you have any idea how much this will all cost? No, it's not right. It's my responsibility."

Helen crossed her arms across her chest. "Who says so?"

"Please, Catherine. Let us do this for you and Michael," Tina pleaded. "He is, after all, my baby brother."

"Yes. We want to. Really, we do," Helen said. "And it's not like we're picking up the tab for the whole wedding. You have enough on your plate."

Catherine opened her arms and enveloped her friends in a group hug. "What would I do without you two?"

Helen patted her back. "That's something, my dear girl, that you'll never have to worry about."

∽

THE EASY WAY for Michael to inform his brother of his choice for best man would be through a phone call. But he knew in his heart that facing up to David in person was the right way to handle it. Besides, coming to the mainland would allow him to ready his house for sale and help Catherine divest herself of her Boston condo in the process. He slipped behind the wheel of his truck, pulled onto the road, and tried to convince himself that meeting with his brother would be no more than a blip on the radar.

As he wound along the Wampanoag Trail in East Providence toward the office park that housed the Benton corporate offices, he knew he'd been kidding himself. This face-to-face meeting might be the right way to handle it, but it would still end up sheer torture. Michael pulled into the driveway, parking in one of the reserved spots his brother had instructed him to take. He shut off the engine, leaned his head against the headrest, and stared at the stone edifice featuring a black granite sign inscribed with large golden letters: Benton Enterprises. Then he popped an antacid to quell the mounting pressure in the center of his chest. "Okay, let's get this over with."

He got out of the truck. Once inside the lobby, a long-term employee Michael had seen in the past looked up from his desk. At first, the man seemed perplexed. Then his face lit up, and he gave Michael a warm smile. "Mr. Benton, how nice to see you. It's been a while..."

Michael glanced at the man's name tag. "Nice to see you too, Henry. I'm here to see my brother. He's expecting me."

"Yes, he mentioned that when he came in this morning." Henry reached into a drawer, then pointed to a sign-in log at the front of his desk. "Sorry, Mr. Benton. It's procedure."

"No problem. It's the world we live in."

After Michael showed his license, received his visitor badge, and affixed it to his shirt, Henry buzzed him in. Michael pulled opened the door. "Is his office still on the third floor?"

"No. Mr. David moved to the executive floor next to your father about two years ago. Suite 420."

Michael was not surprised. They were two peas in a pod. He rode the elevator to the fourth floor and made his way down the hall toward massive double mahogany doors. Then he closed his eyes, exhaled a long breath, and entered.

A middle-aged woman seated at a desk as impressive as the door, asked, "May I help you?"

"David Benton, please."

The woman read Michael's name tag and blushed. "Of course, Mr. Benton. Your brother is expecting you." She stood and motioned for him to follow. "Right this way." She knocked lightly on the door, opened it, and poked her head around it. "Mr. Benton, your brother is here."

"Show him in!" David called out.

Michael entered and stopped in his tracks. He'd hoped not to see his dad, at least not from the get-go. Why was he surprised?

David rose from behind his desk and walked toward Michael. He reached out as if to hug him, but in an awkward move, only extended his hand.

Michael shook it. Then he stepped over to where their father was seated.

His dad didn't stand.

Michael extended his hand.

His father hesitated.

Michael started to withdraw his hand when his father finally reciprocated.

He gave Michael an icy stare. "David and I were speculating about the reason for your visit."

"Michael, have a seat," David offered. "Can I get you something to drink?"

Michael sat. "No. I'm fine."

David returned to his chair and folded his hands in front of him on the desk. "As Dad said, we've been discussing your visit. Not that you're not welcome anytime." Concern coated his face. "You're not sick, are you?"

"No."

A DISTANT LIGHT

"Well, that's a relief." David's look of concern told Michael he meant it.

"Maybe he's finally come to his senses about joining the firm."

The booming tone of voice in his father's statement set Michael on edge. In an effort to remain calm, he glanced around the plush office. Thick cushioned carpeting, wood-paneled walls polished to perfection, a wall of windows with a breathtaking view of the countryside, all arranged to set off the Providence skyline in the distance.

Every aspect of the corner office screamed money, not to mention the private bathroom. Heaven forbid his brother use the public facility across the hall. Even if joining the firm had been the reason for Michael's visit, his father's words and attitude since he'd arrived would've made him turn and run. His stomach seized at the mere thought of sitting behind a desk, wearing a suit, and attending meetings. Maybe this worked for his brother, but it would never work for him.

"I'm getting married," Michael said, anxious to get the discussion underway.

David pulled his head back. "Now, that's a surprise. Congratulations. About time you settled down, old man."

His father huffed. "Probably marrying some fishmonger."

Michael glared at his father and swallowed his contempt. "Hardly. You've met her."

David cocked his head to the side. "Really?"

"Catherine O'Malley. She was at Tina's when you were there for Christmas."

His dad's eyes widened, and he leaned toward Michael as if his son had finally said something worthy of his attention. "The woman who owns the store? The former Boston executive?"

Michael's face brightened. "Yep."

David stood and cupped Michael's shoulder. "Way to go, bro." He winked. "If my memory serves me, she's quite a catch."

"How do you plan to support her?" his father demanded.

"Not that it's any of your business, but I now manage a company on the island and make a decent salary. I'm here to sell my house and use the proceeds to buy something there." He considered saying that Catherine was selling her condo, too, but decided to keep that to himself. What would his father's reaction be to that bit of information?

"What type of company?" his father asked.

Michael sighed. How sad that he had to explain to his father what he did for a living. If they had a healthy father-son relationship, the question would never need asking.

He sat up a bit straighter. "Fishing. The owner has a large fleet, both here and on Nantucket. He treats me very well financially. Down the road, I wouldn't be surprised if he offers me a stake in the company."

"I've never made it a secret that I don't approve of your so-called profession," his father said. "But now that you're going to marry, you need something more dependable than *fishing*."

Michael bristled. Why couldn't his father just be happy for him for once?

"Have you considered that if the country were to suffer a recession, that place would instantly go belly up?" His father's eyes narrowed into a cold stare. "Having said that, at least I approve of your choice in women. Catherine is quite impressive. It looks like what captured my attention wasn't lost on you."

"What's that supposed to mean?"

"She's successful in her own right."

"Yeah, so?"

"So, she must enjoy a comfortable financial position to be able to open a store on Nantucket."

"What are you implying?"

"I'm saying you've found someone other than your sister to support you."

"Let it go, Dad," David said.

Even though Michael was pleased and surprised that his brother stepped in to stand up for him, he couldn't sit idly by. He pushed back his chair and stood, fists clenched at his side. "If you weren't my father—"

Even though the elder Benton continued sitting, David stepped between the two men, as if he thought that Michael might pummel their dad at any moment.

His father bolted from his chair, pushing David aside. "Even though you've never seen fit to take my advice, I suggest this time you reconsider. Think about your future. How long will a woman like Catherine put up with a husband who can't hold a candle to her ambition? And what if you have children? How do you expect to support a family holding down a second-rate job?"

Michael fought to swallow his anger. His chest tightened. He'd give anything for an antacid or a glass of ice water right about now.

"Maybe I should have a talk with Catherine," his father threatened.

"Over my dead body."

Michael's father threw back his head and laughed. "What are you afraid of?"

Michael swallowed. "Look, I didn't come here to argue. Honestly, I didn't intend to speak to you at all." He turned to his brother. "I came to let you know that I've chosen a former crewmate, the captain of the fishing vessel I worked on, to be my best man. I hope you understand."

David's expression became thoughtful.

Michael's heartbeat quickened. He suddenly felt bad for his brother. Maybe he *should've* chosen David, even though they hadn't been close for years. But then he reminded himself that Drake had been more of a brother to him than David ever had.

"*Understand?*" his father exploded. "How does one grapple with disrespect? You choose a coworker over your own brother? If that's not a slap in the face," he huffed, "I don't know what is."

"It's okay," David conceded. "I appreciate you coming to tell me, man to man."

For the briefest moment, Michael saw the older brother he'd once idolized.

David sighed. "I have to say I'm disappointed, though."

"Of course, you are," Michael's father ranted. "Who wouldn't be? All I've ever wanted was for you to be half the man your brother is, but it's apparent living off women is more your style."

Michael stepped closer to the door.

"I'll be the one who says when you may leave." The elder Benton swatted at the air. "Ah, what's the sense? Continue on with your ways, if that suits you, but you better pray that Catherine doesn't become as fed up with you as I am."

Michael glared at him. "Why is it always about *you*?" he asked through clenched teeth. "What *you* think is best. What *you* want, regardless of how *I* feel? If you'd get off your high horse long enough, you'd realize there's nothing wrong with me not wanting to walk in your shadow."

His father's face hardened, and his eyes bulged.

Michael held onto the doorknob. "The wedding is on May 17th. We hope to see you there. But if you decide to come, don't pack your opinions."

MICHAEL'S FINGERS grew numb from gripping the steering wheel as he sped south on I-95 towards Drake's house.

How dare his father insinuate that he'd marry Catherine for her money! And where did he get off saying Michael disrespected his brother? He'd explicitly made the trip to Rhode Island to face David and tell him in person. He understood they hadn't been close for years. That their father's desires had pulled them apart. So why had he driven all this way and planted himself in a situation he knew would be toxic? He had predicted how his father would take the news. But the reality was, it had never been entirely about David's reaction. It was his father's approval he'd sought, he realized. He should've known better.

Oh, what he wouldn't give to welcome back the father he'd known as a child.

After hardly any memory of the thirty-five-minute drive to Drake's house, Michael pulled into the driveway. Drake came out of the garage, wiping his hands with a rag. "Thought I heard you pull up. Your timing's great. I just finished the last item on my to-do list." He folded Michael into a hug. "Come on inside. You look like you could use a beer."

Inside, Drake pulled two bottles from the fridge, popped the tops off, and gave one to Michael. "Have a seat. You hungry?" He held up his hand like a traffic cop. "And before you answer, I don't mind saying I make a mean Italian grinder."

Michael smiled for the first time since he'd left Nantucket. "No thanks. I think I've inhaled too much coffee today." He rubbed the center of his chest. "I've got a wicked case of heartburn."

"I recall you saying that same thing when we were out to sea. Like I said then, you should see a doctor. He can give you something for it."

Michael nodded. "It's to do with the confrontation I had with my dad."

"Your dad? I thought you were going to talk to your brother."

"That's what I'd hoped for. I should've known he would be there, too. David can't use his own private bathroom without letting my dad know. In a way, I'm glad he was there, though, because I made it crystal clear I won't allow him to ruin our day."

"Do you want to talk about it?"

"Nothing much to say. More of the same. Dad rants that I'm a loser. I react. My brother buries his head in the sand." Michael gave a half-hearted chuckle. "Although David did swing into action and stand between us when he thought I was on the verge of kicking my father's sanctimonious butt."

Drake took a swig of beer and put the bottle down. "I'm sorry."

Michael shook his head. "I shouldn't be surprised by what he said. My father always seems to find a way to turn his rhetoric up a notch when I'm around. I thought it had been bad enough at Christmas when he said he wasn't proud of me. As awful as *that* was, he managed to up the ante today." Michael looked Drake in the eye. "Do you know what he had the gall to say?"

His friend shook his head. "I can only imagine."

"He said in no uncertain terms that I'm only marrying Catherine for her money. Can you believe that?"

"Look, I know he's your father, but try not to let him get to you. He wants to wear you down. Manipulate you into coming around to his way of thinking, like he did to your brother. You're a good man. *You* know that, and so does Catherine, and outside of the two of you, no one else's opinion should matter, not even his." Drake clasped Michael's shoulders. "It's not *you* who has a problem. It's *him*."

"You're right, and his opinion shouldn't matter, but it does." Michael put two fingers to the center of his chest and rubbed it in small circles.

"Are you sure you're okay?" Drake asked.

"It'll pass in a minute or so. Always does." Michael stood, forced a smile, and lifted his bottle in a toast. "To my best man."

CHAPTER THIRTY-THREE

Catherine's store cleared out thirty minutes after her scheduled five o'clock closing time. She flipped the sign, leaned against the door, and breathed a sigh of relief.

What a day. Not only had she been busy with customers, but at noon, she'd closed and met up with Michael, Tina, Helen, Bill, and Drake at St. Mary's to rehearse for the ceremony the next day. Afterward, she'd raced back to the store to find a line of customers waiting outside.

She checked her watch. Forty minutes to decompress and transform herself from proprietor to bride-to-be for the rehearsal dinner that Tina was hosting at her house.

On her way upstairs, she thought of Michael's family, and her focus was on his father. When Michael returned from Rhode Island, he'd shared what had happened. Ever since, Catherine had prayed that her future father-in-law didn't cause a scene. If he did, what would that mean for the wedding? Even worse, what would it do to Michael to have his father ruin the day and embarrass him?

She headed to the bathroom and turned on the shower. Unlike her husband-to-be, who cared less if his family—other than Tina—attended the wedding, Catherine would give anything to have her mom and dad there. She'd always dreamed of her father walking her down the aisle and later dancing with him to "Daddy's Little Girl," while her mother shed tears of joy.

She pushed aside the sad thoughts. Michael's family would soon be hers, and she'd do what she could to make the relationship as harmonious as possible, even if it meant dealing with her husband's bear of a father. Maybe she'd be able to mend the fences between Michael and his dad. After all, during her career, her claim to fame was always about building relationships.

After her shower, Catherine stepped into a black sheath dress, another steal from Jennifer's Closet, and wiggled it up and over her shoulders. She applied a hint of makeup, ran a brush through her hair, and let it fall to her shoulders in soft, bouncy waves. Next, she slipped on a pair of black strappy Manolo's. She then heard a knock on the downstairs door. She maneuvered her way down the stairs, gripping the railings. It'd been nearly a year since she'd left her job and abandoned her stilettos for comfort shoes. She didn't need to take a tumble and break something on the eve of her wedding. "Coming!"

She peeked out the window to be sure it was Michael, and opened the door. Catherine almost swooned when she saw him looking more handsome than ever in khaki-colored trousers, a light-blue shirt unbuttoned at the collar, and a navy sports jacket.

"Hi," she said.

He flashed a wide grin. "Look at you!"

Catherine spun around. "You like?"

"You look amazing." He opened his arms. "Come here."

She stepped into his outstretched arms, loving the feel of his embrace. It was like him—strong and steady.

Thanks to Jerry launching intimidation tactics her way like hand grenades, she'd questioned her decision to move to the tiny island and open a store. But falling in love with Michael hadn't garnered a single second thought.

"I love you."

His breath low against her ear made her melt further into his embrace. "I love you more."

Then he kissed her and pulled back. "We better get going. Don't want to leave Tina alone with the big bad wolf for too long."

"What time did they get here?" she asked as he helped her put on a light wrap.

"Tina texted after we left the church to say our family had arrived and were waiting for her."

"So, you've seen them?"

Michael gave a definitive nod. "Oh, I've seen them, all right. Shortly after I got home, David took me aside and assured me that he's okay with my choice for best man. According to him, Dad is still boiling, however. As if I couldn't tell."

"Did your father make a scene?"

"No. But he grumbled about having to come all this way for the wedding and about having to wait ten minutes for Tina to arrive, even though he knew she'd left the door unlocked. Don't worry, my sister shut him down."

"Do you think he'll start anything tonight?"

"Who knows? I've warned him not to, but the only voice he listens to is the one inside his own head."

TINA'S HOUSE seemed near to breaking at the studs when Catherine and Michael walked into the living room. Michael's parents, his brother David, his wife Denise, and their children were gathered and chatting in the living room. Helen and Bill were in the dining room talking to Drake. Catherine had had the pleasure of meeting him at the church earlier in the day.

"Catherine!" Helen called out. She rushed over, hugged her, and whispered, "Heads up. Your future father-in-law hasn't strung more than three words together since we got here. I think he might be getting ready to explode, based on the look on his face." She leaned back. "Though I did hear him say that he's looking forward to talking to *you*, so maybe you'll be able to soften him up a bit."

Catherine briefly closed her eyes. *Oh boy.*

A few minutes later, Michael grasped her hand and led her over to his family. "Everyone, you remember Catherine, the future Mrs. Benton." His face a portrait of pride and joy.

"Of course," Denise said, and wrapped Catherine in a hug. "We're so happy you're joining our family." She glanced at her in-laws and her husband. "Aren't we?"

Catherine liked Denise. She struck her as a woman who wasn't easily intimidated by anyone, including Michael's father. She suspected her soon-to-be sister-in-law would be a good mentor when it came to dealing with her in-laws. "Thank you."

"Yes." Michael's mother stepped forward. "We're thrilled that Michael has decided to settle down, especially with someone like you."

What does that mean? Catherine thought to herself.

Michael's dad grunted through his forced-on smile.

David hugged Catherine. Then he stepped back and focused on Michael. "You're one lucky man, bro."

"Don't I know it." Michael slipped his arm around his fiancée's waist. "Now, if you'll excuse us, my bride-to-be and I need to play host and hostess."

Michael's words raised Catherine's antenna. Did he sense a confrontation brewing? Maybe he knew why his father wanted to speak to her, so he'd whisked her away before his dad had a chance to launch into something.

They headed for Drake, who was engaged in an animated discussion with Tina in the dining room.

Tina was laughing so hard, tears cascaded down her cheeks.

Michael clasped his friend's shoulder and grinned. "What are you saying to cause my otherwise composed sister to double over?"

Tina wiped at her eyes. "He's telling me of your early days at sea."

"You didn't tell her about—" Michael said with mock horror.

Drake grinned. "Oh yes, I did."

Amidst her giggles, Tina shared that the initiation of a new crewmate involved matching tequila shots with the other crewmates the night before they shipped out, and the next morning while nursing a hangover, the newbie had the task of cleaning and filleting fish for that night's dinner. "Michael turned green as an emerald and puked his guts out over the side."

Catherine smiled and stroked the side of his face. "Poor baby."

"I've never been able to eat swordfish since," Michael admitted. He turned to Drake. "Thanks for sharing. I thought you were my *friend*."

Catherine saw why Michael adored this guy. He was everything David and his father were not. Warm and engaging, with a broad smile for everyone. A far cry from the icy stares emanating from her future father-in-law across the room. Maybe once the elder Benton ate, he'd be in a better frame of mind.

Catherine glanced at the table. It brimmed with every kind of food group imaginable. There were bushels of greens, baskets of mixed bread slices and rolls, and warming trays filled with crispy calamari, grilled pork riblets, blue crab fried rice, and roasted root vegetables. They were followed by entrées of Cod Oscar, Beef tenderloin tips, and Chicken Marsala. A separate table nestled in a corner was heaped high with bite-size desserts arranged in triple pyramids.

"Tina, everything looks amazing."

"Is this all your doing?" Drake asked.

"Mostly," Tina replied. "I did cheat a little with some help from a local caterer."

"Thank you, Sis," Michael said. "You've outdone yourself."

"How gorgeous is this table scape?" Helen asked as she oohed and aahed over it. "I may have to hire her to help me at the inn."

Tina raised her hand in the air. "Come on, everyone. Let's eat!"

After dinner, Catherine nudged Michael. "We can't continue to ignore your family," she said quietly. "If you're concerned about an outburst, we may as well deal with it now."

"We haven't ignored them. We spoke to them right after we got here," he said in a clipped tone.

"And if I had blinked, I would've missed it," she retorted. "Come on. I heard your father wanted to talk to me."

"About what?"

So, he didn't know, Catherine thought to herself.

"We're about to find out."

They wove around the kids sitting cross-legged on the floor, their eyes glued to their tablets.

"Where will you be living after the wedding?" the elder Benton asked when they approached.

"At my place." Michael said. "Until our houses sell."

Michael's father shook his head. "You mean Tina's place."

Catherine inwardly winced.

The elder Benton looked at her next. "And you're okay with that?"

Catherine linked her arm with Michael's and leaned into him. "Of course. Why wouldn't I be? As long as we're together, I don't care where we live."

Michael kissed her cheek. "Thank you, sweetheart."

"And we won't be far from our workplaces, so that's an added bonus," Catherine said.

Michael's father looked at him over glasses that had slid halfway down his nose. "If you had a decent job that allowed you to provide for your wife, you'd have a house of your own and wouldn't have to live off your sister."

Michael visibly bristled.

This man riled Catherine's Irish temper. He might be Michael's father, but that didn't give him the right to humiliate the man she loved. She paused, hoping maybe Denise or David, or perhaps Michael's mother, would jump in. But no.

"With all due respect, Mr. Benton—" Catherine started.

"It's okay, honey," Michael said, putting his arm around her. "I'm used to his jabs."

"No, it's *not* okay." She shot her future father-in-law a stern look. "Michael and I won't be living off of anyone."

"I don't believe I was speaking to you. This is between my son and me."

That's it. His attitude had pushed her to the limit. How dare he slight her!

Catherine squared her shoulders. "Oh, I beg to differ. Anything that concerns Michael concerns me." She exhaled. "I don't appreciate how you treat your son, and for the life of me, I fail to understand why you find it necessary to be so mean."

"Who do you think you're talking to?" Benton challenged.

"Do not speak to her like that," Michael warned. "Come on, Catherine. I will *not* let him ruin our evening."

Catherine glared at Michael's father. "I've learned that life is about the choices we make. And Michael and I are quite comfortable with ours. Where we live and what we do is none of your business." She saw the slightest hint of a smile cross Denise's lips out of the corner of her eye. "Life is too short to harbor misguided anger." She shook her head. "It's a pity that you're unwilling to see your son as others do." She tried to quell the tremble invading her voice. "He's a good man. A man I've chosen to create a life with and build our family. A man I'll be proud to call my husband."

Tina hurried over. "Dad, keep a lid on it," she said in a low voice.

Michael's mother laid a hand on her husband's arm. "Tina's right. I thought we agreed—"

Benton shook off her hand. "I agreed to nothing." He locked eyes with Catherine. "It impressed me when Michael said who he planned to marry," he snarled. "I considered you intelligent. But based on your actions tonight, it seems I was wrong." He wagged his finger at her. "I suggest you think about what you're about to do. There's still time to change your mind and save yourself the heartache. Trust me, Michael will take you on a path you'll wish you hadn't traveled."

Catherine fought an urge to slap down his hand. Who did he think he was? She wouldn't allow him to rain on their wedding. If he couldn't keep his comments to himself, he could go home. But before she could suggest that, Drake was by her side.

He extended his hand to Michael's father and nodded in the direction of Michael's mother. "We haven't met. I'm Drake, your son's friend."

"I figured as much." Michael's father didn't extend his hand.

"Nice to meet you," Michael's mother said. "Our son thinks the world of you."

Drake lowered his hand. "I assure you, the feeling is mutual." Then he directed his attention back to Michael's father. "I couldn't help but overhear. As Catherine said, it's a shame that you don't see your son as others do. My advice is to let go of whatever is bothering you and enjoy his special day with him."

"It'll be a snowy day in Miami when I take advice from a fisherman."

"Dad!" Michael stepped forward. "Enough—"

Drake put his arm in front of Michael as a driver would to a passenger when hitting the brakes. "No worries. We men of the sea have broad shoulders."

Although Catherine had just met him, she sensed he wasn't the kind of guy who'd walk away. So, he surprised her when he turned to leave. But seconds later, he glanced over his shoulder.

"I suggest you heed your future daughter-in-law's advice." Then he corralled Michael and Catherine. "Come on. I'm thirsty."

"I'm sorry, man," Michael said when they reached the makeshift bar in the dining room.

"Don't worry. I've been up against the worst. But as Catherine said, life is short. I hope he sees the truth in that before it's too late."

CHAPTER THIRTY-FOUR

Catherine stood in front of the full-length mirror inside the penthouse suite she'd once called home at Sunny Skies and surveyed her wedding day reflection.

Tina fussed behind her, straightening her train and fastening all the buttons.

Catherine looked toward the window. Soon she'd be a married woman. Catherine O'Malley Benton. She ran her hand over the silky material, tilted her head to one side, and marveled at how well the dress fit. Anyone not familiar with the circumstances would have sworn she'd had it custom made. "I can't get over what a find this was. And it's all thanks to you."

Tina peeked around from behind her. "All I did was drive us to Jennifer's. She and the mother of the bride did the rest."

Catherine couldn't have afforded the white satin designer dress if not for the spectacular discount. Even with the price reduction the bride's mother offered, Catherine still couldn't have bought it if Jennifer hadn't stepped in, giving her an even lower price, cutting into her profit.

"I invited both Jennifer and the mother of the bride to attend the church ceremony and reception. It's the least I could do."

"That's nice. I'm sure they appreciate it." Tina straightened. "Where are your pearls?"

Catherine smiled, recalling her mother vacuuming their South Boston apartment while wearing the necklace with her housedress. When Catherine had asked why she wore it while cleaning, her mother said it made her feel pretty. Years later, Catherine inherited the pearls much the same as her mother had. Since then, she'd stored the luminescent orbs in a wooden jewelry box featuring a ballerina that still twirled on its toes when the cover lifted. A gift from her parents on her sixteenth birthday. Thrilled that the necklace would incorporate her mother's memory into the wedding and serve as something old, she fought to hold back happy tears. "On the dresser, wrapped in tissue paper."

Tina draped them around Catherine's neck. "Perfect." Then she went to her purse and retrieved a garter of blue lace. "Something blue."

Catherine sat on the edge of the bed, lifted her dress above her knee, and pulled the garter up.

Tina's eyes misted. "I've always wanted a sister, and soon I'll have one."

"What about Denise?"

"She's nice, great for my brother, and a wonderful mother, but I can't say we've ever connected in the way you and I have."

Catherine stood and hugged Tina. "If I could've custom-ordered a sister, she'd be just like you."

Tina stepped back and chuckled. "We better stop with all this mush, or we'll be redoing our makeup."

Catherine frowned.

"What's wrong?" Tina asked.

"It dawned on me that I don't have something borrowed."

"I'm sure we can fix—"

A knock sounded at the door.

"Quick, step behind the mirror," Tina said. "I wouldn't put it past Michael to try and steal a glimpse of you. The last thing we want is bad luck." She cracked open the door. "All clear. It's only Helen."

"Thanks a lot," their friend laughed. "*Only* Helen."

Tina swatted at her shoulder. "I thought it might be Michael."

When Catherine stepped from behind the mirror, Helen gasped and her eyes glistened. "I promised myself I wouldn't cry, but you're such a vision."

Catherine smoothed her dress. "I hope Michael likes it."

"What's not to like?" Helen brought a neatly folded handkerchief from behind her back and presented it to Catherine. "Here, this is for you."

Catherine's eyes widened as she turned the satiny white square trimmed with lace over in her hand. "It's exquisite."

"I haven't said anything because I wasn't sure I'd have it ready. It's a piece of my wedding gown." She sighed. "I'd always hoped to give my dress to my daughter, but…"

Catherine threw her arms around Helen. "Thank you so much. Now I have something borrowed."

"As I've said before, Bill and I think of you as the daughter we were never blessed with. It seemed only right that you should have it. If I thought my dress would've fit you, I'd have offered it, too. But it would've required extensive alterations, which we didn't have time for, and besides." She stepped back and spread her arms. "This is flawless."

Tears stung Catherine's eyes as she tucked the handkerchief into the bodice of her dress.

Tina picked up the tulle lace veil from the bed. Its pearl-studded comb matched the bodice of the gown, accenting the necklace. "Time to put the frosting on this cake." She centered it on Catherine's head. "Perfect."

CATHERINE WATCHED the downtown stores whiz by as the limo Michael had ordered approached the historic St. Mary Lady of the Isle Church.

Tina pointed. "Look."

A banner stretched across the front window of Catherine's store. "Closed. Getting Married."

Catherine glanced from the sign to Tina. "Michael?"

Tina nodded. "He wanted the world to know."

"You've got yourself one fine man," Bill said.

"I know," Catherine whispered. There was a time when she'd thought she'd never get over losing Jack. Then Michael had come along, and as much as she'd tried to fight off the attraction, she couldn't. His kindness, not to mention his drop-dead gorgeous looks, slowly chipped away at her resolve. And now it was hard to imagine life without him by her side.

The limo turned onto Federal Street and pulled in front of the church.

Helen, Bill, and Tina scrambled from the car.

A minute later, Helen ducked her head into the limo. "All clear."

Catherine gathered up her dress and stepped out.

Like most island structures, thanks to Mother Nature, the church's shingles had weathered to perfection. A stone staircase led to polished double-arched teak doors.

Catherine exhaled. In a few short minutes, she'd be Catherine O'Malley Benton. She took a breath and slowly exhaled as Tina lifted her train from the car.

Helen and Bill opened the church doors.

Tina held the train off the ground while Catherine ascended the stairs.

Inside, Helen and Bill stood on either side of her.

"Before the magic of your day consumes you, we wanted you to know that we wish you and Michael a future filled with an abundance of happiness." Helen kissed Catherine on her cheek and lowered the veil over her face. "You're such a beautiful bride. I can't wait to see the expression on Michael's face when he sees you."

Bill and Helen linked arms with Catherine.

"Ready?" Bill asked.

Catherine puffed out her cheeks. "Yes." She was grateful that they flanked her sides because her legs felt like melting sticks of butter.

Tina positioned herself in front of the trio as they'd practiced the day before, and nodded to a woman standing next to the sanctuary door.

When the door opened, "Mendelssohn's Wedding March" filled the air.

Catherine scanned the pews. Michael's parents, David, Denise, and their three children occupied the groom's side. She assumed that the men seated behind them, along with their spouses or significant others, were Michael's former crewmates. In the next row was Al, the man who had helped haul away the parking signs.

Other than Jennifer and a woman who must be the mother of the bride, the one responsible for Catherine's dress, her side of the aisle was barren. Helen and Bill would be the only ones to join the two women already seated. The stark reminder of how empty her life had become caught in her throat. She breathed in and slowly exhaled. Then a warm feeling came over her. She felt her mother's presence.

Thanks Mom, for helping me find the right path.

Catherine blinked. Carol, the owner of This and That, and Nat, the owner of Nat's hardware store, sat tucked into the last row. Could this be a harbinger of what the future held? A life filled with friends and family? Catherine sure hoped so.

The duo smiled.

Catherine returned the gesture.

Michael, the least formal man she had ever known, stood next to Drake. Movie-star handsome in his three-piece gray-blue suit, white shirt, fun plaid blue-and-white bow tie, he sported a white rosebud boutonniere nestled in his lapel. He looked proud and nervous at the same time.

Drake wore a dark-blue suit. His tie and boutonniere resembled Tina's crimson-colored dress.

Catherine's eyes misted.

Tina started down the aisle.

Catherine tightened her grasp on her bouquet of calla lilies and ivory-colored French tulips.

Dual arrangements of pink roses adorned the altar, while the stained glass windows sprinkled pixels of jewel-like color across the interior.

Catherine stepped onto the satin runner, and an audible gasp filled the air.

∽

Michael beamed happiness as he watched Catherine walk down the aisle. He could hardly believe that this woman he loved beyond measure would soon be his wife.

Drake bumped his shoulder and whispered, "She's beautiful."

Catherine was the woman of Michael's dreams. The woman he'd wake up next to for the rest of his life. And who, if they were blessed, would mother their children. He glanced at his stoic father standing in the front row. Michael had tossed and turned until the wee hours after their clash the night before, imagining his father jumping to his feet and interrupting the ceremony.

They briefly made eye contact.

Then Tina arrived and stood in front and to the left of the priest.

Helen and Bill each hugged Catherine and headed for their seats.

Michael stepped forward. "I love you."

"I love you more," Catherine said.

They turned to face the priest.

He motioned for everyone to sit.

The sweet aroma of the flowers helped offset the faint lingering reminder of incense from the morning mass.

"Dearly beloved, we are gathered together to witness Michael and Catherine declare their intentions to enter into the sanctity of marriage." He looked at the couple. "Have you come here today without coercion, freely and wholeheartedly?"

"Yes," they both responded.

"Are you prepared, as you follow the path of marriage, to love and honor each other for as long as you both shall live?"

"Yes," they both said again.

"Please turn to face one another, join your right hands, and declare your consent before God and His Church."

The priest pivoted. "Michael, do you take Catherine for your lawful wife, to have and to hold, from this day forward? For better, for worse, for richer, for poorer, in sickness and in health, until death do you part?"

"I do."

The priest turned to Catherine.

"Catherine, do you take Michael for your lawful husband, to have and to hold, from this day forward? For better, for worse, for richer, for poorer, in sickness and in health, until death do you part?"

"I do."

"May the Lord in His kindness strengthen the consent you have declared before the Church and graciously bring to fulfillment His blessings upon you." The priest looked to those gathered. "What God has joined together, let no one put asunder."

Then he turned to Drake. "The rings, please."

Drake reached in his pocket and handed them over.

The priest sprinkled them with holy water. "May the Lord bless these rings, which you will give to each other as a sign of your love and fidelity."

He handed Michael Catherine's ring, then nodded at Michael.

"Catherine, I give you this ring as a sign of my love and fidelity," Michael said as he slipped the ring onto Catherine's trembling finger.

The priest gave Catherine Michael's ring, then nodded.

"Michael, I give you this ring as a sign of my love and fidelity," Catherine said, slipping the ring onto Michael's finger.

Then the priest made the sign of the cross. "In the name of the Father, and of the Son, and of the Holy Spirit, I now pronounce you husband and wife." He smiled at Michael. "You may kiss your bride."

CATHERINE PEERED out the back window of the inn to the garden. True to her word, Helen had transformed the area into a magical spectacle.

A large billowy white tent stood off to one side, protecting the tables and food. A three-piece band performed to the left, with a raised platform for dancing in front.

"When you hear the music, come outside," Helen said to Michael and Catherine. Then she motioned to Bill, Tina, and Drake. "Follow me."

Michael leaned down and kissed Catherine. "Are you as happy as I am?" he whispered.

"More." Her heart swelled with love for him.

The music started.

"That's our cue." Michael opened the door, took Catherine's hand, and together they descended the outdoor stairs.

A path strewn with rose petals stretched from the bottom of the stairs to an arch covered with a floral swag of dahlias, peonies, and assorted greenery. Guests lined both sides while Tina, Drake, Helen, and Bill stood like soldiers at the far end, guarding the tent's entrance.

"Ladies and gentlemen!" the band leader announced. "It is my great pleasure to present Mr. and Mrs. Michael Benton!"

Applause broke out, and guests held their phones in the air to capture pictures.

Catherine spotted Michael's parents near the entrance to the tent. Could that be a hint of a smile she saw cross her father-in-law's lips?

Michael shook his father's and brother's hands, then hugged his mother and Denise.

Catherine stepped in and wrapped her arms around her mother-in-law.

"It's written all over Michael's face how happy you've made him."

Catherine wasn't sure how to approach her father-in-law. Should she extend her hand? Attempt to hug him? While she pondered what to do, she leaned over and gave David and Denise a hug. Then, before she could overthink it, she did the same to her father-in-law.

Did he flinch?

"The ceremony was very nice," he said, his manner stiff.

Before she could respond, Helen was at Catherine's side, motioning her inside the tent. "Let's find our seats. It's time for the best man to make his toast."

Michael sat beside Catherine at the head table, as did Tina and Drake.

After they'd settled in, Drake stood and tapped his glass with a spoon.

"I'm not good at making speeches, so this will be short." He cleared his throat. "It's been my extraordinary pleasure to witness Michael and Catherine take their vows. Catherine, I don't have to tell you that your husband's a good man. One who's not afraid to show what's in his heart." He shifted his attention to Michael. "And Michael, although I've been your friend for many years, I can honestly say I've never seen you happier. I may not know Catherine that well, but I consider myself a good judge of character. And man, from what I can tell, your wife's heart is as big as yours. And that's saying something. I'm confident you can trust her to always have your back." He paused. "Catherine, as you so aptly said recently—life is short. So, my wish for both of you is to live each day as if it's your last." He raised his glass in the air. "To a life filled with love and happiness." He winked. "And a houseful of kids." He lowered his glass. "Now, let's get this party started!"

∽

STRAINS OF A LOVE song mimicked what Catherine felt in her heart when she and Michael stepped onto the raised platform for their first dance as husband and wife. She leaned into him and closed her eyes.

Michael lifted her chin and gently kissed her.

Catherine felt the world slip away.

At the end of the song, the bandleader called for Michael to dance with his mother.

When he stepped away to take his mom in his arms, Catherine nearly broke down. If times were different, she'd be dancing with her father, a long-held dream of hers.

A tap on her shoulder pulled her back to the present. She turned to see Michael's father.

"May I have this dance?" he asked, extending his hand.

Really? Was this the same man who had treated her and Michael so nasty the previous evening? Unlike last night, however, today his eyes were soft, and he smiled.

"You may."

The elder Benton slipped his arm around her waist and took her hand. They glided across the raised floor as if they'd practiced for days.

"You were right to say what you did last night. I've been a stubborn old fool," he said. "I hope you'll find it in your heart to forgive me."

Catherine's eyes welled, not only from a sense of relief, but from happiness as well. "Of course, but it's not my forgiveness that's important. It's Michael's."

"Do you think—"

"Come on." Catherine took his hand and led him across the floor to where Michael and his mother danced. When Catherine saw Michael stiffen, she smiled. "Can we make this a group dance?"

"Ohhh…kay," Michael hesitated.

The foursome formed a circle and moved in time to the slow music.

Catherine gave her father-in-law a nod.

He locked eyes with Michael. "I've asked your wife for her forgiveness, and now I seek yours." He stopped moving. "I'm so very sorry for the way I've treated you."

With tears in her eyes, Michael's mother prompted her husband. "Go on, dear."

Michael's father swallowed. "I've only wanted what I thought was best for you." He smiled at Catherine. "But I see now that what's best for you is right here. And if being in the fishing business is what you want, then so be it." He stepped toward his youngest son, slipped an arm around Michael's shoulder, and pulled him in tight. "I love you, son. Always have. Always will."

"Oh, Mr. Benton," Catherine said. "What a lovely wedding gift you've given us."

"Call me Dad," he said.

When Michael stepped back, his eyes were moist. "You have no idea how much I've wanted to hear those words from you. I love you, too."

Tina rushed the platform. "Hey, is this a private party, or can anyone join?"

Michael's father embraced his daughter, then motioned for David, Denise, and the children to join them.

Catherine stepped aside.

"No, no, stay where you were," Michael's dad said. "You're part of this family now."

Catherine smiled and raised her eyes to the heavens.

Thanks, Mom. You were right. I did have more to do.

Drake approached and signaled to the photographer. "Looks like we have a happy family portrait over here."

"That we do," Michael said. "That we do."

THE END

ACKNOWLEDGMENTS

By way of thanks, I must start with Wendy Dingwall, the woman who most recently edited my work. She brought out the very best of my story and removed the rest. Special thanks to The E-book Formatting Fairies for helping me launch this book. Without their expertise and guidance, this story would still reside on my computer. To Susan Busada for her marketing expertise and counsel. I would not be close to promoting my book without her. And finally, to all who have read the story and offered comments and suggestions along the way. Your input is truly appreciated.

This book is a testament to the importance of friendships. For those who I hold especially dear (you know who you are), this book is my way of commemorating our enduring friendships. I hope you know how very much you mean to me.

And finally, but certainly not least, none of this would have been possible without the never-ending support of my husband. Always by my side, he is my love, my staunchest supporter and cheerleader, especially during my dark days of battling cancer.

ABOUT THE AUTHOR

Lorraine resides outside of Tampa, Florida, but will always have a soft spot for New England, where she lived for seventeen years. In addition to writing, she loves cooking and traveling and enjoys watching wildlife roam outside her back window. She is a grateful five-year breast cancer survivor.

Lorraine can be contacted at *lorraine@lorrainesolheim.com*. Please sign up for her newsletter to know when her next book will be available and other interesting information. You may also choose to follow her on Facebook and Instagram @lorrainesolheim, author.

Made in the USA
Middletown, DE
14 January 2022